Murder
with Collard Greens
and Hot Sauce

Books by A.L. Herbert

MURDER WITH FRIED CHICKEN AND WAFFLES

MURDER WITH MACARONI AND CHEESE

MURDER WITH COLLARD GREENS AND HOT SAUCE

Published by Kensington Publishing Corporation

Murder
with Collard Greens
and Hot Sauce

A.L. Herbert

KENSINGTON BOOKS
www.kensingtonbooks.com

KENSINGTON BOOKS are published by

Kensington Publishing Corp.
119 West 40th Street
New York, NY 10018

All Kensington titles, imprints, and distributed lines are available at special quantity discounts for bulk purchases for sales promotion, premiums, fund-raising, educational, or institutional use. Special book excerpts or customized printings can also be created to fit specific needs. For details, write or phone the office of the Kensington Special Sales Manager: Attn. Special Sales Department. Kensington Publishing Corp, 119 West 40th Street, New York, NY 10018. Phone: 1-800-221-2647.

Library of Congress Card Catalogue Number: 2018912504

Kensington and the K logo Reg. U.S. Pat. & TM Off.

ISBN-13: 978-1-4967-1800-6
ISBN-10: 1-4967-1800-3
First Kensington Hardcover Edition: April 2019

ISBN-13: 978-1-4967-1804-4 (e-book)
ISBN-10: 1-4967-1804-6 (e-book)

10 9 8 7 6 5 4 3 2 1

Printed in the United States of America

Chapter 1

"Be careful with that," I say to Latasha as she paints the white cream on Wavonne's hair. "Sometimes I think all that relaxer has fried her brain."

"Now you just shut your mouth, Ms. Naturally Straight Hair," Wavonne says. "Keepin' it short like you do should be a crime."

Wavonne and I are sitting next to each other in front of the long mirrors at Illusions, the hair salon a few doors down from my restaurant, Mahalia's Sweet Tea. Latasha owns the salon and has been cutting and styling our hair for years, even though Wavonne wears wigs much of the time. As Wavonne mentioned, I was blessed with "good hair" that doesn't need to be relaxed, but running a restaurant doesn't leave me a lot of time to fuss with it. So, much to Wavonne's annoyance, I keep it fairly short.

"I like Halia's cut." Latasha comes to my defense. "It frames her face nicely. It gives her a contemporary look . . . makes her look neat and professional."

"What it 'makes her look' is like the sista in those Popeyes commercials." Wavonne turns her eyes to me. "Now, if only your fried chicken was as good as Popeyes'," she adds, an evil grin rising on her face.

Latasha and I gasp in unison.

"You did *not* just insult her fried chicken?! Them's fightin' words," Latasha says with a laugh.

"Damn right, they are." I look at Wavonne. "Don't make me take my earrings off."

"Simmer down, Halia. I'm just messin' with you. We all know you serve the best fried chicken in town." She shifts her eyes to Latasha's reflection in the mirror. "You gotta play to the old girl's ego sometimes," she says. "She ain't got no man, so her fried chicken is all she has."

"Old girl? First you insult my chicken, and then you call me old. Keep it up, Wavonne, and I'll conspire with Latasha to leave that relaxer on your hair until it falls out."

"Calm down, ladies. There'll be no hair falling out in my salon. It's bad for business," Latasha says. "And I certainly don't want any mishaps with Monique Dupree due here in two days."

"Monique Dupree?!" Wavonne exclaims. "Is comin' here?!"

"Yep."

"Get out!"

"Who's Monique Dupree?" I inquire.

Wavonne ignores my question. "Why's Monique Dupree comin' here?"

"She's kicking off a cross-country tour at the Unique Chic Hair Convention in the city this weekend. From there, she'll be traveling all over the United States doing promotional events and visiting salons. We sell a lot of her products, so Illusions made the cut as one of the few stores that she plans to visit before she leaves the DC area. She'll be here on Friday for a meet and greet. My clients are really excited. She's originally from this area, you know. She moved to New York back in the nineties and hit the big time. She only recently took up residence here in Maryland again. Supposedly, she had some grand house custom built in Mitchellville."

"Mitchellville? Swanky," Wavonne says. "I'll have to stop by on Friday . . . and I should get tickets to the convention. They'll probably have some good samples and giveaways. Lately I've been tryin' this new stuff . . . GrowNRestore cream. It has Jamaican Black Castor Oil in it."

"Jamaican Black Castor Oil?" Latasha inquires.

"Yes. It's the latest thing. The package said it stimulates growth and helps repair dry, damaged hair . . . and break-ages. I've only been using it for five days. I hope it kicks in soon."

Latasha and I exchange brief glances via the mirror as both of us know that whatever claims the label of this GrowNRestore cream makes, it could contain holy water blessed by Jesus Christ himself, and it still likely wouldn't grow *or* restore Wavonne's hair, which, much like my relationship with moderation and chocolate cake, is beyond repair. Latasha does the best she can, but between Wavonne's hot iron, cheap home relaxers, and the bargain bin dyes that she uses between salon visits, comparisons between Wavonne's locks and a Brillo Pad are not exactly unwarranted.

"I've never heard of this Jamaican coconut oil stuff. You'd—"

"Castor oil," Wavonne corrects.

"Whatever," Latasha says. "If you don't have any luck with that, I'd recommend Monique's Crème De Curl and her taming balm. We sell the Crème De Curl like crazy. In fact, my stylists and I sold more of it than any other salon in Maryland . . . well, except for one . . . apparently Salon Soleil in Upper Marlboro was her number one seller. I hear the owner, Odessa Thornton, is a personal friend of Monique's."

"Who is this Monique woman?" I ask again.

My question, for the second time, gets lost in Wavonne and Latasha's exchange.

"I've heard of Odessa and Salon Soleil. My girl Melva gets her high bun with a twist done there. It's supposedly off-the-chain luxurious, but you can't get an appointment there to save your life. Melva says that Odessa can *throw down* with a hot comb . . . booked solid through Christmas. I called there. . . ." Wavonne lets her voice trail off as her blabbermouth self realizes she is about to commit a cardinal beauty shop offense by admitting that she was trying to secure an appointment with another stylist. "I called there . . . you know . . . once . . . just *once* when you were on vacation, and I needed my roots touched up."

"Only once, eh?" Latasha questions. "It couldn't wait until I got back?" she asks with a chuckle just to give Wavonne a hard time.

"I don't know. Maybe I had a hot date or somethin' . . . and all my wigs were at the cleaners."

Latasha grins, decides to let Wavonne off the hook, and returns to talk of hair care products. "Well, if you want to go sans wigs more often, you really should try Monique's Crème De Curl. It's meant for curls, but it's a great cream even for relaxed hair like yours. I'll give you a discount on your first bottle."

"Girl, you've already sold enough of Monique's swag to get a visit from her. You don't need to be pushin' her potions on me. Girlfriend does make some good stuff, though." Wavonne pauses for a moment. "Monique Dupree. Comin' here."

"If someone doesn't tell me who this Monique Dupree person is . . ."

"How can you not know who she is, Halia?" Latasha questions, almost as if she's scolding me.

"Pay her no mind," Wavonne says. "Halia's idea of hair care products is some Suave shampoo and a can of Aqua Net."

"Monique is only about the biggest thing to happen in the world of African American hair since Jheri Redding invented the Jheri Curl."

"Oh my," I say. "I remember the Jheri Curl. Boy did people go through a lot of trouble to sport a greasy mop of damaged hair."

"I've seen photos of sistas with the Jheri Curl," Wavonne says. "I'm glad that mess was before my time."

"Call it what you want, and I know you weren't even out of the womb when it was popular," I say to her, "but, back in the day, once Michael Jackson showed it off on the cover of his *Thriller* album, everyone had to have one."

"Believe it or not, I still do Jheri Curls for a few of my customers. I don't think you can buy the actual Jheri Curl brand anymore, but there are other products with the same effect still available. I try to steer customers toward something more contemporary, but, in the end, it's *their* hair . . . you know, the 'customer is always right' and all that jazz. If they insist on looking the same way they did when DeBarge was topping the charts, so be it."

"Do you still use that greasy activator?"

"Yep."

"I had friends in high school with the Jheri Curl. Their hair was so slick it stained everything it came into contact with. Momma didn't even want them sitting on the sofa," I say.

"And it still stains like crazy, but on the plus side, it requires touching up fairly often, so, you know . . . cha-ching, cha-ching," Latasha says, making little cash register noises. "My 'Jheri Curlers,' as I call them, help me make the payments on my Lexus."

"I bet they do." I smile, before, once again, asking about this woman the two of them are so excited about. "So Monique sells beauty products?"

"Halia, you make it sound like she's an Avon Lady." Latasha points a finger toward the shelves by the reception desk. "That entire wall is full of Monique Dupree's line, Hair by Monique. I'm sure you'd recognize her if you saw her. Her infomercials run all the time. They're fun to watch even if you don't buy anything. She's always decked out in loud sparkly clothes, hocking her straightening cream and pomades while drinking martinis and gossiping about Hollywood big shots. She's even had some celebrities on . . . Solange, Robin Givens, Sanaa Lathan . . . that girl that was in one of the *Madea* movies . . ."

"So we're using the term 'celebrity' rather loosely?" I comment.

"Joke if you must, Halia," Wavonne says. "But Monique is the *real deal*. She's worth millions. I can't wait to meet her! What time should we come over on Friday? We'll even whip up some refreshments at Sweet Tea for your guests."

"We?" I ask, knowing that the only thing Wavonne knows how to "whip up" is a peanut butter sandwich.

"It's the least we . . . *you* can do for the chance to meet an icon," Wavonne says.

"If she really is all that, I guess I can put together a few treats if you like, Latasha."

"Are you kidding? I'd love that! And, who knows, maybe you'll get to plug Sweet Tea on television."

"What do you mean?"

"Oh . . . did I forget to mention that Monique is traveling with a camera crew. When she kicks off her *Wear It Straight* tour at the convention center this weekend, she'll be recording the event. Actually, she'll be recording her entire tour, including her stop here—supposedly to gather footage for her TV promotions. But, rumor has it, she is planning to make a documentary about her rise from junior stylist at a local Prince George's County HairPair to the reigning queen of exclusive beauty products for black women. Honestly, I think the whole thing is designed to revive Sleek, her relaxing cream. It's the product that drove her initial success, but as you've probably noticed, more and more sisters are going natural these days, and relaxer sales have been slumping."

"Who cares about the reason as long as we can get on TV!" Wavonne exclaims. "Oooh girl, I better pull Esther out from the wig box . . . this calls for one of my 'good' wigs."

"You have a wig named Esther?"

"I've got names for all my wigs. Esther's my best one . . . real human hair from Eastern Europe. Alma's real hair too, but not quite as nice. Maxine's my party wig . . . she's made of nylon or some synthetic somethin', but she cleans up well and goes clear down to my waist . . . pair her with one of my short sheath dresses and some platform booties, and I'm good for a night at the club. Gladys is more of an everyday wig . . . she's—"

"We'll be here all day, Wavonne," I say, visions of Wavonne's closet, stacked with wig boxes, coming to mind. "I'm sure you'll look very nice in whatever wig you decide to wear if you happen to get on camera." I turn my gaze to Latasha. "How many people are you expecting?"

"Forty or so . . . mostly regular clients. They are all very excited to meet Monique, and I'm sure they'll be thrilled to find that you've brought some of your culinary creations from Sweet Tea."

"I'll think about a menu this evening. We'll bring a nice spread for this *infamous* Monique and your other guests. I must admit I'm a little intrigued to meet her after hearing the two of you gush."

"Thank you, Halia. I think it will be a really nice event."

Latasha places a plastic cap over Wavonne's relaxer-coated head and steps over to me. She reaches for the dryer and curling brush and begins to blow out my hair. As the noise from the dryer halts our conversation I begin to think of what I'll prepare for the event with Ms. Dupree. I'm lost in thought about mini corn muffins with honey butter and chicken salad tartlets with candied pecans when she finally turns the dryer off and starts giving my hair a final once-over with a comb.

"Voilà," she says after giving my hair a light spray.

"Looks great," I compliment as she unsnaps the smock from around my neck.

Before getting up from the chair I take in my reflection. I'm not a beautiful woman . . . cute maybe . . . in a very unassuming way . . . although "cute" isn't really a word used to describe women like me who shop in the plus-size department and have been on the other side of forty for a few years now.

Much like Oprah, I knew early on that my currency in life was not going to be my looks. I'd like to think I'm reasonably attractive, but I've never been a head turner, and, although I enjoy getting gussied up for the infrequent special occasion, I've never really had a passionate interest in fashion . . . or makeup . . . or the latest hairstyles. I decided a long time ago I'd make my way in life with my smarts, a little personality, and a talent for cooking up some of the best soul food south of Sylvia's in Harlem.

As I rise from the chair, I think about how I used the word "unassuming" to describe myself. Then I look over at Wavonne, who's tapping away at her phone with one of her long red fingernails while Latasha removes the cap and runs a comb through her hair. "Unassuming" is so *not* a word I would use to describe Wavonne. Even with her hair lying flat against her scalp as the relaxer works its magic, she's still all flash and glitter—her face made up with a mix of loud eyeshadows, blush, and a shade of MAC lipstick she told me was called Russian Red. She's also sporting these things called double-stacked fake eyelashes. I'd never even heard of such things until she came home with them the other day, claiming they are the same type worn by Nicki Minaj.

Wavonne is on the tail end of her twenties. She's my cousin who has been living with Momma and me since adolescence, when social services deemed my aunt no longer fit to care for her. She has a good heart and I love her, but she's a handful. I employ her as a server at Sweet Tea, but work and Wavonne have never gotten along terribly well. If she weren't family, I'd have sacked her a long time ago.

I read a magazine while Latasha escorts Wavonne back to the sinks for the highly involved process of rinsing and neu-tralizing . . . and conditioning before leading her back to the styling chair. Once Latasha has dried and styled the freshly straightened hair, she removes Wavonne's smock to reveal a Rubenesque figure a size or two larger than mine in a pair of tight black jeans and a snug low-cut top that highlights Wavonne's ample cleavage.

I watch as Wavonne hops out of her chair onto a pair of pointy-toe pumps, which may have come from Payless or could be a designer brand she got off eBay or Craigslist. I can never tell with her purses, either. She buys knock-offs from street vendors, but she also procures "gently used" designer bags online . . . and I seem to remember her belonging to some silly club that lets women rent expensive handbags and trade them out for new ones every month.

"Ready to go to work?" I ask Wavonne as we gather our things and walk over to the reception desk with Latasha to pay the bill.

I look at my watch. It's almost ten thirty in the morning. Laura, my assistant manager, comes into the restaurant at eight, and Momma's probably been there since six doing her baking, but I'd still like to be there when we open in thirty minutes.

"I just got my hair done," Wavonne says. "I hate to waste my new 'do on a shift at Sweet Tea. I guess I'll just have to go out after work and show it off. Maybe I'll get some of the girls together, and we'll go have some drinks. Why don't you join us, Halia?"

I laugh. "Did you *just* meet me?" I ask. "When was the last time I went out for late night drinks on a Wednesday?"

"Live a little, Halia. There's more to life than making waffles and brewin' iced tea. And, Lord knows, you ain't gonna find no man hauled up in the kitchen at Sweet Tea all day every day."

"You *should* go out tonight, Halia, and show off your fresh cut," Latasha says.

"The only thing I'll be doing after work tonight is taking a quick shower and curling up with a good book . . . or a little late night TV."

"That's our girl," Wavonne says. "Party party party."

"I think you 'party party party' enough for both of us," I say, and hand Latasha my credit card, which she runs through the machine. I sign the receipt and give her a nice tip in cash. Then we say our good-byes and head toward the door with Wavonne, once again, grumbling about wasting her "new 'do" waiting tables at Sweet Tea.

Chapter 2

"Hi, Momma," I say as Wavonne and I enter the Sweet Tea kitchen. Five of her famous freshly iced butter pecan cakes are on display on the counter in front of her.

"Those look divine," I compliment, eyeing her creations—decadent cakes made with apple sauce, cinnamon, and finely chopped pecans, which Momma covers with a whipped frosting made from butter, confectioners' sugar, and a touch of cooked caramel.

"They smell good too," I hear Wavonne say while I take a quick spin around the kitchen and greet some of my staff as they busily prepare to open the Sweet Tea doors in a few minutes.

"Thank you, Wavonne," Momma says. "How about giving me a hand with them? If you can finish smoothing out the base icing, I'll go behind you and pipe some final swirls on the top."

"Only if I get to slice into one of these bad boys when we're done."

"Those are for *customers*, Wavonne," I scold, stepping over to the sink to wash my hands. "Why don't you help Tacy with the cornbread?" I nod at Tacy, one of my prep cooks, who's on the other side of the kitchen pouring corn-meal into a large stainless steel mixing bowl. "I'll give Momma a hand with the cakes."

Wavonne groans at me and gives the cakes another look before stepping away. "Maybe we can get Aunt Celia to bake a few of these for Latasha's little soirée on Friday."

"Latasha? Your hairdresser?" Momma asks. "What soirée?"

"Latasha's hosting a little meet and greet thing with some lady that supplies hair care products for her salon," I say casually. "Wavonne volunteered me to make some refreshments."

"Some lady?" Wavonne calls as she lifts the lid off a tub of sour cream and hands it to Tacy, who then adds it to the cornmeal. "She's not *some* lady, Halia. She's Monique Dupree. She's—"

"Monique Dupree?!" Momma asks. "You mean the Monique Dupree of Hair by Monique? That Monique Dupree?"

"None other."

"Oh, I *love* her!" Momma says. "She was on TV last night after my *Living Single* reruns. She's so bubbly and fun. I've been using her relaxer . . . and shampoo and leave-in conditioner for years."

"Really? Well, Wavonne and Latasha seem very excited about her visit."

"Rightfully so. She's lovely . . . so full of energy." Momma scoops some frosting into a pastry bag and gives it a few good twists to keep any from coming out the back end. "She built a hugely successful business from the ground up and"— Momma lifts her eyes from the little drop flowers she's piping along the outer edge of one of the cakes and steadies her gaze on me—"even *she* still found time to get a husband. If Monique Dupree can run a multimillion-dollar beauty empire and still land a man, one would think you could find some time to work on doing the same."

"Yes, Momma," I sigh, not looking up from the spatula in my hand. "I'll get right on that 'finding a man' thing just as soon as I can. But, at the moment, I've got a restaurant to open for the day." I step closer to her and change the subject. "These cakes really do look gorgeous. I bet we sell out." My words are offered mostly to distract Momma and get her to shut up about the lack of any romance in my life, but I mean them just the same. Momma really is a talented baker, and I'm grateful every day that she agreed, so many years ago, to make the desserts for Sweet Tea. And I'm even *more* grateful that she comes in very early to create her delights and is usually gone from the restaurant shortly after I arrive for the day. I love Momma, but I already share a house with her and Wavonne. I'd been out of my parents' house for years when I agreed to move back in about fifteen years ago when Wavonne came to live with Momma a few years after Daddy died. Wavonne was too much for her to handle alone, and the two of us have been trying to keep her out of trouble ever since. Between us living together and our few overlapping hours at Sweet Tea each day, during which I get an earful about my lack of a husband (and Momma's lack of any grandchildren), I get more than enough "Momma time."

Sometimes I worry that, at her advanced age, it's too much responsibility for her—to come in six days a week and be on her feet all morning preparing the desserts that make my customers swoon. But she shows no signs of or interest in slowing down anytime soon and claims that baking keeps her young . . . it also adds to her many means of keeping tabs on me and my goings-on.

"I think we'll have enough desserts to go around. I made red velvet cupcakes and apple cobbler this morning, too. And we have a few slices of sour cream coconut cake left over from yesterday."

"Red velvet cupcakes," Wavonne calls to Momma from

the other side of the kitchen. "That's what you should make for Latasha's reception on Friday."

"I don't think I'm inclined to make *anything* unless I'm extended an invitation to attend the gathering," Momma decrees.

"I'm sure Latasha won't mind if you come," Wavonne offers. "Especially if you bring some desserts."

"I'll call Latasha and let her know there will be three of us attending."

"Oh how fun," Momma says. "I'm going to meet Monique Dupree and get to tell her how much I love her products."

"Speakin' of products, I hope she brings some freebees. I could use some of that stylin' milk I saw her hockin' on TV last week . . . and some of her hair butter, too," Wavonne says.

"Styling milk? Hair butter?" I ask. "Why do her products sound like they belong in the dairy aisle at the Harris Teeter?"

"That shouldn't be any surprise," Wavonne remarks. "She got her start whippin' up creams and potions from ingredients in her kitchen . . . right here in Prince George's County, Maryland."

"Is that so?"

"Have you honestly never heard her rags to riches story?" Wavonne asks. "She's always talkin' about it on her infomercials . . . those things run on late night TV all the freakin' time. Many nights, after I watch me some *Martin* or *Bernie Mac* reruns, I'll click around and come across Monique peddling her wares. She's usually doin' a demo of one of her products and talkin' about her bygone days as a local hairdresser and her bygone nights sitting at the kitchen table testin' hair remedies."

"It was the topic of conversation last night while she was running a hot comb through a model's hair, showing off one of her conditioners . . . or her pressing oil . . . I don't remember. She—"

Wavonne cuts Momma off. "Aunt Celia, you act like Halia knows what pressin' oil is. She ain't never used a hot comb in her life."

Momma laughs. "She got that naturally straight hair from her late father's side of the family," she says while both she and Wavonne enviously eye my hair.

"I know what pressing oil is, Wavonne, but never mind about that. You were saying about Monique?"

"That she got her start making hair creams in her kitchen. Her first conditioner was made from avocados and honey . . . and yogurt, I think . . . or sour cream."

"That must have smelled nice on a hot day."

"Hush, Halia," Momma says. "Sleek, her flagship relaxer—the one I've used for years—still has avocado and olive oil in it. Leaves my hair really soft." Momma pauses for a moment and looks up from her pastry bag. "Oh, I simply can't wait to meet her! What do you think I should prepare, Halia?"

"I think cupcakes or tartlets would work out well."

"Maybe my pink lemonade cupcakes . . . or red velvet like Wavonne suggested. I've been toying with a chocolate bourbon pecan pie, but the recipe is not quite ready for prime time . . . still tweaking that one."

"Your chocolate marshmallow cake is always a hit. Why don't you use that recipe and make cupcakes with it?"

"Hmm . . . maybe . . . I wish I knew what Monique liked. I think I'll do some research and see if she's mentioned some food preferences in any interviews. I know she likes cocktails. She's always sipping those on TV, but I've never—"

Momma stops midsentence as she and I both take note of Wavonne, who has abandoned her duty assisting Tacy and is pulling jars from the shelves—mayonnaise, honey, coconut oil—and plopping them down on the counter. She's doing something she typically does not do—*hurry*—which has both

Momma and me perplexed. I'm sure Momma, like myself, is wondering why Wavonne, who only moves quickly when things like discounted shoes or all-you-can-eat buffets are involved, is scurrying around the kitchen.

"What are you doing?" I ask as she scuttles toward the walk-in refrigerator and opens the door. She doesn't answer as she steps inside and quickly emerges with some avocados and Greek yogurt.

"Monique hit it big making her own hair care products, right?" Wavonne places the avocados and yogurt on the counter. "We've got a whole kitchen full of stuff that's good for hair. I'm gonna concoct somethin' for Monique's visit and sell her the formula," she says, opening one of the jars in front of her and looking under the counter for a bowl.

I'm about to reprimand her, remind her that we are about to open, and tell her to make hair potions on her own time, but I figure she'll lose interest once the first batch of whatever she's throwing together is a bust and move on to the next thing.

Momma and I take a break from finishing up the butter pecan cakes to stand and watch the spectacle that is "Wavonne on a Mission." I see her dump a heaping tablespoon of mayonnaise into the bowl and squeeze in some honey. As she starts to slice into the avocado I have the same thought I have at the start of most of my dates: *This is not going to end well.*

Chapter 3

"What is that foul odor?" Momma asks as we step outside the restaurant on a chilly October afternoon.

"I don't know." I scrunch up my nose. "It smells like a can of opened cat food that's been sitting out too long."

"I think you need to call the property management company. Maybe that trash can needs to be emptied." Momma nods her head in the direction of one of the small receptacles dotted along the front of the shopping center that houses Sweet Tea.

"I'll call Tacy from the salon and ask him to empty it. It could be hours if we wait on the leasing company to take care of it," I respond, before turning my attention to Wavonne. "Be careful with those," I say to her. "I don't want you dropping them." She's carrying a tray of deviled mini potatoes as we hurry toward Illusions with the refreshments for the Monique Dupree Welcome Party. The salon is a few doors down from Sweet Tea, so we're only going a short distance, but Wavonne, unsteadily teetering along the sidewalk in a pair of high heels while holding my carefully crafted hors d'oeuvres, is making me nervous.

I thought her towering shoes were peach, but Wavonne corrected me and instructed that they are "coral" in color—one could argue whether or not the shoes are peach or coral, but I think all would agree that they are *absurd*. They are open-toe with a series of straps that start behind her brightly painted red toenails and go well past her ankle. She's paired them with a snug mint-colored minidress adorned with a zipper that runs from the plunging V-neck to the hemline—one unzip and all of Wavonne's voluptuous "parts" would spring out like a jack-in-the-box. Oddly, she is without a wig this afternoon, and her God-given hair is styled in a much more subdued fashion than usual.

"Your hair looks nice, Wavonne," I say even though that is not entirely true. It *is* an improvement from her usual teased-up styles, but, even slicked back behind her ears (a sort of "wet look") you can tell that her hair has tussled a few too many times with do-it-yourself Dark and Lovely relaxers.

"You think so?" Wavonne asks, a hopeful tone in her voice.

"Of course. It's very chic."

"It's my own hair potion . . . perfected it last night."

"Is that what all the racket was in the kitchen after I went to bed?"

"Sorry. I had to run the food processor to grate the carrots."

"Carrots?"

"Uh-huh. I was makin' carrot oil. I saw online that it's good for your hair."

"I wasn't aware you even knew how to work the food processor."

"I figured it out. It ain't that hard."

"You left a mess on the counter," Momma offers, walking along behind Wavonne and me with two brown butter lemon poppy seed cakes, stacked, one upon the other, in plastic cake carriers. I'm toting a tray of spicy crab balls to go with the potatoes in Wavonne's hands and the cheese puffs I dropped off at the salon about an hour ago.

"I'll clean it up when we get home," Wavonne moans. "I was too tired by the time I finally got it right last night."

"So what is it that you finally got right?"

"I made my own smoothing cream with coconut oil, avocado, carrot oil, eggs, and some apple cider vinegar . . . and a hair gel from some gelatin and olive oil. I dampened my hair a little bit with water, worked in some of the smoothing cream with my fingers, and then brushed in the gel to slick it back." Wavonne turns and looks at Momma and me. "Looks pretty fly, eh?"

"Looks pretty 'like it might attract some flies,' " Momma says under her breath to me before adding, louder and uncomfortably, "Yes, it's very . . . um . . . yes . . . *fly*." Momma looks down from Wavonne's hair to her dress. "How about pulling that zipper up a little higher, honey? You're one wrong move away from a . . . what are they calling it these days? A wardrobe malfunction?"

"Fine." Wavonne lifts the zipper between her cleavage about a millimeter. "I do want to stand out from the crowd, but it's my *hair* I want on parade this afternoon, not my bazoombas . . . lovely as they are."

"Your hair?"

"Yes. I want Monique to ask about it, so I can tell her about my concoctions. Who knows, she may want to buy the formula."

"Wavonne, she probably has a team of chemists at her disposal. I don't think she's going to be interested in some mush you threw together in the food processor," I advise as we approach the entrance to Illusions.

"I'm still getting that smell," Momma says before Wavonne has a chance to respond to my comment.

"It must not have been the trash can over by Sweet Tea if we're smelling it all the way over here. What do you suppose it is?" I ask while balancing my chaffing dish of crab balls on my hip freeing up a hand to open the salon door.

I hold it open and Momma walks through followed by Wavonne : . . and that's when I realize where the dreadful odor is coming from. As Wavonne patters through the door past me the highly unpleasant scent wafts to my nostrils.

"Wavonne!" I say in a strong whisper as I step inside. "It's your hair."

"What's my hair?"

"It's your hair that stinks."

"It does not! I don't smell nothin'."

"Well, you're the only one," Momma says. "You can't meet Ms. Dupree with your hair smelling like the cheese section at Wegman's."

"No, she can't," I agree. "That ingenious purée of oils and vegetables you put on your head has started to spoil, Wavonne. Fortunately, we're at a salon. You can wash your hair before Monique gets here."

"I ain't washin' nothin'. It doesn't smell that bad."

I'm about to insist that Wavonne walk herself to one of the shampoo chairs pronto, when Latasha approaches. "Hey, ladies," she says to me and Wavonne, before greeting Momma. "Mrs. Watkins, so good to see you. What have you got there?" she asks in reference to the cake containers in Momma's hands.

"Two of my special—"

Before Momma can finish her sentence, I see Latasha's eyebrows narrow. "Something smells . . . um, I'm sure it can't be your food, Halia . . . but . . . do you smell that?"

"Smell what?" Wavonne takes a few steps back from Latasha.

"What do you mean *what*? It smells like the dumpster behind Long John Silver's." Latasha looks around. "My God. I hope there isn't a gas leak on today of all days."

"There's no gas leak, Latasha," I assure. "Wavonne was experimenting with some homemade hair creams last night and tried a sample of her creations today. Clearly, the formula still needs a little work . . . maybe some preservatives. But she's going to wash it out before Monique gets here." I shift my eyes in Wavonne's direction. "Aren't you?"

"You heifers go ahead and hate, but I'm still perfectin' my miracle creams. Don't expect me to share any of my millions with the likes of you when I sell the formula to Monique."

"Unless she's looking for something to attract mosquitoes, I wouldn't start counting my money just yet, Wavonne," I say. "Now go wash it out. I don't want that stench around my food."

"I can't wash it out. I don't have any of my wigs, and I can't get my hair restyled before Monique gets here . . . and how am I gonna sell her my formula if I can't show her how well it works?"

"Wavonne, sweetie," Latasha says, "Monique Dupree, the *queen of all things hair*, is paying a visit to my salon . . . *my* salon." Her tone is measured, but there is no doubt that she means business. "You're a good friend and a good customer, but I will not have you smelling like a carton of spoiled milk in her presence." She pauses for a moment, before adding, "You head back to the sinks, or you head out the door."

Wavonne lets out a heavy breath, rolls her eyes, and reluctantly creeps toward the back of the salon.

"Just go have a seat," Latasha calls behind her. "Kerry will wash it for you as soon as she's done helping us set up . . . then we'll find you a hat . . . or turban . . . or *something*."

Chapter 4

Latasha's VIP clients begin to trickle in, and their excitement around meeting this Monique Dupree woman, someone I'd never even heard of a few days ago, is palpable. While Latasha greets her guests, I work with Kerry, one of the shampoo girls at Illusions, to get the refreshments table ready. Once all the trays of hors d'oeuvres are in place, I light the little tins of ethanol gel underneath them to keep everything hot and help Momma transfer her cakes from their travel containers to the table. I'm rearranging some napkins when I notice Latasha's staff members and clients rush toward the front windows.

"Oh my God!" I hear someone say. "Look at that!"

Curiosity gets the best of me, and I scurry toward the windows with everyone else and take a look outside. I hadn't given much thought to the mode of transportation in which Monique would arrive at Illusions, but, if I had, I would have guessed a limo or maybe a black SUV. Apparently, I would have guessed wrong . . . *very* wrong. As we look through the glass panes we are treated to a sizable bright pink tour bus winding its way through the parking lot on no fewer than ten wheels. It must be over twelve feet high and maybe forty or fifty feet long. Monique Dupree's face is plastered on the side of the bus along with the Hair by Monique logo and the words WEAR IT STRAIGHT!

The bus comes to a stop across a row of parking spaces, and we eagerly look on as the door flips open, and a stocky man with a professional video camera steps out from the vehicle. He takes a few long strides before turning to face the bus and focus his camera on the door from which he just emerged. He holds the camera's focus on the empty bus stairs, and, just when you think no one or no thing could compete with the brilliance of the brightly colored vehicle, a figure that can't possibly be anyone other than Ms. Dupree appears in the threshold. My eyes are first drawn to the glittering silver heels she uses to carefully descend from the bus like a First Lady disembarking *Air Force One*. Her flashy shoes complement an equally flamboyant knee-length black skirt with some sort of sparkle woven into the fabric. She completes the look with a white silk blouse and a wide silver belt that matches her shoes. It's a look that might appear a bit garish on some women, but the way Monique carries herself, while followed by an entourage of minions, lets any onlookers know that she wouldn't wear anything but the best.

She's a large woman in both height and stature—more thick than fat . . . the sort of woman Momma would call "big-boned." She's about five nine, but, at the moment, in her shimmering heels, she clears six feet. As she nears the salon, a wide smile never leaving her face, the cameraman walks backward in front of her, filming her every move. While she gives her fans an excited wave from the other side of the windows, I get a closer look at her jet-black hair, and, I must say, it is *fabulous*, falling in waves past her shoulders with long swept side bangs. I also get a better look at the big silver hoops dangling from her ears and what Wavonne would call some "serious bling" around her neck—a large pear-shaped red stone (I'm guessing a ruby) surrounded by what I assume to be pavé-set diamonds suspended from a silver chain.

The cameraman steps into the salon before Monique and continues to film as she crosses the threshold to be greeted by Latasha.

"Welcome to Illusions, Ms. Dupree. It's truly an honor to meet you," Latasha says, extending her hand.

"Girl, I don't do handshakes," Monique says in a boisterous voice before leaning in and giving Latasha a hug followed by a kiss on each cheek. "You must be Latasha." She pulls away and warmly grips Latasha's hands. "What a lovely space you have here. No wonder you're a top seller of Hair by Monique. You're gorgeous . . . your salon is gorgeous. . . ." She turns her attention from Latasha to the rest of us. "And your clients are gorgeous."

Monique removes her wide-rimmed sunglasses, revealing kind eyes below expertly painted lids and lush fake lashes. "Hello, everyone," she says, easily taking command of the room without waiting for an introduction. "I look forward to meeting each of you and personally thanking you for making my Hair by Monique line such a success. I'm nothing without your support." She looks down at her clothes and shoes before extending her arms as if she's presenting herself to the crowd. "As Dolly Parton says, 'It costs a lot of money to look this cheap.'" She pauses while the crowd laughs and takes us all in. "It's good to be home. You guys know I'm a local girl, don't you? Born and raised right her in PG County. That's right . . . I hung out at PG Plaza after school, went to the movies over at Andrews Manor . . . I even ran the blender at the Orange Julius in Landover Mall while I was in cosmetology school."

You occasionally hear about how some people have "presence," but, until now, I'm not sure I had ever met anyone who actually had such a thing. She definitely has an *energy* . . . an *aura* about her that makes people instantly like her. Though larger than life with her perfect hair and makeup, flamboyant fashions, and expensive jewelry she somehow still comes across as unpretentious and relatable.

Latasha escorts Monique through the crowd and introduces her to her customers and employees, who, along with Momma and me, have formed a makeshift receiving line. While Momma and I patiently wait for our introduction to Monique, my eyes shift toward the gentlemen who followed her into the salon. There is a handsome, though somewhat gruff-looking black man with a neatly trimmed Afro and a solid build. He's wearing a conservative dark suit and appears to be giving directions to the cameraman. The other man in Ms. Dupree's entourage is a portly white man with heavily gelled light hair. He straddles the line between stylish and ridiculous in a pair of tight patterned pants that I would call "leggings" if they were on a woman, a purple sweater with black trim, and a pair of shiny black boots with purple buckles. I can't help but stare at his quirky footwear for a moment or two before diverting my attention back to Monique, watching her move from person to person. I'm listening as she graciously expresses her gratitude for her fans' support, when a familiar, though unpleasant, odor begins to waft around me. The scent has barely had a chance to register when Wavonne wedges herself between Momma and me.

"Good grief, Wavonne!" I say. "Latasha told you to stay back there until we can get your hair washed."

"I ain't missin' my chance to meet Monique."

I'm about to insist that Wavonne return to the rear of the salon when Latasha and Monique appear before us.

"This is Halia Watkins," Latasha says. "She is responsible for the fabulous refreshments on hand today."

"So nice to meet you," Monique says, and reaches out to

hug me, a gesture that seems a bit intimate from someone I've never met before, but if anyone can get away with such a thing, it's Monique.

"And this is Wavonne." Latasha hesitates for a moment, clearly unnerved to see that Wavonne has defied her instructions. "She's been a loyal customer for years." Latasha keeps a stiff smile, but simultaneously shoots Wavonne a potent glare, the kind a mother gives a petulant child when she is misbehaving in public . . . one that says, "I can't whoop your ass right now because there are witnesses, but just you wait until we get home."

Monique leans in to embrace Wavonne, and the smile she's been wearing since she stepped off the bus abruptly disappears. "What is that odor?" she asks, looking around the room for an angry skunk. "My God! It smells like Bourbon Street during Mardi Gras."

Chapter 5

Wavonne leans in toward Monique. "Girl, the smell is rank, ain't it? I think it's comin' from sista girl over there." Wavonne directs her eyes toward one of Latasha's stylists. "Now why, when we have all that good food on the refreshments table, did she go and wolf down a tuna fish sandwich and some Doritos? Somebody best get her a breath mint before we *all* pass out."

Monique narrows her brows and offers Wavonne a bemused nod. She is about to continue down the line when Wavonne, fearful she may miss her only chance to engage Monique, blurts out, "Do you like my hair?"

Monique takes a step back and gives Wavonne's hair a look. "Ummm . . . *hmmm* . . . it's quite . . . quite *slick*."

"Thank you! I invented my own cream."

"Really?"

"Yes. And my own gel, too. Pretty nice, huh?"

"Um . . . well, it's *unique*."

"It's a secret formula," Wavonne boasts, lightly patting her hair. "But, you know, I might be willing to share it for the right price."

Monique laughs graciously. "Is that so? Well, I wish you

much luck with it." Monique places a finger under her nose and lifts her eyebrows as another rush of the unpleasant aroma radiates from Wavonne's head. "I might suggest adding some rosemary oil extract . . . or vitamin E to that secret formula. They will help keep it . . . keep it from . . . *turning*," she adds, her eyes rapidly blinking as one's eyes do when they begin to water.

"What a great idea. Maybe Wavonne can try out her potions another time after she's made them a bit more . . . shall we say *shelf-stable*," Latasha suggests before calling to the shampoo girl. "Kerry, can you take Wavonne back to the sinks and freshen her up a bit. *Now*, please."

"But I haven't had a chance to tell Monique about—"

"*Now!*" Latasha insists through clenched teeth.

"It was very nice to meet you, Wavonne. You keep working on your creams," Monique says right before Kerry gives Wavonne a tug on her arm, and she grudgingly allows herself, much like a cat on a leash, to be led toward the washbasins.

"Good Lord, that girl is stubborn," Latasha says to me while Monique proceeds down the line to Momma.

"You have *no* idea."

Latasha is about to introduce Monique to Momma, when the man in the suit who followed Monique into the salon brusquely invades our space with the cameraman following. Based on the way he's been milling about the store and giving direction to the videographer, I assume he is the de facto director of whatever it is Monique is trying to capture on film. Rather than introducing himself or saying hello, he simply points at me and spouts off to the cameraman, "This one. She has nice hair. Let's get some footage."

Next thing I know there is a microphone in my face and Monique, who I notice already has a lapel microphone on her blouse, goes into reporter mode. With the camera centered on us, she slides closer to me and puts her arm around my waist.

"Hello to all of my Hair by Monique fans," she begins. "We are kicking off my cross-country Wear It Straight tour here in the Washington, DC, metro area. Today we're at Illusions in Prince George's County, Maryland."

I notice that the director fellow is holding up a cue card of sorts with the words "Illusions" and "Prince George's County, Maryland" printed on it as if Monique needs reminding of where she is. I guess this makes sense, given that she will be visiting hundreds of salons all over the country, but you'd think she'd remember where she is while in her hometown.

"This is my new friend Halia," Monique says just after the director flips to another cue card with my name on it. I didn't even know he was within earshot when I was introduced to Monique, but it must be his job to keep track of names for her as well.

Monique turns toward me. "You have truly exquisite hair. So soft and silky. What Hair by Monique products do you use?"

"Oh . . . umm . . . I keep it simple . . . a little Johnson's Baby Shampoo and some conditioner that was on sale at CVS . . . Pantene, I think. Sometimes I add a little—"

"Cut!" yells the director, a cross expression on his face. "Halia, is it?" There is clear annoyance in his tone. "*What* are you doing here if you don't use Hair by Monique products?"

"Relax, Nathan," Monique says. "I've been told that Halia supplied the refreshments for the event." Nathan looks at Monique crossly—the way a mother might look at a child that just got smart with her. And, just for a second, I sense a crack in Monique's jovial veneer.

"Yes," Latasha says. "Halia owns her own restaurant . . . Mahalia's Sweet Tea, a few doors down from here. Best soul food in town. She kindly prepared a few treats for us."

Nathan is not impressed and, rather than expressing any enthusiasm or gratitude for my catering, he points to Momma. "Who's that? She has nice hair as well. Does *she* use Hair by Monique products?"

"This is Halia's mother and baker extraordinaire, Celia Watkins. Wait until you try her brown butter lemon poppy seed cake," Latasha says.

"*Butter* and *cake*. Two of my favorite words," Monique replies, leaning in toward Momma for a hug. "Lovely to meet you, Celia."

"We're not here for a bake sale," Nathan bemoans, his eyes going from Momma to me and then back to Momma again. "Hmmm . . . a mother and daughter, both with nice hair, raving about Hair by Monique. Now that would be some great marketing." He waves his hands at Momma and me. "Can you make some space for Monique in the middle?" He says this in the form of a question, but it's really more of a command. "We'll have Monique ask you a few questions. We merely need you to gush about her products. You," he says to me as Monique slides in between Momma and me. "You'll say how much you love her thickening and texturizing mousse. And you," he barks at Momma. "You'll rave about her deep moisturizing shampoo."

"I actually use Ms. Dupree's moisturizing shampoo . . . and her relaxer and restoring conditioner," Momma says. "I've got a bathroom full of Hair by Monique products."

"Perfect. Mention them all. We can edit it down later."

"Maybe it's best if Momma does this alone," I say. "I'm not sure I'd know what to say. I'm certain they are very nice products, but I've never used that mousse you mentioned."

Nathan sighs. "It's not rocket science, lady. Just say you've been using it for years . . . that you love the product . . . that it leaves your hair soft and shiny with lots of body, blah blah blah."

"I think I have to pass," I say flatly, in part because I don't want to make up lies about a product I've never used, but more because this Nathan guy is rude and condescending.

"Ignore him, Halia. Nathan went missing the day God was handing out manners," Monique says, getting yet another heated look from Nathan. "How about I have my own personal stylist give your hair a quick touch-up with some of my products. Then you'll have an idea of how good they are and can offer some honest comments." She then calls to her associate in the purple shirt and man-leggings. "Maurice," she beckons toward the other side of the reception area. Maurice walks toward us, and, without waiting for me to agree to her plan, Monique says to him, "Can you give Halia here a quick style? Maybe work in a little frizz-free mousse, quickly blow it out, and give it some staying power with my flexible hold spray."

Maurice says nothing before reaching for my hair, separating a few strands, and running his fingers through them. "How much time do I have?" he asks, a displeased expression on his face. "I can take it to a B-minus in about twenty minutes, but it would be hours to take it to an A-plus." He turns to me. "No offense, sweetie. Your hair is very nice, but you know the ole saying: 'I'm a beautician, not a magician.'"

Before I have a chance to say that I, in fact, am not familiar with that saying, Monique intervenes. "Don't be so dramatic, Maurice. She has lovely hair. Just give it a quick restyle for the camera."

"Fine, fine," Maurice sighs, and looks at me. "Come with me. Holly, was it?"

"Halia," I correct as I follow him back to one of the chairs.

"Like 'hell yeah?'" He snaps his fingers.

"Um . . . no. Like *Halia*. It's short for Mahalia."

"Oh . . . like the gospel singer. Mahalia Jackson. Got it. They were playing a remix of 'Respect' at the club last night."

"That's Aretha Franklin."

"Huh . . . I guess you're right." He stops next to a vacant styling chair. "This one is as good as any."

He gestures for me to sit in the chair, looks around, and raises his voice to no one in particular. "Can I get a smock, please?"

Kerry, who has finished combing out Wavonne's freshly shampooed hair, rushes over with a cape and snaps it around my neck. "May I get you anything else?" she asks.

"Ummm . . ." Maurice starts rifling through the tools on the counter. "I suppose I can make do with this . . . this *paraphernalia*," he adds with an upturned nose. "Can you bring me some of Monique's mousse? The frizz-free . . . not the texturizing."

"I didn't realize people used mousse anymore. I thought it was a thing of the eighties," I say.

"Monique has reformulated it and brought it back. It's nothing like the canned fluff from back in the day. Monique's mousse adds volume and calms frizz without making your hair crunchy. You'll love it."

As Maurice begins spritzing my hair with a water mist sprayer, I see Wavonne's curious reflection in the mirror.

"Oh Lord . . . here we go," I say quietly as she gets up from the shampoo chair and walks over, clearly wanting to know what's going on and how she can become a part of it.

"What's happening over here?" she asks, finally free of any offensive odors.

Maurice ignores Wavonne as he runs a comb through my now-damp hair and grabs a bottle of what I guess is Monique's frizz-free mousse from Kerry.

"Maurice is giving my hair a quick style. Monique wants to

interview Momma and me about her products. I guess Maurice is trying to make me presentable for the camera."

"Camera?!" Wavonne says. "I wanna be on camera. How do I get in on this?" she asks Maurice.

"And you are?" Maurice inquires, dispensing a dollop of fluffy white mousse into his hand and beginning to work it into my hair.

"Wavonne. Wavonne Hix. I'm Halia's cousin. We brought the food."

Maurice momentarily takes his eyes off my hair and turns toward Wavonne. He runs his hand down the side of her head to feel her hair. "Oh sweetie, we're trying to promote Monique's products. Not have them banned in all fifty states."

Wavonne's mouth drops, but before she has a chance to offer Maurice a few choice words, he makes a peace offering. "I'm only joking," he says. "Your hair is quite . . . well . . . it has . . . *potential*. We simply need to get you on a program . . . some keratin, some emollients, some hot oil treatments . . . there's hope for you yet. We'll talk later."

"So you and Aunt Celia get to be on TV, and I don't?"

"I'm afraid it looks that way, Wavonne."

"Maybe we can work you in somehow," Maurice says. "We'll put you under a dryer and say you're in the middle of a deep conditioning or something. Now run along and find Maurice a cocktail, would you?" Maurice says before flicking the switch on the dryer and beginning to blow out my freshly moussed hair.

I watch in the mirror as Wavonne weighs her options. She doesn't like taking orders from anyone, so, under normal circumstances, she would likely tell Maurice to go get his own damn cocktail. But he has offered to work her into Monique's video and possibly help her with her hair, so perhaps she has decided to keep herself on his good side . . . or maybe it's only because there is no point in her protesting any further as even her loud mouth can't compete with the roar of the hair dryer. But, for whatever reason, Wavonne refrains from making any biting replies and departs in search of an adult beverage for Maurice.

Chapter 6

"Wow," I say, marveling at my newly styled hair, thanks to that certain "way" stylists have with a circular brush and a hair dryer. It's not like I don't have a collection of brushes and my own dryer at home, but no matter what acrobatics I put myself through when combing out my hair, it never looks as good as when a professional stylist does it.

"Much better," Maurice says while spraying my hair, using a bottle with the Hair by Monique logo on it that reads "Flex Finish Style Lock." He's unsnapping my cape when Wavonne reappears with a glass of champagne and hands it to Maurice. "This is the closest thing I could find to a cocktail."

"I was hoping for a dirty martini, but I guess this will have to do." Maurice takes the flute from Wavonne and quickly gulps down its contents. "Only the one?" he asks, then lifts the empty glass toward me. "You may want to down a few of these too before going on camera with Nathan directing. A glass or two of bubbly will make dealing with him slightly more bearable."

I hop out of the chair. "He isn't terribly pleasant, is he?"

"I've met angry pit bulls that are more enjoyable to be

around," Maurice says as Wavonne and I follow him toward the front of the salon where Nathan and the cameraman have been filming Monique's interactions with Latasha's staff and clients.

"I've done what I can," he says to Nathan. "This is as camera-ready as I can get her in the time allotted."

Nathan nods at Maurice, and, after he calls Monique over to join us, I hear him say, "Where's the old lady?"

"I'd thank you not to refer to my mother as an old lady," I reprimand, even though I guess it is a technically accurate term. Momma is a lady, and she is old.

"Your mother then? Where is she?"

"Momma?" I call over toward the refreshment table where Momma is slicing her lemon cake and putting it on plates. "Let's do this. I need to get back to the restaurant."

After Momma makes her way toward us, Nathan tells us where and how he'd like us to stand, what products to plug, and reminds us to look at the cue cards if we have any trouble remembering the names of the items he wants us to mention.

"Time is money, people. Time is money," he says before filming begins.

Once he shuts up, the camera starts rolling, and Monique begins asking us questions, things move along with relative ease. Monique, clearly a pro at this sort of thing, makes us feel comfortable and knows how to phrase a question to get the answer she wants, which makes things pretty simple for Momma and me. I talk about the volume that Monique's mousse gave my hair while keeping it soft and, at Monique's urging, Momma gives a run-through of her morning hair routine and all the Hair by Monique products involved. Ultimately, our product-plugging interview turns out to be fairly painless and is over in less than ten minutes.

"You did great, ladies," Monique says while Nathan fails to comment on our performance at all. "I say we turn the camera off for a few minutes, so I can check out some of these refreshments I keep hearing about."

Momma and I lead Monique toward the assortment of treats, and I hand her a plate.

"Oh my, I shouldn't partake. I could barely get this skirt buttoned this morning, but it all looks so good. I'll just have a little taste." Monique starts adding items to her plate. "A little taste of these," she says grabbing a few spicy crab balls. "And a little taste of these." She picks up three deviled potatoes. "And I *have* to have a little taste of these," she adds, lifting several cheese balls from their tray. "Oh my! What do we have here?" she asks when she comes upon Momma's cake. "I certainly can't miss out on a little taste of this," she announces, using a pair of tongs to reach for a slice of cake. "Girl," she says to me. "In one afternoon, you're going to take me from a size twelve to an Old Navy–size twelve with all these goodies."

"You'd look lovely at any size," Momma says.

"Wow. This is heavenly," Monique says, bypassing the more savory hors d'oeuvres and diving right into the cake. "So moist and lemony . . . and this *glaze*! I may need to pack a few slices of this to go . . . you know, for a *friend*," she adds with a laugh before addressing Momma individually. "So you are the baker?"

"Yes. It's been a hobby of mine for years, and, when Halia opened Sweet Tea, I came on board to make the desserts."

"Sweet Tea sounds fabulous although I may need to bring a seamstress along to let out the waistline of my clothes while I eat."

I chuckle. "We'd love for you to come by sometime."

"You must try it," Latasha says, appearing next to us and starting to fix herself a plate of food. "All of this is only a sampling of the yummy food Halia makes at Sweet Tea. You have not lived until you've tried her sour cream cornbread."

"I do love cornbread."

"Why don't you have dinner there tonight?" Latasha suggests.

"Much as I'd love to, I don't think I can work it out tonight. I have another salon to visit, and my personal chef already has dinner in the works back at my house. Maybe I can squeeze a visit in after the hair convention wraps, and I'm back in town after the tour."

"Of course," I say. "You're welcome whenever you can make it. We may not have my smothered pork chops on special like we do tonight, but we'll have something equally good."

"Smothered pork chops?" Monique asks.

"Served with homemade biscuits," I entice.

"Oh girl . . . no need to mention the biscuits . . . although they are a plus. You had me at smothered pork chops. I'll call Alex, my chef, and ask him to halt dinner preparations. How about we arrive at about seven? That will give me time to change into something with an elastic waistband."

"Perfect. If you can let me know how many people we should expect in your party, we'll have a table waiting for you."

"Well, me, Nathan, Maurice . . . and I guess I probably have to ask Odessa." She appears to have some distaste in her mouth when the name Odessa comes out of it. "She owns the next salon I'm going to . . . Salon Soleil. And I suppose I should ask Alex, since I put the kibosh on his meal preparations." She turns to Latasha. "And would you like to join us?"

"Absolutely. I don't turn away invites to Sweet Tea."

"Great. So that's six of us, right?"

"Yep. Would you like me to reserve a table for you in the back of the restaurant so you can be a bit discreet . . . so no one bothers you?"

"*Discreet*? Girl, Monique does not do discreet. Do you think I'd be wearing all this razzle dazzle, standing on six inches of heel, and have all this paint on my face if I was looking to be incognito?"

I laugh. "No, I guess not. We'll make sure your table is front and center."

"Sounds like a plan."

"Then it's all settled. We'll see you later this evening at Sweet Tea." I turn to Momma. "We should really get going. Where's Wavonne?"

"She's in the back under a dryer. That hairdresser fellow told her they would film her."

I look toward the rear of the salon and see Wavonne under a dryer, anxiously awaiting the camera.

"Were you going to get some footage of my cousin?" I ask Nathan and Maurice. "I think she's waiting for you under the dryer."

"I did tell her we'd try to work her in," Maurice says to Nathan.

"Isn't she the one whose hair smelled like that Chinese restaurant back in New York . . . the one shut down by the health department?"

"Yes," Maurice says. "But it's been washed. I have her under the dryer with Monique's Heat Rescue conditioner. Just ask her a few questions and tell her to wave to the camera. From my limited interaction with her, I sense it's easier to just let her have some camera time. If we don't do it here, she might show up at the next salon with some fresh hell mix of mayonnaise and horseradish on her head."

"One of those?" Nathan asks. "Reality TV has made everyone think they should be famous." He gestures for the cameraman to follow him toward Wavonne.

Momma and I watch as Wavonne is completely tickled to get some time on video. She's smiling and moving her hands around as she talks. At one point, she seems to have trouble hearing Nathan and tries to lift the dryer, only to have Maurice push it back down again, making sure to keep her hair out of the shot.

When they are done filming, Nathan moves on with the

camera guy, and Maurice lifts the dryer from over Wavonne's head. He then runs a comb through her hair. I think Wavonne was hoping for a full blowout from him, but he only offers her some final tips and sends her on her way.

"Tonight should be interesting," I say once the three of us are finally out the door and on our way back to Sweet Tea. "Celebrities in the restaurant always make for an eventful night."

Truth be told, I'm not that keen on having famous people in Sweet Tea. They just create a frenzy with my other guests and even my staff. I get local celebrities in the restaurant all the time . . . politicians, local newscasters, players from the Redskins, and the Wizards, and the Nationals. Most of them are okay and fairly easy to deal with, but every now and then we get the occasional pop singer playing at the Capital One Arena or a Hollywood actor filming on location. That's when paparazzi creates a nuisance outside the restaurant, and we get demands about clearing out the bathroom for celebrity use or all sorts of other inconveniences to my staff and my customers.

"Do I get to wait on the table?"

"Sure." I don't usually have Wavonne wait on VIP guests, as she is, at best, a mediocre server, but I know I'll never hear the end of it if I refuse, so I don't even bother saying no.

"Monique's nice enough," I say. "And I guess Maurice is okay, but that Nathan—I wish she hadn't included him in the dinner."

Momma and Wavonne exchange looks following my remark.

"What? What did I say?"

Momma and Wavonne look at each other again before Wavonne responds, "I doubt she'd come to dinner without her husband."

"How do you know that he's her husband?"

"He pops up on her commercials sometimes."

"Seems like she could have any man she wants," I say. "I wonder why she chose him."

"You could take a lesson from her, Halia," Momma says. "Sometimes you can't wait for the absolute *perfect* man. Sometimes you have to accept some flaws and just work with them if you ever expect to give your momma some grandchildren."

"Momma, I'm well into my forties. Man or no man, I think your grandchildren ship has sailed."

"We'll see about that," Momma replies when we reach the restaurant. "I'm going home. Good luck tonight," she adds, before stepping away.

"Thanks," I say, opening the door to Sweet Tea and thinking of all I have to do to get ready for the usual Friday night dinner rush and the added commotion of a celebrity guest. "I'll need it."

Chapter 7

"They're here!" Wavonne calls as she peers out the front window. Fortunately, she seems to have already lost interest in her homegrown hair potions and is back to sporting one of her wigs.

I walk over to her and look over her shoulder. I'm thankful that, for this visit, Monique has left her flashy tour bus behind, and all the parking spaces it takes up, as I watch her and her entourage exit a midsize SUV.

"Is that a . . . ?"

"A what?"

"Oh my God!" Wavonne says. "It is! It's a Bentley Bentayga."

"Is that a nice car?" I ask.

Wavonne looks at me like I've been living under a rock for the last ten years. "Last I heard, it's the most expensive SUV you can buy . . . like more than two hundred thousand dollars. Chris Brown has one, and I saw on TV that Rick Ross bought one for his daughter's sweet sixteen."

"Wow," I say, as the group approaches the front door, more about how crazy it seems to spend so much money on a car than about being impressed by the vehicle in any way.

As Ms. Dupree and her guests make their entrance into Sweet Tea, conversations cease throughout the restaurant, and all eyes are on Monique. She's changed clothes since the gathering this afternoon and is now wearing a pink skirt, a white jacket trimmed with pink fur, and white heels with pink polka dots.

"Hello, hello!" she calls with a smile as she waves to my customers, who are either busily asking their tablemates who she is or busily telling their tablemates who she is.

"It smells wonderful in here. Thank you so much for having us," she says to me. "You know Nathan and Maurice . . . and Latasha," she adds before limply gesturing to the striking woman next to her. "This is Odessa Thornton. She owns Salon Soleil in Upper Marlboro." Monique makes Odessa's introduction with little warmth or enthusiasm, and something about the body language between the two ladies makes me think they are not the best of friends.

"Hello. I'm Halia, and this is my cousin Wavonne. Welcome to Sweet Tea." I extend my hand to Odessa. She's quite beautiful but has a much more subdued presence than Monique. Her light brown skin is a shade or two paler than Monique's, and her petite figure seems slight next to Monique's more robust frame. In contrast to Monique's waves of flowing black hair, Odessa has a simple, yet elegant side swept bob with subtle copper highlights. And while she's stylishly dressed in a pair of form-fitting dark jeans, an off-the-shoulder beige blouse, and nude patent leather pumps, her taste in fashion is clearly much more understated than Monique's.

"Thank you," Odessa says. "I'm excited to be here."

She shakes my hand and then reaches for Wavonne's. Wavonne accepts her grasp, but I notice her eyes looking over Odessa's shoulder while she greets her. When my own eyes follow the focus of Wavonne's attention, I see an extremely good-looking young man with dark brown skin, a finely developed physique, and a trendy haircut that I only know is called a Low Fade with Twists because there was a gentleman next to me at the salon a few weeks ago getting the same style, and Latasha gave me the lowdown.

"And this is Alejandro Rivas, my personal chef," Monique says of the handsome man with much more zeal than when she introduced Odessa. "His cooking is the reason I get those peculiar glares from the salesgirls if I happen upon the petite section at Neiman Marcus. I always tell them I'm passing through on the way to the *real* women's clothing section." She looks Odessa up and down. "Who wants the body of a twig anyway? So *not* sexy."

Odessa rolls her eyes. "I've never really been in the *real* women's section at Neiman's. Don't they usually keep it hidden and out of the way . . . somewhere in the back of the store? And isn't there a barn door or something you have to go through to get to it?"

Monique laughs as if she's more amused by Odessa's comments than annoyed. "Oh Odessa, you can be quite witty when you stay on your meds."

There's a momentary silence while the rest of us try to make sense of the exchange of barbs between the two women. I get the feeling Odessa is about to offer yet another counter dig, but, fortunately, Alejandro cuts in between them before she has a chance and extends his hand to me.

"You can call me Alex," he says with a noticeable accent that I recognize as Dominican.

"So nice to meet you." I turn my head toward Wavonne. "This is my cousin Wavonne."

Wavonne shakes his hand while grinning from ear to ear. Then, without releasing her grip, she leans in closer to me. "Girl, forget the pork chops. I'm suddenly in the mood for some mofongo," she whispers.

With all the introductions completed, I lead Monique and

her associates to their table. Once they get settled in, order some drinks, and begin reviewing the menu, the general fascination exhibited toward them from my other diners seems to diminish a bit.

"Monique," Maurice says, looking at my list of specials. "Why did you bring me here? This is going to completely blow my diet."

"Take a night off, Maurice. You can go back to celery sticks and protein shakes tomorrow," Monique says.

"I'm going to Key West for Christmas, and I *will* have all this extra weight off by then," I hear Maurice reply as I walk with Wavonne to the bar to put in their beverage order—white wine for Maurice, a Blue Moon with an orange slice for Alex, a Corona with a lime for Nathan, and a Diet Coke for Odessa. And for Monique, a Pink Lady, one of our signature drinks, which I added to our bar menu in honor of my grandmother, who taught me how to cook.

My grandparents rarely went out to restaurants or bars—they didn't really have the financial means for too many nights on the town and only a handful of establishments were welcoming to African Americans in the fifties and sixties—but I have fond memories of Grandmommy talking about the occasional night out to the Lincoln Theatre or Bohemian Caverns along the U Street Corridor in DC. Grandmommy would warmly refer to it as Black Broadway, a nickname bestowed upon the area due to the plethora of legendary African American singers who performed at the theaters in the neighborhood. Grandmommy never drank at home (or so she said), but on those nights out, she said she always ordered a Pink Lady. I was initially surprised by its popularity when I first put it on the menu. I think it fell out of fashion in the seventies, and, typically, vodka-based cocktails are much more popular these days than gin-based libations. But all it takes is for one person to order a Pink Lady, and other diners start asking about the pretty pastel drink with a hint of foam on top, garnished with a cherry. I think the glasses we serve them in, the old-fashioned shallow champagne glasses (technically called champagne coupes), give rise to nostalgia, further adding to the allure of the cocktail.

Wavonne is officially the server for the table, but I check in here and there to help out and make sure all is going smoothly . . . and, okay, I'll admit it, to sneak the occasional peek at Alex . . . the man is *fine*. Monique seems to do most of the talking at the table. Her gregarious voice carries throughout the restaurant, and while the rest of her party, and even other patrons seated nearby, laugh heartily at her frequent musings, Odessa seems quite cool to her quips, and I catch her occasionally scowling like a toddler who's jealous of a new baby getting all the attention.

In between refilling drinks and delivering entrees, I hear snippets of the conversation and have to make a conscious effort not to groan when I hear Monique complain about her lifestyle of the rich and famous—the inconvenience involved with the renovations to her New York apartment, the aggravation of Nathan's Tesla being in the shop because it's been making a faint rattling noise, that inadequate massage she got at the Gold Door Spa earlier today, and how Neiman Marcus had the audacity to try to put her on a waiting list for something called the Fendi Aubusson-Print Chain Shoulder Bag.

"*Try* being the operative word," Monique says with a sly smile as she reaches next to her and holds up a cream-colored leather bag decorated with floral print.

"The Aubusson bag! I think I would need to sell my house to buy one of those," Latasha says.

"You don't want that gaudy bag . . . it's too busy," Odessa says. "If you're going to buy a designer purse, it should at least be tasteful. Something like this." Odessa gestures toward her Coach purse, a simple, yet elegant, suede shoulder bag in beige.

"Oh yes. Coach," Monique says. "Isn't their tag line something like, 'Coach: For girls who can't afford Fendi'?"

"They're both very nice," Latasha says before Odessa can respond. "Seems you two have come a long way since your rumored days at HairPair so long ago. I doubt Fendi and Coach were being flung over your shoulders then."

I set another Pink Lady down on the table for Monique. "HairPair?" I ask, referring to the local hair salon chain that went bust about twenty years ago. "I used to get my hair cut at the one in Clinton when I was in high school."

"Word is that Monique and Odessa ruled the chairs at the one in Camp Springs."

"That we did," Monique says. "Ah . . . the old days. We were like a fine-tuned machine turning out finger waves and sock buns by the dozen."

"Girl, you ain't lyin'," Odessa says with the first smile I've seen on her face all night. She turns to me. "That was the nineties. We were fresh out of high school and just getting started. I was the go-to girl for micro braids for all the sisters that wanted to look like Moesha, and Monique did the box braids for all the ladies trying to look like Janet Jackson in *Poetic Justice*."

Monique laughs. "Yep. Everyone came in with a cutout from a magazine. They wanted T-Boz's mushroom . . . or Aaliyah's swoop and wrap . . . or Toni Braxton's pixie cut."

"Remember all those girls that came in with their nappy hair, thinking we could make them look like Whitney Houston in *The Bodyguard*?"

"Girl!" Monique exclaims. "I remember wanting to tell them, 'I can't pull a rabbit out of a hat or turn water into wine . . . what makes you think I can make your burnt tips look like the wig Whitney Houston wore in a movie?'"

Odessa laughs. "But of course we never actually said things like that. The worse the shape of the hair, the more promises we'd offer . . . and the more money we'd make . . . not that it was ever very much back then."

"We *had* to upsell the hot oil treatments and deep conditioners. How else were we going to have some extra bucks to buy some cocktails at Zanzibar or concert tickets to see the Fugees?"

"Yeah . . . money was tight, but boy did we have some fun."

"Cutting and relaxing . . . and curling and blow-drying with Brandy's 'Sittin' Up in My Room' blaring from the speakers." A wide smile of nostalgia comes across Monique's face.

"We rocked out to all the greats: Jodeci, Montell Jordan, Boyz II Men . . . Bell Biv DeVoe—"

"Oooh, girl! I have not thought about Bell Biv Devoe in years." Monique slides closer to Odessa. I watch as they lean in toward each other and break out in song. *"That girl is Poooiiisson!"* they croon in unison before breaking up in laughter.

I'm perplexed by their behavior. A few minutes ago they were trading barbs, and now it's like they're best friends. I'm curious how much longer this little lovefest will continue when Odessa makes me wonder no more.

"Yep," she says, looking down toward the seat of Monique's chair, then back up at her face. "Never trust a big butt and a smile."

Monique throws her head back and laughs. "Don't be hatin'," she says. "My big butt and my smile are some of my best assets."

RECIPE FROM HALIA'S KITCHEN

Celia's Butter Pecan Cake

Cake Ingredients

2 cups finely chopped pecans (reserve ¾ cup after toasting for icing)

1 cup softened butter (¼ cup for toasting pecans, ¾ cup for cake batter)

3 eggs

1 cup sugar

1 cup applesauce

½ cup whole milk

1½ teaspoons vanilla extract

2½ cups all-purpose flour

1 teaspoon of cinnamon

1½ teaspoons baking powder

½ teaspoon baking soda

¼ teaspoon salt

- Preheat oven to 350 degrees Fahrenheit.
- Generously grease and lightly flour two 9-inch round cake pans.
- Place pecans and ¼ cup butter in oven safe pan or baking dish. Toast pecans in oven for 10–12 minutes, stirring every 3–4 minutes; set aside and let cool.
- Lightly beat eggs; set aside.

- Cream sugar and ¾ cup of butter together with mixer on high speed for 1 minute. Add eggs, applesauce, milk, and vanilla extract. Mix on medium speed for 30 seconds.
- Combine flour, cinnamon, baking powder, baking soda, and salt.
- With mixer on medium speed, slowly add combined dry ingredients to creamed mixture until well blended.
- With mixer on low speed, add 1¼ cups toasted pecans to batter until fully incorporated.
- Pour batter into prepared pans and bake for 25–30 minutes, until a tooth pick comes out clean.
- Cool in pans for 10 minutes, then turn out onto rack and cool completely.

Icing Ingredients
1 cup softened butter
⅓ cup brown sugar
2 tablespoons evaporated milk
6 cups confectioners' sugar
2–5 tablespoons whole milk
1½ teaspoons vanilla

- Add 2 tablespoons of butter, brown sugar, and evaporated milk to a small sauce pan. Heat to boiling over low-medium heat for three minutes, stirring constantly to make caramel. Remove from heat. Set aside.
- Cream remaining butter with confectioners' sugar.
- Add caramel to butter and sugar mixture and blend on low speed for 1 minute.
- Add milk, one tablespoon at a time while continuing to blend. Stop adding milk when icing reaches a spreadable consistency.
- Add vanilla and remaining pecans and mix on low speed until well blended.

Chapter 8

"That was perfect," Alex says as I clear the empty plate sitting in front of him. He and the rest of the gang have finished their entrées and moved on to dessert.

"Momma's caramel cake," I say. "It never disappoints."

"Maybe your mother can share some of her secrets with me . . . about what makes her cake so good. I've got to make one for a party Monique is throwing tomorrow night, and now I'm afraid it's going to pale in comparison."

"Well, I'll share the biggest secret to all of Momma's desserts . . . which really isn't so secret. *Butter* . . . lots of butter! I order it by the case . . . thirty pounds to a case, and she goes through it like crazy."

"It's worth it. That was one good cake. Moist and rich and not too sweet."

"She's a master baker. I can fry up some of the best chicken you've ever had or broil a smothered pork chop that will fall off the bone, but baking has never been my thing. That's why I'm grateful Momma runs the dessert operation around here. I don't know what I'd do without her."

"I suspect you'd manage. From what I've seen tonight, this place runs like a well-oiled machine. I worked in a lot of restaurants before I signed on with Monique, and Sweet Tea has them all beat by a mile. You're clearly very good at what you do."

"That's very nice of you to say," I respond, and feel my face getting hot. At some point in the conversation, his tone appeared to shift. At first it seemed like casual banter between us, but there was something about the way he said "you're clearly very good at what you do" or the way he looked at me when he said it that makes me wonder if he's flirting with me.

No, the idea is ridiculous, I think to myself. He's a beautiful man and probably a good ten years younger than me. I'm likely misreading his Latin charisma and charm. I'm sure he talks to all women that way.

"I'm not just saying it. It really was an exquisite evening . . . delicious food, prompt service . . ." He looks at me in that peculiar way again. "And an enchanting host."

I smile. "I'm glad you enjoyed it."

"I think *everyone* enjoyed it," Alex says, and nods toward his fellow diners, who, at this point, are leaning back into their chairs, sipping on cappuccinos. I see nods of agreement around the table from Monique and her other guests. Their conversations have quieted, and they look almost serene after an evening of cocktails and comfort food. It's a look that says "yeah, I overindulged, but it was worth it."

"If I may, I'd love to see your kitchen."

"Sure," I respond. "We're in 'closing down' mode back there at the moment, but I'd be happy to show you around."

I try not to let my eyes linger as I watch Alex lift his taut frame from the chair before I turn toward the kitchen with him following.

After we come through the swinging doors, I stand next to Alex and notice his gaze moving around the room, taking in the spectacle of constant activity—no one is ever still in the kitchen of a busy restaurant . . . what we call the "back of the house." It's such a contrast to the dining room (the front of the house). The dining room is designed first and foremost to create a fun, festive atmosphere and to ensure the comfort of my customers. The lighting is designed to be soft and flattering, the warm beige walls allow the artwork to really pop, and the rich cranberry carpet in the main dining room was chosen to act as a contrast to the more subtle hardwood floors and maple accents in the bar area. When I was designing the interior of Sweet Tea, I wanted the space to be vibrant and energetic but not so loud that patrons have to shout at each other to be heard over the constant boom of background noise. So, in addition to the rich color it brings to the restaurant, I had the carpet installed to serve as a sound-absorbing mechanism as well.

Every detail of the front of the house is about ambience. The kitchen, on the other hand, is about function . . . function, function, function. The overhead lighting is bright and harsh, the floor is a series of simple white tiles surrounding a handful of strategically placed drains, and stainless steel abounds throughout the entire space. There is a constant hodgepodge of noise—running water, clanking dishes, loud voices, humming exhaust fans, spinning mixers—bouncing off the wealth of hard surfaces. It's a lot to take in and brings the words "sensory overload" to mind.

I give Alex a chance to get his bearings before introducing him to some members of my kitchen staff and showing him around the various stations that make up what we call "the line." My team is in kitchen-closing mode and eager to go home, so we have to carefully navigate through the space as they hurriedly sweep the floor, brush the grill, sanitize surfaces, and manage a wealth of the other activities to put the kitchen to rest for the night. When I give the occasional tour of the Sweet Tea kitchen to others, it generally involves a quick look around that lasts a few minutes, but, as Alex is in the business as well, I go into more detail about the various stations and machines. I show him the steam table, the grill, the sauté station, and some of the other setups and contraptions that help us churn out our delicious delights. As I give him the ins and outs of why I chose specific types or brands of appliances, and how I've changed the setup of the line over the years to make the kitchen operate more efficiently, he takes note of the sense of pride and enthusiasm I have for my restaurant, and what it takes to keep it running smoothly.

"You really know your stuff," he says. "It's obvious how much you care about this place."

"Thank you. I do my best," I say before continuing the tour and the verbal cascade of details and specs about my beloved kitchen devices. I'm probably boring him, but I can't help myself. I'm a bit of a kitchen equipment geek. If you want to get me excited, forget discussions of perfume or jewelry or fashion. Instead, ask me about my Arctic Air two section solid door reach-in refrigerator or my Vulcan natural gas double deck convection oven. I could go on about them for hours.

Alex is either a good actor or is actually keenly interested when I show him what may be the most important piece of machinery in my kitchen—my state-of-the-art deep fryer. No fryer equals no fried chicken . . . and Mahalia's Sweet Tea without fried chicken is like Taco Bell without tacos or IHOP without pancakes. I paid nearly twenty grand for it, and it's worth every penny, but when I catch myself rambling on about its stainless steel eighty-five-pound-capacity fry tank and hear words like "thermal units" and "twin fry baskets" coming out of my mouth, I think that maybe I've shared enough minutiae about my kitchen operations and decide to give it a rest. Much as I'd like to show him my walk-in cooler and the pantry . . . and the broiler . . . and the dry storage room, I decide to wrap up my little dog and pony show and let Alex get back to his dinner companions.

"Well, I'm sure I've gone on long enough," I say. "More than you ever wanted to know, right?"

"Not at all," he says. "I really enjoyed seeing the inner workings of this place. It's like getting a peek backstage at a concert or touring the tunnels underneath Disney World." He looks around the room. "I miss this sometimes: working with a team and all. Being a personal chef can be isolating. I love the clamor back here . . . it's invigorating . . . a thing of beauty, really." His Dominican accent makes talk of my kitchen operations seem sensual.

I smile. "I guess it is."

He smiles back at me. "A beautiful restaurant run by a beautiful woman."

My first response to his compliment is a quick laugh. I'm not sure what to say. I'm terrible at flirting. "Aren't you sweet," is the best I can come up with. "Should we get you back to your friends?"

Alex is about to respond, when Tacy approaches him with a five-gallon container of lemonade and abruptly calls, "Behind you!" Tacy's loud deep voice startles Alex, and he involuntarily backs into him. The splatter of lemonade on his back propels Alex toward me, and the two of us end up in a bit of a compromising, but not necessarily unwelcome, position with Alex pressed against me as I steady myself against the counter.

He hovers over me for a brief period, his arms on either side of me, as he grabs the counter to regain his footing. He looks into my eyes, and I can feel his chest, all solid and hard, against my body. This definitely feels like a "moment" between us, and it makes me feel both invigorated and uncomfortable at the same time.

"I'm so sorry." He releases one hand from the counter as he pulls himself upright and then moves the other.

An awkward laugh escapes my mouth and I fidget with my shirt as I try to compose myself. "That's okay. These things happen back here." I notice some members of my kitchen staff suddenly looking away from us. Clearly, I was not the only one who sensed a little *something* was going on here. "I'm sorry about your shirt. Let me find you a towel."

"No need. I'll run to the men's room and get cleaned up."

"Okay." I gesture for him to follow me and point to the restrooms once we're back in the dining area. Alex thanks me and makes his way toward the far end of the restaurant, crossing paths with Monique and Odessa as they head in the other direction.

As the men's room door closes behind Alex, I see Wavonne emerge from the ladies' room and barrel toward me. "Oooh girl, Diana Ross and Mary Wilson just had a *throwdown* in the bathroom," she cackles, eyeing Monique and Odessa. They both look a little unsettled as they take their seats back at the table.

"What are you talking about?"

"I happened to overhear them—"

I cut her off. "You *happened* to overhear them? You mean you lifted your feet up in the stall the moment you heard someone enter the bathroom in hopes of getting some good gossip?"

"Don't hate on my curiosity, Halia. You are just as interested in the four-one-one around here as I am."

"What were they fighting about?" I ask, realizing that Wavonne may be right—maybe I am just as interested in gossip as she is.

"I'm not sure. I only got bits and pieces . . . fruits and nuts. I heard Monique say, 'You're done hustling me, Odessa. Find someone else to leech off.' Then Odessa said, 'I'm not done with *anything*. Cut me off and I'll—'" Wavonne takes a breath. "Then Monique interrupted her . . . didn't let her finish . . . and said, 'You'll what? You'll *what*, Odessa?! You make any trouble for me, and I'll blow the lid off your entire operation.' Odessa didn't say anything back. She just stormed out of the ladies' room with Monique following."

"Hmm. Wonder what that's all about. Sounds like those two ladies weave a bit of a tangled web," I say, and notice Monique and her guests begin to gather their belongings. "Oh well. As long as Monique paid the bill, I'm not too concerned about whatever happenings are going on between her and Odessa. She did pay the bill, didn't she?" I ask.

It's been my experience that a significant number of famous personalities think they can run up a tab from here to next Tuesday and then skip out on the bill—like I'm supposed to comp a few hundred dollars' worth of food and drinks because they have graced my restaurant with their presence. As you can imagine, my response to that nonsense, if I may borrow from Wavonne's lexicon, is: "Oh hell to the no!"

"Yeah," Wavonne says. "She paid with an American Express Black Card. Only the second one I've seen since I started working here."

"Good," I say. "Looks like they are getting ready to skedaddle. Why don't we go say good night?"

"Thanks for joining us. It was a pleasure to have you," I say to Monique as she pushes in her chair.

"The pleasure was all ours," Monique replies. "The smothered pork chops were to die for. And that banana pudding?!" She leans in toward me and lowers her voice so Nathan doesn't hear her. "Girl, Idris Elba could have been standing here shirtless, lookin' all fine . . . wanting to take me home, and I would have said, 'Honey, that's cool, but not until I finish this pudding.'"

I laugh. "Can I pack you a serving to go?"

"I better say no. There's a fine line between voluptuous

and plain old fat. One more piece of cake, and I may find myself on the wrong side of that line."

"Take the cake, Monique," Odessa says. "The way that
button on the waist of your skirt is straining, you may as well
go up to the next dress size. I've been afraid all night that it's
going to pop off and take someone's eye out."

"Pay her no mind," Monique says to me rather than responding directly to Odessa. "Spindly man-less girls like Odessa
are always hating on real women like us."

Us? Who's us? It takes me a moment to realize that she's
referring to her and me. I guess my size fourteen self, according to Monique, must qualify me as a "real woman."

"Well, if you two are real women then I'm Queen Real
Woman!" Wavonne says, opening her arms to showcase her
impressive frame. "I got lumps and bumps that make all the
guys wanna—"

"Wavonne! Behave yourself," I scold.

Monique and Odessa laugh.

"Girl, you got it going on," Odessa says to Wavonne. "And
you and your restaurant are both lovely," she says to me. "I
would never, as Monique put it, hate on either one of you. I
save my hates for this one." She flicks her eyes in Monique's
direction.

"I think we can agree that all of you ladies are beautiful."
Maurice gets up from the table and steps toward us. "Now
go to your corners and don't come back until you can play
nice," he says to Monique and Odessa. "I just nibbled on
grilled fish and broccoli while the rest of you indulged in
pans of cornbread and fried chicken . . . and pork chops covered in gravy. If anyone's going to be bitchy, it's going to be
me," he adds. "Those two," he quips to Wavonne and me.
"I've seen wet cats be more pleasant with each other."

"Speaking of wet," Monique says as she catches sight of
Alex coming back to the table with a lemonade stain on his
shirt. "What happened to you?"

"Nothing. A little accident when Halia was showing me the kitchen. I dried off as best I could in the men's room. I'll throw the shirt in the washer when I get home. Hopefully, there'll be one free."

"One free?" I ask.

"Yeah. I live over at Iverson Towers in Temple Hills. We have a central laundry room, and sometimes one or two people take up all the washers."

"Did you spill somethin' on him on purpose, so he'd take his clothes off?" Wavonne whispers to me as Alex puts a light jacket on over his sullied shirt.

I ignore her question before, once again, apologizing for the spill.

"No worries. Really," he says, and turns toward Monique and the rest of the group. "I guess we'd better get moving. We have an early day tomorrow."

"We certainly do. I want to be at the convention center by seven a.m.," Monique says. "I need to be on-site while they set everything up."

"Oh yes, the big hair convention is tomorrow," I say. "Maybe I'll see you there. We're running a food stall at the event. I'll be there in the morning to help my team set up."

"How nice. I hope you can sneak away and visit my exhibit. We'll be there all day."

"I'm sure we can," Wavonne responds before I have a chance. "I'm guessin' there'll be a lot of free samples?"

"Of course . . . samples, prizes, items for sale."

"We should really be leaving," Nathan says. He then grabs Monique's hand and starts to lead her toward the door. "It's getting late. You need your rest." His words are innocuous enough, but there's something in his tone and the way he grabbed her hand that makes it seem like he's giving commands to Monique.

Wavonne and I walk the group to the exit and say some final good nights to everyone. Nathan and Monique head out first, followed by Odessa, Maurice, and Latasha. Alex momentarily lingers behind and, before he heads out the door, he looks at Wavonne. "It was very nice to meet you, Wavonne." He then turns to me and takes each of my hands in his. "Thank you for the tour. I'll be at Monique's exhibit tomorrow. I really do hope you'll come by and say hi." He then raises my hands to his full lips for a brief kiss. "Good night, Halia," he says.

"Um . . ." I say, a little befuddled. "Good night."

He turns to leave and the door has barely swung shut behind him when Wavonne starts with the questions. "What was *that* about? What happened during your little kitchen tour? If I didn't know better, I'd think Rico Suave was into you."

Chapter 9

"I have never seen anything like this before in my life," I say to Wavonne and Momma. We just finished helping some of my staff set up our food stall at the Unique Chic Hair Convention, and Wavonne has coaxed us into taking a look around before we head back to the restaurant.

As a woman who doesn't fuss much with my hair, I'm in awe of the sheer magnitude of the event as we walk down the aisles of the 2.3-million-square-foot Walter E. Washington Convention Center in DC. There are thousands of products on display, makeshift salons set up in neat rows along the convention center floor, hair care books and DVDs on sale, booths featuring local radio personalities, and other exhibits showing off wigs, and weaves, and cosmetics, and salon equipment. On the lower level, there is a lengthy catwalk for models showing off the latest hairdos. I hear the announcer describing their styles as the ladies strut down the runway. Words like the "Pretty Pixie," the "Short and Sassy," the "High Bump and Straight Ponytail," and "Peek-A-Boo Highlights" come over the speaker as I take a moment to look through the program and see that the stage will be used later in the day for all sorts of demonstrations and competitions. With so much going on in every direction, the place is a bastion of overstimulation.

"Come here, Halia," Momma calls, having gotten ahead of me while I was flipping through the event guide.

I approach Momma while Wavonne hangs back, shoving as many samples as she can in her purse.

"This is Karl," Momma says to me, gesturing toward a tall middle-aged man as he runs some clippers up the side of a young man's head. "What is it you're demonstrating again?" Momma asks him.

"This is called the 'Frohawk,'" Karl says, laying down the clippers and starting to comb the hair of the young man in the barber chair in front of him. "It's a great cut for men who want to keep things short and neat, but not too conservative. We clip the sides and fade them nicely into the curls on top. It's a great look with tight curls . . . or, sometimes, we finish it with wide ringlets."

"It looks very nice," I say.

"This is my daughter, Halia. She's a business owner, too." Momma shifts her eyes in my direction. "Karl owns his own barbershop in Waldorf. And he's single."

"That's really great." I'm trying to hide my embarrassment as Momma attempts to move me like I'm about to go on clearance.

"Why don't you take one of his cards." Momma picks up a business card from the table next to Karl and hands it to me.

"Sure." I accept the card and offer an apologetic smile to him.

"Halia owns Sweet Tea . . . the restaurant. Do you know where it is? In the King Shopping Center off of—"

"I know where it is," Karl says. "I've heard great things about it."

"I'm glad. I hope you'll come by and try it sometime," I

say, and, honestly, as much as I don't care for Momma's pushiness, I wouldn't mind if he did. He appears to be only a few years older than me, and he's a nice-looking man with kind eyes, and, apparently, a steady job. I could do worse.

"Give him one of your cards, too, Halia."

"He said he knows where Sweet Tea is, Momma," I respond, but start looking through my purse anyway. I dig out a card and hand it to him. "Clearly, you're busy, Karl. We'll let you get back to work. And I should really do the same. It was nice to meet you."

He takes the card, while Momma looks on, quite pleased with herself.

"We really should get back to the restaurant," I say as Wavonne rejoins us.

"Let's find Monique's display before we go," she insists.

We've all had our eyes out for Monique's booth since we got here, but have yet to come across it.

"Do you happen to know where the Hair by Monique display is?" I ask Karl. "We've been up and down most of the aisles and haven't seen it."

Karl doesn't have a chance to answer before a woman doing a banana braids demonstration next to him lets out a loud laugh. "You all must be new here," she says. "Monique Dupree has not had a paltry exhibit on the main floor in years."

"Really? I thought she was supposed to be here promoting—"

"Oh, she's here," the woman says. "Not on the main floor though." She lifts her comb and points up and to the left.

Wavonne, Momma, and I turn our heads in unison to find a large neon sign over a set of double doors at the far end of the aisle. The sign reads: MONIQUE'S HOUSE OF STYLE.

I thank the hairdresser for pointing out what was in plain

sight all along, and the three of us begin to work our way through the crowd. When we reach the double doors we see that there's a line of more than fifty people waiting along the wall to get inside whatever the hell Monique's House of Style is. A burly man in a tuxedo is letting small groups in as others exit. Momma and I are about to take our place in the queue, when Wavonne makes a beeline for the bouncer.

"We're friends of Monique," she says to the man. "Surely we don't have to wait in that line with all those sad-lookin' heifers."

A curt "End of the line, please," is the bouncer's reply.

"This is my cousin," Wavonne says, motioning toward me. "Monique had dinner at her restaurant last night."

"End of the line, please."

"Come on, Wavonne, let's get in line," I say.

We are about to join the masses when Odessa approaches. She's wearing a short beige skirt and a silk white blouse with a plunging neckline. What little of her breasts that the shirt leaves to the imagination are clearly being kept at bay with some double-sided tape.

"Well, hello, ladies. Thank you for such a wonderful dinner last night. And who is this?" Odessa asks, looking at Momma.

"This is my mother, Celia Watkins." I turn to Momma. "Momma, this is Odessa. She owns a salon in Upper Marlboro."

Odessa shakes Momma's hand before focusing her attention on the bouncer. "Don't worry. They're with me," she says to him, and gestures for us to follow her through the doors.

"Whoa . . . wait a minute! And you are?" the bouncer asks Odessa as she starts to step away. Odessa looks her flawless figure up and down, gives her hair a quick toss, and lightly rests the back of her hand on the bouncer's cheek.

"Does it really matter?" she coos before pushing one of the doors open and casually walking through without incident. Momma, Wavonne, and I quickly follow while we have the chance.

Chapter 10

"If you'll excuse me, ladies," Odessa says to us, "Some of my stylists are working the tables, and I need to check on them."

"Of course," I reply. "Thanks for helping us jump the line."

While Odessa walks away, Momma, Wavonne, and I look around and take in the scene . . . and I think it's safe to say we are all quite impressed. The crowd control happening on the other side of the doors, along with a string quartet softly playing in the far corner of the spacious ballroom make Monique's House of Style a tranquil oasis away from all the commotion on the main floor. The tables displaying the multitude of Hair by Monique products are draped in varying shades of pink fabric. Fresh flower arrangements are strategically placed between the hundreds of pink boxes, bottles, and tubs of follicle-boosting serums, scalp infusion treatments, hair lotions, deep conditioners, and, of course, Monique's marquee product, Sleek. The displays are manned by attractive young women sporting tailored sleeveless dresses made from the same pink-colored fabric used to cover their respective tables. I see Odessa chatting with one of them.

At the front of the room, Monique is busy posing for photos

with fans while Nathan directs the same cameraman who filmed at Latasha's salon yesterday, making sure he gets footage of Monique interacting with her adoring public.

We're each handed a flute of sparkling cider while we peruse the room and look at the displays. We move from table to table, getting an earful from the attendants about the products on sale and the magic they will work on our hair. One of the attendants, a salesgirl really, talks Wavonne into buying Monique's Moisture Growth Shampoo and another one persuades Momma to purchase her Nourishing Deep Conditioner. They both pick up a few more items and are probably out more than a hundred bucks between them by the time we stumble upon Alex. We find him manning a refreshments table. He's talking in Spanish with one of the maintenance workers. They seem to be trying to fix an issue with the electrical cords for one of his chafing trays.

"Mmmm," Wavonne hums as we approach the table. "Free snacks."

"Hey there," Alex says to us as Wavonne begins to fill a plate. "So glad you came by."

"It's nice to see you, too," I reply, introduce him to Momma, and check out his food. "What a great spread you've got here," I say, although I don't really mean it. The table is a mix of basic fruit and veggie trays, crackers with a salmon spread, various chips and dips, and a couple of chafing dishes filled with some sort of cheese-based concoction—it all looks fine, but certainly nothing to write home about.

"Thank you," Alex says. "Are you enjoying the event?"

"Yes. It's quite something. Honestly, I've never seen anything like it. There are hair products on display that I didn't even know existed. I'd never heard of a humidity shield or a scalp exfoliator before today."

"Well, clearly you don't need any of them. You have beautiful hair."

I see Wavonne and Momma exchanging glances after that remark, which falls from Alex's lips like honey. His rich voice and Dominican accent make everything he says sound sensual, but compliments are particularly emotive.

"So you're Monique's private chef?" Momma asks. "Does that entitle your wife to a discount on her products?"

I give Momma a look that she pretends not to see. I already caught her checking out his left hand to see if a wedding band was on it, but I guess she wants to be sure he's unattached before she starts playing matchmaker. You'd think her trying to fix me up with the barber on the main floor would be enough humiliation for one day, but apparently Momma does not see it that way.

"I'm not married."

"Girlfriend?" Momma asks.

Alex laughs. "No. Monique keeps me pretty busy. There isn't much time for all that."

"You'll just have to make time," Momma instructs. "I'm always telling Halia here that she needs to make time for a love life, too. Maybe the two of you could make some time together."

"Momma!" I say, mortified.

"What? You two clearly have a lot in common. You're both in the food service industry."

"Yes," Wavonne chimes in. "And one of you is in his thirties, and one of you *was* in her thirties . . . like a million years ago," she says just out of Alex's earshot. Then she starts with "Rock-a-bye Baby" in a barely audible hum.

"We do have a lot in common." Alex says this to Momma, but he's looking at me. "I suspect I could learn a lot from you after tasting some of your wonderful food last night."

I swallow hard after that comment. This beautiful man *is* actually flirting with me. "That's nice of you to say."

"Not at all," he replies as another technician appears with

an extension cord. "Can you excuse me? I need to take care of this."

"Certainly. We need to get back to Sweet Tea anyway."

"Come by the restaurant anytime," Momma says to Alex as we turn on our heels. Then to me, in a hushed voice she adds. "You should have given him your phone number."

"He knows where to find me, Momma . . . and I'm old enough to be his . . . well, not quite his mother, but I suspect I've got a good ten years on him."

Momma purses her lips to respond when I hear Maurice's voice at the front of the room. "Okay. Ladies . . . ladies," he calls, trying to quiet down the room. "We're going to start the demonstrations." He looks around at the crowd. "Who would like to volunteer to take part?"

"I wouldn't have worn a wig if I'd known Maurice would be doin' demos."

"So take it off," I say.

"I'm not takin' my wig off in front of these people. My hair's all matted down underneath this thing."

"Our volunteer will get a free bottle of Monique's Crème De Curl and a fifty-dollar gift card toward Hair by Monique products."

It takes about a nanosecond after Maurice mentions the words "free" and "gift card" for Wavonne to have her wig off her head and in her hands. "Here, hold Gladys." She hands the wig to me and hurries toward the front of the room before anyone else has a chance.

"You again," Maurice says when Wavonne reaches him. "What was it? Waverne? Whayette?"

"Wavonne."

"Oh yes." He runs his hands through Wavonne's hair, looking like he just swallowed something distasteful. "Well, I do love a challenge," he says. "Please, have a seat, dear." He raises his voice to the audience. "So this lovely young lady's

hair has a . . . a *bit* of damage . . . from chemicals, probably."
He slides a lock of hair up through his fingers and says something about it having too much "porosity," whatever that is.
Then he goes on to demonstrate the use of a deep conditioner
using an oversize plastic comb with widely spaced teeth. He
talks about how he would normally have Wavonne sit under
the dryer for several minutes, but since they do not have one
available at the event, he proceeds to the application of what
he calls a "heat-infused strengthener." He applies a second
cream to Wavonne's hair in much the same manner as he did
the conditioner and begins to glide sections of it through a
flat iron. "This is the Hair by Monique iron," he says. "It has
ceramic rather than metal plates, which helps prevent damage. It's on sale here today for $79.99."

When Maurice is done with the iron, he adds a little mousse
to Wavonne's hair, and gives it a quick style, more with his fingers than the comb, and, I must say, the result is quite nice. He
hasn't worked any miracles, but her hair looks much better
than it did when she first pulled Gladys off her head.

"I want you to repeat this process once a week and to only
use Sleek to relax any new growth," he says to Wavonne.

As Wavonne admires herself in the mirror that Maurice
handed her, Monique takes a break from her fan photo ses-
sions and approaches Momma and me. She's looking fabulous in a bright purple pantsuit with ruffles along the sleeves
and the lower part of the legs.

"I'm glad you stopped by," she says to me. "Your restaurant was absolutely perfect. We had such a nice evening.
Now that I'm living back in the area, you may see a lot of me
and my entourage there . . . after the tour, of course."

"So you're living in Maryland full-time now?"

"I still have the apartment in New York, but home base is
here now . . . in Mitchellville. We've barely been in the new
house for a year and, with my hectic work schedule and

travel . . . and planning for the upcoming tour, it took me most of that time to get the place furnished and decorated. It's finally ready for prime time, which is good, as I'm hosting my annual white party there tonight," she says. "You should come." She looks at Momma. "And you as well."

"And me." Wavonne hurries over at the first word of a party, the mirror Maurice offered her still in her hand.

"Of course," Monique says. "Starts at six p.m. Ends promptly at ten p.m., so I can get my beauty sleep."

"A bunch of black folks throwin' a white party . . . ain't that somethin'?" Wavonne says. "I think—"

"Thank you, Monique," I say, interrupting Wavonne. "But I have to work tonight. Saturdays are super busy."

"Well, I don't," Wavonne says. "I'd love to come."

"You're on the schedule, too, Wavonne. I need you there."

"Do you not realize what we've just been invited to, Halia? This party will be the biggest social event Prince George's County has seen in years. I'll be damned if I'm gonna miss it."

"That Alex fellow," Momma says to Monique before I can respond to Wavonne. "Will he be at the party tonight?"

"Yes. He'll be supervising the food."

"In that case, Halia," Momma says to me. "I'll cover for you at the restaurant, so you can go. And I'm sure you can find someone to take Wavonne's shift."

"I don't have anything to wear to a party like that."

"How about I make a deal with you?" Monique asks. "You bring a few of your Sweet Tea creations for the buffet table, and I'll ask Maurice to take you shopping for something fabulous to wear to the party . . . and Wavonne, too. My treat."

"Oh no. I can't ask you to do that."

"Of course you can," Monique says.

"Yeah," Wavonne agrees. "Of course you can."

"No, really, it's not necessary," I say, eyeing Wavonne as

she gives me a pleading look. "Given that Wavonne will likely never forgive me if I deny her this party, I suppose I'd better accept your gracious invitation, but I insist on paying for our outfits."

"Then I insist on paying for your catering services."

"I guess it's a deal."

"Maurice," Monique calls in his direction. "We'll get one of Odessa's stylists to do the rest of the demos," she says to him as he steps toward us. "I'd like you to take these two shopping . . . help them find something suitable for the party tonight."

"Okay," he says. "Let me get a few things set up for the demos before we go." He pulls his phone from his pocket and hands it to me. "I'll be a few minutes. Why don't you give me your phone number, and you can walk around until I get things wrapped up. I'll text you when I'm ready to go."

"Okay," I say, and type my number into his phone and hand it back to him.

"So I'm tasked with dressing the two of you," he says, taking the phone from me and giving both Wavonne and me a good once-over before looking at Monique. "I guess I did just say that I love a challenge."

Chapter 11

"I thought we could start at Macy's," I say after I've parked the van in the parking garage of the Fashion Centre at Pentagon City, a multilevel mall just across the bridge from Maryland in Arlington, Virginia.

"Macy's?!" Maurice bemoans as if I suggested we shop for outfits at a flea market. "You may enjoy sorting through heaps of marked-down clothing flung all over the place, but I prefer stores that don't look like the Tasmanian Devil had a sudden need for a tunic and a discounted pair of leggings."

"Yeah . . . Macy's all ghetto these days," Wavonne says as the three of us step out of the van and walk toward the entrance. "Can't never find anyone to wait on you, and they all funky-monkey about their returns. I tried to take back that Michael Kors dress I bought there a few months ago—you know, the green sheath dress with the studs on the sleeves . . . the one I wore to Melva's wedding . . . and to Linda's birthday party . . . and my date with that cheap-ass brotha that took me to that nasty Cici's pizza buffet—although I will say macaroni and cheese on pizza crust is not the *worst* idea in the world. *Anyway,* the heifer behind the register wouldn't take the dress back . . . somethin' about how the tags had been removed, and it had clearly been worn. It was a *hundred* dollars. I can't afford a hundred-dollar dress."

"Well then, maybe you shouldn't have purchased it in the first place."

"Save the lecture, Halia," Wavonne replies as we approach the mall directory. "At least I was able to sell it on eBay . . . got forty bucks for it. So I'm only out sixty, but I'm done with Macy's for the time bein'."

"Everyone at Macy's will be so hurt that you've taken your 'buy, wear, and return' routine to their competitors."

Maurice ignores our bickering as he eyes the map and sighs. "What kind of place is this? No Neiman's, no Saks . . . no Prada, no Burberry . . . no Chanel. We may as well be at one of those outlet malls where women shop in sneakers and sweat pants," he laments about what I always thought of as at least a *semi*-upscale mall. There may not be a Tiffany & Co. or Cartier, but there's a Banana Republic, and a Zara, and a Hugo Boss . . . and Coach and Kate Spade . . . it's way nicer than any of the malls we have on the other side of the river in Prince George's County.

"At least there's a Nordstrom." There's a sound of resignation in Maurice's voice. "I guess it will have to do." He turns to us. "I'm sorry. I need an attitude adjustment. It's just that I've been on this low-carb diet for two weeks now, which means I've been chronically hungry for two weeks now," he says, before turning on his heel and heading toward the south end of the mall. "Hurry, I think I smell Cinnabon! I can only resist for so long."

Wavonne and I follow Maurice through the busy mall corridor, and, when we cross the threshold into Nordstrom, he stops to speak to the first salesperson we encounter.

"May I help you?" the young man asks.

"Yes." Maurice looks Wavonne and me up and down then back at the sales associate. "Where's the Encore section?"

"Encore?" I ask Wavonne as the sales guy directs Maurice. "It's Nordstrom's fat lady section."

The salesclerk overhears Wavonne. "Not at all. It's our department for plus . . . um . . . *full-figured* women."

"Well, that's me. I'm definitely full-figured." Wavonne looks down at her ample bosom. "My girls ain't gonna fit in nothin' petite—that's for sure. Oprah and Gayle," she says, looking at her left breast and then her right, "need room to breathe."

"I'm sure you'll find some great fashions over there with plenty of room for . . . um . . . Oprah and Gayle."

Maurice thanks the young man and the three of us set off for, as Wavonne put it, "the fat lady section."

"Hello," a smartly dressed middle-aged woman says when we reach our destination. "What can I help you with?"

"I need to find something suitable for these two . . . for an exclusive event . . . a white party," Maurice says. "What's your name, dear?"

"Susan."

"Okay, Susan. Well, she looks to be about a fourteen." Maurice points to me. "And she's a sixteen," he adds with a finger toward Wavonne.

"Sixteen?" Wavonne scoffs. "I'm a fourteen, too."

"Wavonne, sweetie," Maurice replies while waving his hand from her neck down to her feet. "Just because, with a little vigor and a lot of Vaseline, you can finagle all that into a size fourteen, doesn't mean you *are* a size fourteen."

"I've been telling her that for years."

"Don't be hatin' on all my jelly. I like a fitted look."

"There's *fitted*, and then there's buttons hanging on for dear life," Maurice says. "Let's just plan to go for a . . . um . . . a *less fitted* look for the white party. Trust me. I'm highly experienced at dressing generously proportioned women. I've been styling Monique for years." Maurice turns back to Susan. "I want something formal for both of them, but still fun and stylish." He points to me again. "Let's go a bit more conservative for this one . . . maybe something from Alex Evenings or Adrianna Papell . . . or Eileen Fisher." Then he looks at Wavonne. "This one . . . she's more Mac Duggal or City Chic."

"Sure . . . sure," Susan says. "Why don't I get you both set up in the fitting rooms, and I'll bring some selections to you."

Susan is about to lead us to the dressing area when Maurice speaks up again. "They'll need some Spanx, too . . . and not just the tummy ones . . . tummy *and* thigh."

Over the next thirty minutes or so, Susan helps Wavonne and me into these sort of torture devices called Spanx to smooth out our curves and begins bringing dresses to us. We try them on while Maurice sits on a stool outside the stalls and provides commentary.

"No," he says to Susan, exasperation in his voice, as I model a Pisarro Nights beaded gown trimmed with something Susan calls "sheer-illusion lace." "Why didn't you tell me that dress had a drop waist? Anyone can see she's a pear!"

"A pear? What does that mean?" I ask.

"It means you have small titties and a fat ass," Wavonne says. She's standing next to me admiring herself as we share a mirror. "*I*, on the other hand, am an hourglass."

I give her a quick look. "More like an hour and a half glass."

Wavonne scowls at me in the mirror as Maurice looks me over once again.

"Dear God," he grumbles to Susan. "If the dress was purple, she'd look like that slow-witted creature in the McDonald's kiddie commercials."

"He's talkin' about Grimace."

"I *know* who he's talking about, Wavonne," I respond as Susan unzips the back of the dress, and I head back into the dressing room.

"Bring me something flowy with a softly fitted waistline," Maurice commands before I have a chance to close the curtain and finish getting out of the dress. "Something sparkly above the waist and plain below . . . we need party on the top," he says, gesturing toward my upper half before lowering his finger in the direction of my waist and thighs, "and all business on the bottom."

"He's trying to draw attention away from your big behind," Wavonne quips, paying me back for my "hour and a half" comment.

I close the dressing room curtain without bothering to respond. As I step out of the dress, I hear Maurice make a few comments about the outfit Wavonne is modeling before sending her back into the changing room for another round as well.

A few minutes later, Susan brings me yet another frock. I try it on and dare to think that we may have finally found a keeper. It's an ivory-colored knee-length dress by Adrianna Papell with a slightly lower hem in the back than in the front, a scoop neck, and something Susan called flutter sleeves. It ties loosely at the waist and is actually quite flattering.

"Now we're getting somewhere," Maurice says as I step out of the fitting room. He walks a complete circle around me, adjusts the neckline, and redoes the tie so the bow sits more to the right of my waist than the middle.

His eyes meet mine in the mirror, and he smiles. "Lovely! I think we have a winner."

I smile back at him and decide that maybe he's not quite as snarky and irritating as I originally thought.

"*Very* nice." Wavonne gives me a long look as she steps out of her stall in Susan's latest selection. "Girl, they better turn off the detectors, 'cause you smokin'!"

I laugh. "Thank you, Wavonne. You look very nice yourself."

"Hmmm," Maurice says, scrutinizing her dress, a floor-length white gown with silver sequins dotted throughout. "It just sort of pours down your body, doesn't it?" He circles her like he did me a few minutes ago. "I'm not sure about the plunging neckline. That's a lot of décolletage for a party that starts early in the evening."

"Décolletage?" Wavonne asks.

"I think he's talking about your cleavage."

"It's not awful, but I don't think this is it. Maybe we need to go in another direction." He turns his neck. "Susan," he calls out toward the main shopping area, prompting her to appear. "I saw a red jumpsuit on one of the mannequins. Do you know which one I'm talking about? That might be a good look for Wavonne if you have it in white."

"Yes. That's by Marina. I think we do have it in white. Let me check."

As Susan returns to the racks I see Maurice look at his watch. "Let's try the jumpsuit. If it's not *you*, we'll go with this one. We're getting short on time. I've got to get Monique dressed, and only God knows what sort of drama will be going on in that house by the time I get to there."

"Drama?" Wavonne asks. "What sort of drama?"

"Oh nothing . . . let's just say I may be her stylist, but half the time I feel more like her therapist. There's always something going on between her and Nathan that I have to hear about and help her process. The man is a total sleaze."

"Really?" I say. "I can't say I particularly cared for him based on what little interaction I've had with him."

"You're not the only one. He's always up to no good."

"What sort of 'no good' are we talkin' about here?" Wavonne asks.

"I'm not one to gossip," Maurice replies in that way people who love to gossip speak right before they're about to start gossiping. "You name it. Drinking. Women. And, lately, gambling. Monique will not even tell me how much of their fortune he's lost over at MGM." Maurice is referring to the swanky Las Vegas–style casino that opened to great fanfare a couple of years ago in National Harbor, a multi-use waterfront development that has become Prince George's County's haughtiest neighborhood. "He's a regular in the high-limit room. I've heard rumors of him losing more than a hundred thousand dollars in a single day."

"A hundred thousand dollars?!" I bellow. "Oh my."

"A few weeks ago the *Enquirer* published a photo of him meeting with Rodney Morrissey."

"Who's that?"

"He's a well-known crime boss . . . a high-dollar loan shark and a very, *very* bad man. More than one person associated with him has turned up dead over the last few years."

"Why doesn't Monique get rid of Nathan if he's gambling away all her money and getting involved with dangerous people?"

"Your guess is as good as mine. Monique is a smart, beautiful woman, but when it comes to relationships, she makes bad decision after bad decision."

"Speaking of relationships, what is up with her and Odessa?"

"Those two." Maurice shakes his head. "They've had a . . . shall we say *tenuous* relationship since I've known them. They started out in the cosmetology trenches together . . . low-paid styling jobs at chain beauty shops . . . and, while Odessa has certainly had some success with her salon, Monique just surpassed her by leaps and bounds and became this nationwide phenomena. I don't think Odessa can handle it. She's jealous."

"So why did Monique invite her to dinner last night if they don't get along?"

"I don't know. Their whole deal is complicated. They go way back, and they have a mutually beneficial relationship.

From what I know, Odessa sells more of Monique's products than any hair salon in the country, so Monique gives her some discounts on the wholesale prices. They are both making a lot of money for each other."

Maurice pokes his head outside the dressing area. "Where is that salesgirl?"

"I'm not sure we need her," Wavonne says. "The longer I wear this, the more it grows on me."

"It's okay, but it would need a little tailoring to make it a perfect fit and it might be a little too glittery . . . with the silver sequins and all."

"There is no such thing as too glittery when it comes to Wavonne."

"Not for *Wavonne*," Maurice says. "For *Monique*. She'll get testy if she knows I helped Wavonne select something that, even for half a second, takes any attention away from her."

"Is that even possible? For anyone to take attention away from Monique?" I ask, although I guess, if anyone was going to do such a thing, it would be Wavonne. "Monique would be the belle of the ball in a potato sack. And I'm sure whatever she's wearing to the party will be in a league all its own."

"It will be. Monique would settle for nothing less," Maurice says. "She's had a custom-made gown in the works for months . . . mermaid silhouette . . . bateau neckline . . . hand-sewn beads . . . it's gorgeous . . . just *gorgeous* . . . worth every penny of the four thousand dollars she's paying for it."

"Four thousand dollars?!" Wavonne shrieks.

"Wow. That must be some white dress," I say.

"*White*?" Maurice responds. "Aren't you cute." He's talking to me as if I'm a naïve child. "Now, how do you expect Monique to be the undeniable center of attention in a *white* dress at a *white* party?"

Wavonne and I stare back at him, perplexed.

"That's Monique's *thing* . . . every year she throws a white party and insists that all her guests wear white . . . then she makes a grand entrance in a bold-colored dress. This year she is wearing a vivid Larimar blue evening gown."

"Sounds like it will be quite something."

"Yes, and if I don't get over to her house and help her get into it soon, I'll never hear the end of it." Maurice looks at his watch once again. "I'm going to go find Susan. We need to get a move on."

"Larimar?" I ask Wavonne as Maurice steps away. "Must be one of those trendy designers my unfashionable pear-shaped self has never heard of."

"How can you not have heard of him, Halia? He's dressed Halle Berry and like a million other celebrities."

"Really? That's—"

"Here we are," Susan says, reappearing with Maurice and handing a white jumpsuit to Wavonne.

"Try it on and let's see how it looks," Maurice instructs. "We are out of time, so if this is not a good look for you, we'll go with the dress you have on. I've got to get over to Casa Monique and help her get ready . . . and help her deal with whatever antics that husband of hers has been up to."

"Wow, it sounds like working for Monique is quite the roller-coaster ride," I say as Wavonne steps into the dressing stall and closes the curtain.

"It's certainly never boring," Maurice says. "Never ever boring."

Chapter 12

"A large, purple creature of indeterminate species with short arms and legs. He was first introduced by McDonald's in—"

"I *know* who Grimace is, Wavonne. I don't need you looking him up on Wikipedia or whatever you're reading from," I say to her as she puts her phone back in her lap. We're in my van on the way to Monique's party. After our shopping excursion with Maurice, Wavonne and I went back to the house to get ready and then stopped by Sweet Tea to pick up the items my staff prepared for the event. I must say I have the best team in the business—in only a few hours they prepared quite the spread for us to take with us.

As Wavonne and I maneuver through Saturday night traffic, the smell of chafing dishes filled with my famous corn fritters, mini waffles topped with little nuggets of crispy fried chicken, and buttermilk biscuit bites permeates throughout the vehicle. I suspect the main reason Monique invited us to this haughty affair is because she wanted my culinary contributions on her buffet, so I went with time-tested party food that always goes over well rather than daring to try something new. I'm sure her guests will enjoy the creations we have in transit—they really are delicious on their own, but, in my never-ending quest to take things up a notch, I've brought along a few accompaniments to make them even tastier: a little powdered sugar to dust the corn fritters, praline syrup for the fried chicken and waffle hors d'oeuvres, and house-made pineapple red pepper jelly for the biscuits.

"That food sure smells good," Wavonne says as we turn off the highway and continue to follow my navigation system, which leads us to a winding back road.

"I didn't know there were this many trees left around here," I say as the robotic voice coming from my speakers tells us we are approaching our destination. Prince George's County is a densely populated Maryland suburb across the line from DC, so, even though I've lived here my whole life, I'm surprised by the area we've found ourselves in—it has an almost rural feel to it. We're in Mitchellville, one of the more affluent areas of the county. I don't get over this way much, but, based on the few times I've passed through recently, I thought it pretty much consisted of high-end tract housing developments and shopping centers. I didn't realize there were still wooded sections in the area with houses that sit on multiple acres rather than a fraction of one.

"Me either," Wavonne says. "These are some big-ass houses . . . on some big-ass pieces of land. People are spendin' *money* for these places."

"I'm sure they are," I agree as we close in on Monique's driveway. I know it must be hers because it's safeguarded by two young men who look like they just stepped out of an episode of *America's Next Top Model*. They're both African American and wearing crisp white pants held up with thick silver belts, snug white shirts, and white pageboy hats. There's a bit of a chill in the fall air, so I imagine they must be cold without any jackets on.

"Ooh, girl," Wavonne says as I make the turn, and one of

the young men motions for me to stop. "I need to get me some of that praline syrup you got back there. I know what . . . I mean *who* I'd like to pour it all over."

"They are quite handsome, but aren't they a little young . . . even for you?"

Wavonne is barely shy of thirty, which sounds positively youthful to my forty-something self, but these guys look like they're barely over eighteen.

"As long as they are old enough to vote and enlist in the army, ain't nothin' wrong with dippin' your toes into the Generation Z pond here and there."

"I think I'll let you dip your toes in that pond solo," I say as one of the young fellows reaches my van, and I let the window down. I'm about to greet him, but before I have a chance to speak, his eyes catch sight of the chafing dishes in the back, and he says, "I'm sorry. The help is supposed to use the back entrance."

"The *help*?!" Wavonne barks from the passenger side. "Do we look like freakin' Aibileen and Minny? We are guests of Ms. Monique Dupree. I know you'd better get out our way . . ."

"Oh gosh . . . I apologize," he says. "May I have your names please?"

I give the young man our names, he checks for them on his list, and gives us the okay to continue up the long driveway that leads to Monique's house.

"Wow." Wavonne takes notice of the stately home, which, based on Monique's bright pink tour bus and flamboyant taste in fashion, is a bit more conservative (in style, not size) than I expected. It's an enormous (I'm guessing upward of five thousand square feet) red brick home with a series of long white columns, staggered dormers, and a double-door entry. The trees along the driveway and the shrubbery in front of the house have been strung with what must be thousands and thousands of twinkling white lights—the effect is quite spectacular.

The driveway loops into a circle in front of the house, and I stop the van near the main doors. I figure I'll park it out of the way once we've unloaded the food, but I've barely stepped the vehicle when a young man, dressed in the same outfit as the guys at the other end of the driveway, hands me a ticket and looks for me to give him my key.

"Valet parking? Look at Ms. Dupree keepin' it classy," Wavonne says as she rounds the corner from the other side of the van. "Is this a home or a country club?"

After I explain to the gentleman that I need to bring the food into the house before he parks the car, he calls over another attendant. They offer to help us carry in the trays, and all four of us walk up the front steps with our arms loaded.

When we reach the front door, an older woman greets us and introduces herself as Lena, Monique's housekeeper. We step into a grand foyer at the base of an imposing curved staircase as a little toy dog, a Pomeranian, I think, yaps at our feet. It has some sparkly stones on its collar, and I can't help but wonder if they are actual diamonds.

"Please tell me those are not real diamonds on that dog's collar," Wavonne says to me as Lena, with an air of authority, instructs several attractive young ladies, garbed in the most bizarre catering uniforms I've ever seen, to take the chafing dishes from us and carry them to the kitchen. They are all wearing white minidresses with a lace overlay and four-inch white leather pumps. The only reason I know they are staffing the party rather than attending as guests is the small half apron tied around their waists with the Hair by Monique logo embroidered in pink across the front. The outfits look beautiful, but are clearly highly impractical for working a party—I guess, when she decided on the apparel for her party staff, Monique, much like God when he created the Kardashians, valued appearance over any real utility. I suppose it makes sense—she is in the beauty business after all. But as the daintily clad women, who look vaguely familiar to me, walk away with my food, I find myself afraid they might stumble on their ultra-high heels and corn fritters and fried chicken will go flying all over Monique's pristine granite floors.

"You can drop your coats in Monique's den," Lena says, and leads us to, when compared to the grand nature of the rest of the house, a fairly modest room with a large flat-screen television, a fireplace, and a taupe leather sectional on which coats are already piling up.

"There's a full home theater in the basement, but this is where Monique tends to relax in the evenings. We're using it for jackets and purses this evening."

"It's very nice . . . cozy," I say as Wavonne and I remove our coats and lay them on the sofa. "If you can show us toward the kitchen, I'm happy to help set up my trays."

After Lena points us in the right direction and excuses herself, Wavonne and I exit the room.

"I love that jumpsuit on you," I say as we navigate the cavernous home in search of the kitchen. "Maurice had the right idea when he picked it out." My compliments for Wavonne are not always altogether sincere (honestly, much of the time, she doesn't give me a whole lot to work with), but this time I do really mean what I've said. Maurice's selection for Wavonne is quite striking—it's formal enough for the occasion, but the way it drapes over only one shoulder with a sleeve that drops slightly above her elbow and flows from a loose-fitting midsection into what Maurice called "palazzo pants" (apparently, a fancy way of saying bell bottoms) gives the ensemble a sense of whimsy and fun that fits her . . . and the little cutout along the bustline revealing her cleavage is so *Wavonne*. Of course, it took some persuading to get her to agree to take it home in a size six-teen rather than a fourteen, but with many words of encouragement and a few digs from Maurice (I recall some-thing being said about "sausage" and "casing") she eventu-ally relented.

"Thank you. It's growing on me." She looks down at her-self. "All white and flowy . . . I'm thinking I can add some wings to it and be an angel for Halloween," she says as we bypass the same cameraman who was at Odessa's salon yes-terday. He appears to be getting ready to film the festivities.

"Well, that's one idea," I reply just before we reach the kitchen and come upon Alex. He has his back turned to us and is in the midst of removing his chef's jacket. I hate to admit it, but I think Wavonne and I are both too enmeshed in the view of Alex's V-shaped back muscles protruding through the tight-fitting T-shirt he has on under the outer layer, that we fail to announce ourselves. Assuming he's still alone, he removes the T-shirt, and Wavonne lets out an audible sigh, alerting him to our presence.

"I'm sorry," he says. "I thought I was alone."

I smile, trying to look at his eyes rather than his defined bare chest. "Oh . . . no need to apologize."

"Apologize?" Wavonne says. "You should charge a fee. If anything need cheese on it tonight, we can grate it on your abs."

Alex laughs, which sends a ripple through his chiseled stomach. "I was putting the finishing touches on the cake in the living room and made a little mess on my chef's coat. Monique wants us lowly staff members to wear these shirts anyway," he jokes, and grabs a short-sleeve white linen shirt from the counter (the same type the attendants at the gate were wearing) and quickly slips it on. "Did you *have* to do such a great job with your contributions to the buffet? I'm afraid my efforts are going to pale in comparison."

I smile again. "That's nice of you to say. Has my food been put out already?"

"Yes. Some of Odessa's girls helped me set them up in the dining room." He gestures toward the threshold on the other side of him. "Would you like to see the buffet?"

"Sure," I say as Alex leads Wavonne and me to the dining room. "What did you say about Odessa's girls?"

"Some of her stylists are working the party . . . taking coats . . . serving drinks . . . passing out hors d'oeuvres in addition to what we have on the buffet . . . just standing around looking pretty."

"That's why I recognized them. They were staffing the tables for Monique at the hair show today."

"Yes. I think Monique pays them quite well to do a little moonlighting for her. Tonight I believe they are supposed to somehow bring up which hair products they use while passing around trays of champagne," Alex says, and then nods toward the table, which could easily seat fourteen people if the dining chairs had not been removed so it can act as a serving station. It's draped in a white taffeta cloth that could easily be repurposed as a train for a designer wedding dress. A crystal vase with more than a dozen white roses graces the center of the table and several long taper candles are glowing among the food displays.

"Your items are at that end." Alex points to his left. "And here we have my spinach dip with marble rye bread, shrimp cocktail, and mini quiches," he says before going through the rest of his handiwork, which includes a cheese board, some vegetable trays, meatballs, and a few other, mostly uninspiring, edibles.

"It all looks delicious," I say, trying to muster some enthusiasm as I eye the mini quiches that look like the frozen ones you buy at Costco.

"Sure does," Wavonne agrees, and grabs a plate.

"Wavonne!" I snap. "I don't think the buffet is officially open. The guests have barely started arriving."

"*I'm* a guest, and I'm here . . . and if I'm gonna start wearin' a sixteen I may as well eat up."

"Put the plate back, Wavonne. Can you at least wait until the party is actually underway before attacking the food?"

"Fine." She puts the plate back on the stack. "I'm going to find the little girls' room, and see if I can adjust these Spanx." She wiggles around uncomfortably. "I think my pancreas has been shoved up into my neck."

"What are Spanx?" Alex asks.

"Essentially a modern-day girdle."

"Sounds painful," Alex says, and looks me up and down. "Seems unnecessary to me. I personally think women should celebrate their curves, not try to hide them."

"Aw . . . that's sweet. All the fashion magazines would disagree with you, but it's nice to know that there are some men out there who appreciate women who look like *women*."

Neither one of us seems to know what to say next, so to break the silence and steer the conversation away from women's shapewear I ask, "So, how long have you been working for Monique?"

"A few months. I cook for her and Nathan three or four nights a week, and they're taking me on the road to cook for them during the tour. I'm figuring out how to make the best use of that little kitchen on the bus now."

"Must be very different from working in big commercial kitchens."

"Yes, but mostly in good ways. Monique pays me well, it's definitely less hurried and stressful, and she and Nathan still spend a lot of time in New York, which amounts to many days off for me."

"Sounds like a good gig. Where do I sign up?" I joke. "How long have you been a chef?"

"About six years. I came here from my home country on a student visa and studied at L'Academie de Cuisine in Gaithersburg. From there, I worked as a sous chef at a number of restaurants before working my way up to head chef at the little bistro where I met Monique. She enjoyed my food and asked to meet me. She was looking to hire a personal chef as she doesn't have time to cook and is trying to eat healthier. We got to talking and eventually worked out a deal. So far, it's working out pretty well."

"Your home country is the Dominican Republic?"

"Yes. How did you know?"

"One of my employees is from the DR so I recognized the accent, which is lovely by the way," I say. "Where are you from in the DR?"

"Villa Jaragua. It's on the western side of the country next to Lake Enriquillo," he says. "Would you like to see some photos?"

"I'd love to."

Alex retrieves his phone from his pocket and begins to show me some pictures. "These are from my last trip back home in August. It's cheaper to go in the summer months when tourism slows down." As he swipes through images, I see him with an array of other young men and women mostly in bright-colored clothing suitable for tropical weather. There are lots of palm trees and blue skies in the backgrounds . . . and apparently a beer called Presidente that comes in a green bottle is very popular on the island—it seems to be the beverage of choice for most of the people in the photos. He shows me his mother and a brother . . . and some cousins, and, even though Momma grilled him about it already, I must admit I have my eye out for anyone who seems like a girlfriend in the photos, but I don't see anyone who fits the bill.

"These are great," I say as Alex continues to swipe. "Looks like a beautiful country."

"It is . . . not as much wealth and opportunity as there is here, but I do miss it." He's about to continue through the collection when we hear the doorbell ring. "Sounds like more guests are starting to arrive." He lowers the phone. "I guess I'd better get back in the kitchen."

"Okay," I say. "I'll go find Wavonne and try to keep her out of trouble."

The doorbell rings again as I step away. And, just like that, Monique's white party is underway.

Chapter 13

"We got the who's who of PG County in da house to-night." Wavonne looks around at Monique's guests while I watch her place her long-stem glass underneath the champagne fountain on display in the foyer. I must say I'm impressed by the crystal champagne glasses—clearly Ms. Dupree is having nothing to do with those "assembly re-quired" plastic flutes from the Party Store I see at most events.

"That's your third glass, Wavonne."

"I know how to count, Halia. Thank you very much."

"Don't you think it's a little early in the evening to be on drink number three?"

"These glasses don't hold much and, if you haven't no-ticed, Halia, this is a *party*." She takes my glass, my first of the evening, which is not even half-empty, and plunks it under the fountain as well. "Take a few swigs. It'll do you some good." She hands it back to me, filled to the rim. "Seems that Puerto Rican brotha in the kitchen really does have a thing for you." Wavonne pauses for a moment. "It is okay to call a Puerto Rican a brotha, right? You know, if he's black and all?"

"I don't know, Wavonne, and I don't particularly care . . . and he's Dominican, not Puerto Rican."

"Dominican . . . Puerto Rican. Tomayto . . . potahto."

"That's not even how the saying goes, Wavonne. It's tomato . . . oh, forget it."

"Whatever. They're both on the same island."

"No, they aren't. Puerto Rico is its own island. The Dominican Republic shares an island with Haiti."

"Well . . . aren't you just Jenequa Geography." Wavonne shifts her weight on her high heels. "Either way, he's sexy as hell. And why his hot self is into you and not me, is for only God, Jesus, and Dionne Warwick's Psychic Friends to know."

"I don't think he's *into* me," I respond, even though I do actually think he might be. "He's so much younger than I am. We just have the cooking thing in common, so he's chatty."

"Maybe . . . maybe not. But if you want to go flirt with him in the kitchen, and see if you can get you some, I won't be mad atcha," Wavonne offers. "I can go off on my own and scope out the other eligible men. There are some *money'd* folks at this party, Halia. I recognize a lot of faces from the social pages."

By "social pages" Wavonne is referring to the obituaries in the *Washington Post*, which she occasionally peruses for the death of women who were married to rich men; *Washingtonian* magazine, which she flips through looking for articles about the communities' most successful businessmen; and a host of other periodicals and online social media outlets that follow the lives of the local elite and help Wavonne keep tabs on bachelors with fat bank accounts. Her attention, however, is not limited to single men—she monitors couples as well, keeping a watchful eye for impending separations and divorces. If Wavonne hears of a wealthy couple splitting or the untimely demise of a rich man's wife, she uses any connection at all to the affected gentleman as an excuse to be the first to darken his door with a casserole (that I'll have to make), a low-cut blouse, and some comforting words. Unfortunately

for her, she has to get in line with all the other shameless op-
portunists.

"I think I'll stay put for the time being," I say. "I'm sure
Alex is busy, and I sort of like this spot, but feel free to mingle while I hang back."

We've mostly been hovering in the dining room or the
foyer since the party started. At one point, we tried to muscle
our way into the main living room, but, despite the generous
size, it was super crowded—a sea of mostly brown skin and
pale clothing . . . everyone very chic and elegant in expensive-
looking white fashions. We could barely get through the
threshold and ended up spilling back into the foyer where
we've been chatting amongst ourselves and a few other guests
as they partake in the flowing champagne. We've also done a
fair amount of people-watching as Monique's guests pass
through the foyer from the living room to the dining room to
refill plates.

"Okay, I may circulate in a few minutes and—" Wavonne
stops talking as a stream of guests, likely wanting a little
space, begin to exit the living room and congregate in the
foyer. "Look," she says, nodding her head in the direction of
a handsome older gentleman. "That's Charles Norman. He's
a county executive or sits on the council or somethin' . . .
made a ton in real estate." Wavonne then eyes the mature
woman next to him in a snowy silk gown. "Unfortunately,
that is a *Mrs.* Norman," she adds before less than discreetly
pointing in another direction. "That's Cedrica Harper. Remember, we catered a Fourth of July party at her house. That
lucky heifer married Clarence Harper, who owned a bunch
of small bidnesses . . . laundromats, pizza places, hair salons.
He croaked a few months after they got married. She sold
most of his companies and made a bundle. And over there"—
Wavonne eyes another couple making their way into the
foyer—"that's Tim and Treena Simms. They own the Oasis Spa

in Bowie and some other salons around town. Word on the street is that their marriage is on the rocks. My girl Melva gets her weave done at one of their salons, and her stylist said that the two of them bicker like crazy. If they're headed for splitsville, maybe I should go over there and introduce myself." Wavonne adjusts her breasts. "Are my girls even?" she asks.

Before I have a chance to answer, she pulls a little spray bottle from her evening bag and hands it to me. "Give me a quick spritz, would ya?" She sticks out her chest.

"No!" I say. "Go in the bathroom and do that yourself."

"Oh, just do it, Halia. Hurry. Treena is steppin' away."

I groan but accept the bottle, grudgingly angle it properly, and give her cleavage a quick spray of glitter.

"Thank you."

I hand the bottle back to her, and she tries to slink away, but more guests keep piling into the foyer, tightening the space. That's when I realize that Maurice is the impetus for the migration toward the base of the grand staircase. It's the first time I've seen him since we arrived. He's engaging with other party attendees, gesturing for them to enter the foyer.

"This way, ladies and gentlemen," he says over the loud murmur of voices. "Monique is about to make her entrance."

I chuckle quietly to myself. I have catered more parties than I can count, but I've never been to one during which the host makes an *entrance*. The over-the-top nature of this party . . . the-over-the top nature of *anything* related to Monique is a bit comical to me.

"Shhhhhhh." Maurice puts a finger to his lips, the party quiets down, and the chandelier dims . . . and, I kid you not, a young man wheels in a spotlight. *You've got to be joking . . .*

"Girl is about to *throw down*," Wavonne says, deciding against homing in on Mr. Harper for the time being.

Before I have a chance to agree with Wavonne, the lights

go black, and Bruno Mars's "24K Magic" begins to boom from some speakers mounted in the corners of the walls. Someone flicks on the spotlight and directs it to beam toward the top of the steps. Monique strides into the light just as the song switches from its slow-pulsed intro to its upbeat groove.

"I doubt Eva Perón made this much of a fuss when she came out on the balcony of the Casa Rosada."

"Casa who?" Wavonne asks.

"Never mind."

Monique waves and begins sashaying back and forth along the landing like she's just been crowned Miss America, her yappy little dog following behind her while the cameraman films the whole thing.

"I'm surprised Ms. Thang doesn't have a tiara on her head," Wavonne says as Monique continues to strut back and forth with occasional stops to pose in the gown that Maurice described to us earlier . . . and I must say, Maurice was right—it is gorgeous!

For anyone else, this whole spectacle would be obscenely ridiculous . . . *embarrassing* even. I don't think I've seen as much posturing when they run the red carpet footage before the Academy Awards. But Monique has a way about her that makes her antics at the top of the steps endearing. It's like she's in on the joke—she knows how silly she's being, and she knows her guests know the same. But everyone is having a great time, so it's all good. We're all laughing as Monique places one hand behind her head and the other on her hip, posing like Jessica Rabbit. But we're laughing *with* her, not *at* her.

As the music fades and the lights go up, Monique slowly descends the steps and stops mid-staircase.

"Hello, hello!" she calls to us. "Thanks so much for coming. You know I always try to put on a grand affair and tonight is no exception. Is everyone having a good time?"

There are some claps and a mix of affirmative words before she speaks again.

"Now how about this dress?!"

More claps and a few cheers.

She looks down at her bright blue gown. "Oh my!" she says facetiously. "Was this a white party? No one told me."

We all laugh again as Monique throws her hands up to her cheeks and drops her jaw in mock horror. "Oh well. I was never one to blend in," she offers with a broad smile before lightly fluffing her tresses. "And the hair?"

More applause.

She teases us with a look of disappointment, insinuating that we can do better with our show of appreciation for her famous mane. "You guys do know I'm in the hair business? What does it take to get some love?" she playfully asks before repeating her question. "And the hair?!"

Stronger hand claps . . . more cheers and a loud "*Fierce!*" from Wavonne.

Again, this would all seem absurd coming from anyone else . . . like a sad Real Housewife of Atlanta demanding compliments at her own party, but Monique makes it work.

"Tonight we celebrate past successes for Hair by Monique," she says when we've quieted down, "and look to the future for—"

The doorbell rings and a "Who dares interrupt me?" expression appears on Monique's face.

All eyes look toward the door and then back up at Monique, who is still for a moment before nodding at her housekeeper to answer the door.

As instructed, Lena moves toward the front door and swings it open, treating Monique's guests to yet another splash of color amidst masses of stark whites, ivories, and creams. Odessa is standing in the doorway in a dress the color of a fire engine. She carefully steps into the foyer in a dramatic red gown adorned in sequins and finished with a thick band of feathers at the bottom. She plants herself right next to Wavonne and me before uttering the same words used by our hostess moments earlier . . . the same words I suspect Monique uses every year when she debuts at this event. "Oh my!" Odessa says, an evil twinkle in her eyes. "Was this a white party? No one told me."

The light from the overhead chandelier reflects off the sequins, creating a sparkle that mesmerizes the entire room. Everyone is quiet as they try to make sense of Odessa's entrance. Even the dog seems bemused by her clear attempt to upstage Monique at her own party.

All eyes are on Odessa until they realize that the look on Monique's face as she glares at the new arrival might be the more interesting view. Gazes lift back toward Monique, who only momentarily lets the scorn show on her face before making a quick recovery and reclaiming her winning smile.

As Monique purposely descends the stairs I think about what Maurice said about her distaste for anyone taking attention away from her and can't help but stare as she reaches the bottom of the staircase. Her heels meet the granite tile and nimbly click along the stone in Odessa's direction.

As she leans in to embrace Odessa and give her a kiss on the cheek, Wavonne and I are the only ones close enough to hear her say, through gritted teeth, "I'm going to get you for this, you evil bitch."

Chapter 14

Everyone at the party knew that Odessa would have hell to pay at some point in the future, but once it became clear that, in the here and now, Monique was going to handle Odessa's attempt to so boldly upstage her with measured grace, the crowd lost interest in the pair. They began to disperse throughout the main level before Monique got a chance to restart her welcome speech.

After their forced embrace and the exchange of a few stony pleasantries to keep up appearances, Monique and Odessa parted company. Monique sauntered off to hold court in the living room, and Odessa made her way to the dining room.

At the moment, the foyer has mostly cleared and, as Wavonne has crept off to prey on some unsuspecting couple's failing marriage, I find myself standing next to the champagne fountain alone. I'm a pretty social person—I enjoy being with people and don't generally struggle with mingling—but I feel a bit out of my element at this "see and be seen" affair. Everyone is so attractive and wealthy . . . and likely on the hunt for the next person they think can do something for them—so *not* my people.

I'm trying to decide what to do with myself when I see Maurice emerge from the living room and walk over to him.

"Thank you for all your help today. I'm not much of a fashionista. God knows what sort of white ensemble I would have come up with if left to my own devices."

Maurice takes a quick look at his watch before responding. "You're welcome, hon. It's what I do. It's all about accentuating the positive and bringing out someone's personality. When you look good, you feel good. And you, my dear, are looking quite fetching in that dress."

Maurice turns to one of the servers who has just approached with a tray of hors d'oeuvres. "No, thank you. Dieting," he says to the young lady before she teeters off on her high heels. Between her svelte figure, long legs, and flowing chestnut hair, she looks more like she should be at a photo shoot for some high fashion magazine rather than schlepping finger food from room to room at a party.

"She's one of Odessa's stylists?" I ask Maurice.

"Yes. I believe so."

"Alex mentioned they were working the party. I think I may have seen her at the convention this afternoon, too. So, what are all these beauticians doing manning tables at hair conventions and passing out nibbles at white parties?"

"Making some money," Maurice says as if the answer is obvious. "I'm sure they make a decent living doing hair at Odessa's salon, but, you know, life is expensive, so they moonlight. And when you look the way they do, opportunities abound."

"They are all quite striking."

"Yes . . . well, that is sort of Odessa's 'brand.' The same way Abercrombie and Fitch only hires attractive sales associates, Odessa only hires beautiful woman to work at her salon, and she occasionally helps them land moonlighting gigs. I assume she takes a cut of their fees. Extremely good-looking people are always in demand. They do car shows, and local fashion shows, and even host open houses with real estate agents . . . anything that can benefit from a pretty face.

Monique prefers that her event staffers have a certain look . . . valuing their level of attractiveness over any catering experience, so Odessa hooked her up . . . another example of their mutually beneficial relationship."

"I thought you said Monique didn't like people being prettier than her?"

"No, I said she didn't like people taking attention away from her. You can be prettier than she is . . . or younger . . . thinner . . . just don't *outshine* her . . . don't try to snuff out her star. It's only when you mess with Monique's sparkle . . . with her glitz . . . that you get into trouble."

I think of how Odessa tried to do just that tonight—how she tried, and perhaps succeeded, in out-glittering the self-proclaimed queen of glitter, when I see Wavonne emerge from the dining room and stagger toward me. Clearly, the abundance of champagne she has consumed is taking its toll.

"That Treena's stickin' to her man like glue," she says to Maurice and me. "Which confirms that they are on the skids, and she thinks he has a wanderin' eye. I just need to get him away from her, lay on a little sugar, and, who knows, I may get me a spa in Bowie. If you're nice to me, Halia, maybe I'll let you get a facial or a massage at a discount."

I catch Maurice looking at his watch for the second time this evening. "Much as I'd love to get the scoop on whoever Treena is and what the deal is with 'her man,' I'm afraid I need to excuse myself, ladies," he says. "Things to do . . . people to see."

"Sure. No worries. It was nice to see you and thanks again for your help today."

"Yeah . . . thank you, Maurice," Wavonne says, her words slurring together. "I'm diggin' my jumpsuit."

"You're quite welcome . . . just remember what we talked about, Wavonne . . . about the tight clothing—only shopping bags and bank accounts should be bursting at the seams."

Maurice withdraws from our little trio, and Wavonne

starts laughing way more heartily than his little "bursting at the seams" quip calls for.

"How much have you had to drink?"

"I don't know, Halia. A few glasses of champagne here . . . a gin and tonic there. Who can keep track." Wavonne reaches for a champagne glass. "Yo! What is your problem?" she asks when I take the glass from her and set it back on the table.

"You've had enough, Wavonne. Take a break for a little while. Let's get you a glass of water."

"Halia, sometimes you sure do know how to put the poop in party pooper."

"I do try my best." I nudge her toward the dining room, sneaking a peek into the living room on our way. There's a parting in the crowd, and I catch a glimpse of Nathan on the sofa. One of Odessa's stylists-turned-cater-waiters is sitting on his lap.

"Am I drunker than I think I am or is that leggy blond white chick all up in Nathan's bidness?"

"Yes and yes. You *are* drunker than you think, and that young lady *is* sitting on Nathan's lap."

"And there's another ho-bag curled up next to him." Wavonne takes note of a woman sitting inappropriately close to Nathan. She's also a server for the party and, much like the woman on his lap, is quite beautiful.

"How come I never get to sit on the sofa and mingle with guests when I work parties for you?"

"Because I'd fire you," I say, even though we both know that if I was going to fire Wavonne, I would have done it many years ago on numerous occasions on which it was warranted. "Come on, let's get you a big glass of water . . . and maybe a cup of coffee."

As I lead Wavonne back to the dining room to try to sober her up, another exodus from the living room begins, and guests start to pass by only to disappear through a doorway down the hall.

"Where's everyone goin'?" Wavonne asks no one in particular.

"The dancing is starting in the basement. Monique has flown in James DeShawn to DJ," a random guest says to Wavonne.

"James DeShawn?!" Wavonne says. "Come on, Halia. Let's go downstairs and shake a tail feather."

"Is there water downstairs?" I ask the same woman who told us about the dancing.

"I'm sure there's a full bar, including bottled water."

"Full bar," Wavonne says. "Nice. I can get me another gin and tonic."

"Fine . . . fine," I say, and move with Wavonne and the rest of the crowd toward the basement. I have no intention of letting Wavonne indulge in another cocktail, but I figure we can tackle that issue once we get downstairs.

RECIPE FROM HALIA'S KITCHEN

Halia's Smothered Pork Chops

Ingredients
1 teaspoon salt
½ teaspoon black pepper
1 tablespoon onion powder
1 tablespoon garlic powder
1 teaspoon paprika
½ teaspoon allspice
¼ teaspoon cayenne pepper
½ cup all-purpose flour
4 one-inch-thick pork chops
⅔ cup olive oil
1 large onion sliced into thin rings
1 clove minced garlic
¼ cup butter
1 cup water
2 cups chicken broth
½ cup sour cream

- Preheat oven to 300 degrees Fahrenheit.
- Combine dry ingredients (salt, black pepper, onion powder, garlic powder, paprika, allspice, cayenne pepper, and flour). Set aside.
- Heat oil in a 12-inch pan over medium-high heat until it

begins to lightly smoke. Pat pork chops dry and lightly salt them. Dredge each chop in flour and seasoning mixture. Add to pan and fry until golden brown (about 2 minutes on first side, 1 minute on second side). Remove chops from pan and place in glass or other oven-safe 12-inch casserole dish.

- Reduce heat slightly. Add onions to pan and cook until tender (about 6 minutes). Remove onions and set aside.
- Add minced garlic to oil, cooking until fragrant (about 30 seconds).
- Add butter and remaining flour mixture to pan. Stir constantly until bubbly and slightly pasty. Add water and chicken broth. Continue stirring until a gravy consistency is attained. Remove from heat and add sour cream. Stir well.
- Pour gravy over chops. Cover casserole dish with foil and place in preheated oven. Bake for 1.5 hours. Remove from oven, uncover and place sautéed onions over pork chops, recover with foil and bake for an additional 30 minutes.

Chapter 15

Once we descend to the basement and stroll past a home theater, an enclave with a pool table, and an actual in-home bowling alley, we reach a large open area with a mirrored disco ball spinning overhead and colored spotlights beaming in random order from the corners of the ceiling. I have no idea who James DeShawn is, but when I hear the dance remix version of Whitney Houston's "Heartbreak Hotel" blaring from the speakers, I decide I like him.

Wavonne is so inebriated that when I return from the bar and hand her a plain glass of tonic water with a lime and tell her it's a gin and tonic, she doesn't notice it's devoid of any alcohol. Over the next several minutes, I bring her two more and, even in her current intoxicated state, I find it odd that it doesn't occur to her how out of character it is for me to be plying her with cocktails.

Pleased with my ability to get a little liquor-free hydration into Wavonne, I agree when she suggests we hit the dance floor. The DJ is playing a mix of pop and R & B music, much of it from the eighties and nineties. Wavonne is always telling me I'm too uptight and conservative, but when the music is good, I can shake my groove thing with the best of them—by *good*, I mean music with words and a beat you can move to as opposed to that pulsing electronic devoid-of-vocals nonsense they play at many of the clubs these days, or so I'm told.

I'm doing my usual fairly basic dance moves while Wavonne, much like Suzanne Somers in *Three's Company*, is the "jiggle in the show." We're both having a good time on our little piece of dance floor real estate, bopping around to some oldies from Janet Jackson and Salt-N-Pepa . . . and some more current tunes from Rihanna and Drake and The Weeknd . . . when Wavonne catches sight of Tim and Treena Simms dancing next to her. It's not long before I see her give Tim a seductive smile and shimmy her shoulders in his direction to Mary J's "Family Affair." Then she brazenly starts mouthing the words at him . . . something about "a dancery," and "I'mma make it feel all right."

It's not long before Wavonne begins inching farther away from me and closer to Tim and Treena. She dances near them for a few minutes before completely invading their space. Despite Treena's looks of extreme displeasure, Wavonne holds her ground and eventually manages to maneuver herself in between the two of them. At some point she turns around and presses her body against Tim's, something he does not seem to mind at all. Treena, however, clearly minds—her eyes expand with anger before she stomps off the dance floor in disgust. My guess is that she expects Tim to chase after her with a profuse apology, but Tim, who appears to be as drunk as Wavonne, stays put.

"I guess Felicia's goin' bye," I hear Wavonne say to Tim over the loud music.

My first instinct is to intervene and try to pull Wavonne away from Tim, but *she's* drunk and *he's* drunk, and I don't feel like causing a scene. And, seeing how I've lost Wavonne as my dance partner, I figure I may as well go back upstairs and see if Alex needs any help before the evening starts to wind down. Neither Wavonne nor Tim notices when I depart the dance floor for the main level of the house.

I'm almost to the top of the steps when I hear Monique and Odessa talking in low voices . . . *arguing*, really. They are to the left of the doorway that leads to the basement, so they are unaware that I'm within earshot.

"I told you, our little arrangement is over, Odessa! I'm not the only one with secrets," Monique says, somehow managing to yell and whisper at the same time. "I don't know which one of your multiple personalities thought it would be okay to show up at my house and try to upstage me, but you will pay for that little stunt. How dare you come all up in my house looking like some dollar-store hooker in that tacky red dress . . . dropping cheap feathers all over my house. And then you think you can continue to wheel and deal with me—you've bled me of the last penny you'll get from me."

"We'll see about that, Monique. And you think *my* dress is tacky? What look were you going for in that gaudy blue number? Ghetto Smurf?" Odessa retorts. "I didn't realize Five Below was selling evening wear these days."

Oddly, I hear Monique laugh at Odessa's quip rather than respond.

"And as long as we are talking about discount stores, is that where you got that sad necklace?" Odessa asks. "I think my cleaning lady wears one like that when she's scrubbing my toilet."

"Yeah, like you can afford a cleaning lady," Monique sneers.

This time it's Odessa who laughs. "I'd say something about my cleaning lady being your momma, but I like your momma too much. How is she doing, by the way?"

"She's good. I can't get her out of that crap house I grew up in. I want to move her into someplace nice in a better neighborhood, but she won't hear of it," Monique responds, the anger in her voice a few moments earlier mostly gone.

"Well, tell her I said hi and will come by for a visit sometime soon." Odessa, too, seems to have lapsed from insult mode into casual conversation. "Would be great for her to move somewhere nicer, but I'd hate to see her sell that house. Boy, did we have some *times* within those walls."

"Girl, you ain't kiddin'," Monique replies. "I remember a house party or two back in the day . . . when Momma and Daddy were out of town . . . beer kegs in the backyard, bongs in the basement, Lydia Kingston dancing on the coffee table flashing her boobies to everyone. Kid 'N Play had nothing on us."

"Remember our motto? 'As long as no one got killed or pregnant it was a good party.'"

They both erupt in laughter.

Bemused by the dichotomy of their interaction, I'm contemplating how they went from the terse belittling of each other to friendly conversation and shared laughter over the course of about a minute, when I see some guests starting up the staircase behind me. This forces me to climb the last two steps to the hallway on the main level and make myself known to the ladies.

I offer a quick smile as I walk past the pair, giving the necklace Odessa mentioned a brief look. It's a fairly simple piece—a silver chain with a large stone that matches the bright blue of Monique's dress. It's not as flashy as I'd expect from Monique, but it looks nice enough to me.

Monique and Odessa return my smile but don't attempt to engage me as I stride by them.

"How's it going?" I ask Alex, stepping into the kitchen. He's at the sink with his back toward me.

"Good." He turns around. "Although I must say that I'm feeling a little slighted. We are clean out of every morsel of food you brought, but some of my chafing trays are still half full."

I chuckle. "I think we may have started with larger quantities of your food."

"Maybe so." He puts down the tray he was wiping when I came in the room. "Are you having a good time?"

"I am, but I think it's almost time to call it a night. Wavonne's overindulged in all the free-flowing liquor. She's stirring up trouble downstairs."

"Stirring up trouble?"

I'm about to explain when Monique swaggers into the kitchen. She's all smiles and appears to have regained her affable demeanor, which was clearly absent when I heard her arguing with Odessa in the hallway.

"Everything was lovely. Thanks so much . . . to both of you," she says to us, before looking at Alex. "I think you can start taking down the buffet in a few minutes. Nathan and Maurice are trying to move folks upstairs, so we can cut the cake, and then send everyone on their way. I've got a big day tomorrow with the tour launching and need to be up early. I want everyone out of here by ten."

"Sure."

"I'm happy to help before I leave."

"Please don't, Halia. You're a guest."

"I don't mind. I'm sort of partied out . . . it will give me something to do."

"Have it your way," she says. "I'm going to go upstairs and freshen up a bit. Don't cut the cake without me."

"As if that would ever happen," Alex jibes as Monique leaves the kitchen, and he and I make our way toward the dining room to begin clearing the buffet.

I've barely grabbed a few items from the table when I hear Wavonne's voice coming from the foyer. "Like it's my fault when a sista can't keep a man," she croons.

I can't see her, but it's clearly her voice booming from the right of the dining room entrance. Afraid that she's talking to Treena, I scurry into the next room to rein her in before the situation escalates. To my surprise, she's not talking to Treena . . . or any human.

"We were only dancin'. There was no need for her to get so salty," Wavonne continues. She's sitting on a chaise lounge using one hand to hold a half-full martini glass and the other to pet Monique's little froufrou dog that has hopped up on the lounge with her to, apparently, receive a play-by-play account of what happened in the basement since I came upstairs.

"I think it's time to hit the road, Wavonne."

She looks away from the little dog and up at me. "What? Why?"

"Because you've had too much to drink, you're causing strife among the guests . . . and, currently, you're having a one-way conversation with a Pomeranian."

"I was just telling little Rover here about Treena. When Tim didn't go after her, that heifer came back to the dance floor and gave it to him good." She looks back at the dog and starts talking to him again. "And then she started throwin' me all sorts of shade . . . actin' like she's all better than me. Well, I told her," Wavonne says, lifting the dog from under his front legs so his eyes are level with hers. "You know what I said?" She seems to be giving the pup a moment to respond to her question. When he doesn't, she continues. "I said, 'Stop talkin' like you all high and mighty . . . just cause you got hot sauce in your bag, don't make you Beyoncé.' Then she got her weave all in a tangle and—"

"Give him to me," I say, cutting her off. I reach for the dog and gently place him down on the floor before returning my attention to Wavonne. "You stay here while I go settle things with Monique. Then we're going home."

"Home? But I heard there's cake."

"Maybe we'll get you a slice to go," I offer before strengthening my tone. "And I mean what I said—*stay here* and out of trouble."

As I walk up the steps, I see that damn dog jump up on the lounge with Wavonne again and pick up my pace. I'd like to collect payment from Monique as quickly as possible and minimize the amount of people being treated to Wavonne conversing with a canine as they come upstairs for cake.

I wouldn't normally approach a client in her bedroom, but through years of catering experience, I've learned the hard way that if you don't get paid before you leave an event, you may very well never get paid at all. It's always nice when a customer simply hands you a check or a credit card without your even having to ask. And maybe Monique intended to do just that later in the evening, but Wavonne's already causing mayhem, and I'd like to get her home before more chaos ensues, so up the stairs to Monique's lair I go.

Chapter 16

I head down the long hallway on the second floor of Monique's home. Most of the doors I walk past are closed, which, I admit, disappoints me. I'm up here to collect my catering fee, but getting a sneak peek at a few more rooms of this fabulous house would have been a nice bonus.

At the far end of the hallway, I see a trace of light sneaking past a barely ajar door. I figure it's my best bet for finding Monique, so I stride in that direction. Before knocking on the door, I look through the small space and see Monique seated in front of a dressing table removing her makeup. I watch as she thoroughly wipes her face before placing the cleansing pad on the table and giving herself a long look in the mirror. Maybe it's just the lighting coming from little bulbs surrounding the reflecting glass, but from where I'm standing, she appears to have some bruising under one of her eyes.

I know I should announce myself but, honestly, I'm as captivated with Monique's cosmetic-free image as she seems to be. Without all her war paint on, she's barely recognizable and has a certain vulnerability about her. The longer Monique continues to stare at her reflection, the more her poise and general exuberance seem to fade. Her mouth slowly turns downward, and I look on from the hallway as a lone tear falls from her eye.

Feeling like I'll be entering into "creepy voyeur territory" if I peek through the open door any longer, I announce myself with an "ahem" and a knock on the door. Startled, she catches sight of me in the mirror and quickly wipes away the droplet of moisture on her cheek.

"Hello," she says. "Come in . . . come in. Close the door, please." She adjusts her posture and slaps on a smile. "Just reapplying my makeup. All the dancing made me a little misty." She catches me looking at the bruise under her eye. "I guess I'm busted," she admits, beginning to dab concealer under the affected eye. "I had a little work done on my eyes. My surgeon assured me the bruising would be gone by now, but I must be a slow healer. Oh well . . . I guess no one really believes I look this fabulous without a little help anyway."

"You do look fabulous," I offer, feeling like I interrupted something by stepping into the bedroom even though she was the only one in here. "Your dress is simply amazing."

"Thank you," she says. "Seems a waste to only wear it this one time, but once I've worn something at a high-profile event like this, I can't really don it again. Although, I guess if I did, it might get me a little press in one of those glossy trash mags . . . in the 'She Wore It Twice' section." She's finished applying the concealer and reaches for a little jar of foundation and a makeup brush. "When you're the face of your products, you've got to keep that face in tip-top condition. Right?" As she begins brushing on the cream, I wonder why she has not yet asked me why I came upstairs and approached her in her bedroom. "You know, Halia." She says this to my reflection in her mirror. "People think I have it all, but sometimes I look at a woman like you, and I'm envious."

A loud laugh blurts from my mouth. "Envious? Of me?!"

"Yes. You're lucky to be a normal woman." She stammers a bit, afraid she may have offended me. "Well, not *normal* . . .

not that you're *not* normal . . . or *abnormal* in any way." She takes a breath. "You know what I mean . . . sometimes having a life with some anonymity would be such a treat." She sighs. "Like I was saying about not being able to wear the same dress twice . . . and being up here during my own party reapplying makeup because I'm afraid someone may snap a photo of me when I'm not at my best. Being *on* all the time can wear a sister out."

Monique and I barely know each other, so I find it peculiar that she is sharing such personal information with me, but maybe I shouldn't be surprised—apparently, I just have one of those faces that make people bare their souls. It happens all the time. People just start talking to me. Maybe I simply have a kind face or come off as very nonthreatening or something. Sometimes it's a positive quality. Like now, I find it interesting to hear about how there is another side to the marvelous Ms. Monique Dupree. Other times, like when restaurant patrons want to tell me their life story when I have a few hundred other things that need tending to, it can be a bit of an encumbrance. Don't get me wrong—I enjoy engaging with my customers, but I've had to master the art of exiting a conversation gracefully when patrons want to gab for extended periods during the lunch rush.

"Look at me going on and on." Monique sets down the makeup brush. "Things okay downstairs? Can I help you with something?"

"Things are fine. It's been a wonderful party, but I have an early day tomorrow, too, so I should get going."

"And I owe you a check," she says. "Can you hand me that folder?" She points to a leather portfolio on the dresser next to the door.

After I retrieve the folder and hand it to her, she starts rifling through it, flipping through a number of business-size checks. "Here you go."

I take a quick look at it and fold it in half. "Thank you. It really was a delightful party."

"Please! I should be thanking you for agreeing to help cater the affair. Your food was delicious."

I smile. "Well, I'll collect my trays and whatnot, and Wavonne and I will be on our way."

"No need to take them now. Lena can wash them for you, and you can pick them up another time."

I'm about to decline the offer when Nathan abruptly opens the bedroom door and pokes his head into the room. "Everyone is waiting," he says impatiently to Monique. His words or his tone, or maybe just his presence, shifts the energy in the room—there's a sudden tenseness in the air.

"Okay," she replies. "I'll be down in a minute."

"Um," he says, looking at me. "Your niece, is it? In the jumpsuit?"

"Wavonne? She's my cousin."

"Well, your cousin is downstairs telling our guests how unfair it is that our dog wears better jewelry than she does."

A quiet groan comes from my mouth. "Oh my. I guess it's time for me to get her home. Maybe it is best if I pick up the catering supplies later."

I thank Monique one last time and begin to exit the room. Nathan moves to the side of the doorway, offering just enough space to let me pass, which I do hurriedly, trying to escape his negative energy as quickly as I can.

I'm halfway down the stairs when I'm treated to a vision that immediately reminds me of an old *Sex and the City* episode—the one where the girls visit the Playboy Mansion. They had been there for a while with various antics ensuing when Carrie and Miranda stumble upon a grotto with a bunch of naked women cavorting in a hot tub. Miranda takes in the scene and says something about "tit soup," and Carrie, a defeated look on her face, says, "It's time to go home."

Wavonne has gotten up from the lounger and the dog is at her feet, looking up at her with puzzled eyes. Dogs have always taken a liking to Wavonne—I think they figure that, with her curvaceous girth, there's bound to be some treats around. She's swaying from side to side with her shoes in one hand while using her other hand to twirl some sort of fabric or garment over her head. She looks like she might stumble over at any moment while guests pass by on their way to the living room. It's only when I notice how much more Wavonne's "parts" are jiggling than they were on the dance floor, that I realize it's her Spanx that she's whirling around in the air.

"Halia!" She spots me on the steps, which by no means prompts her to end the little show she's putting on. "I feel so free. I think I was about to cough up a kidney in these things."

I scurry down the rest of the steps, praying that she went in the bathroom when she removed her shapewear from underneath her jumpsuit and didn't disrobe right there in the foyer. When I reach her, I take hold of her shoulder with one hand and gently place my other hand under her elbow to keep her steady as I lead her back to the lounger and make her sit down.

"Stay here! I'm going to have the valet get the van and then fetch our coats."

"We're leaving?"

"Yes. Do *not* leave that seat until I get back. You're making a complete spectacle of yourself." As I give her the same eyes Momma used to give me when I was a kid and she wanted me to know she *meant business*, the dog hops up on the cushion with her. I look at her, lazily petting the dog with one hand, while her Spanx hang limp in the other . . . and I think of *Sex and the City* . . . and Carrie and Miranda . . . and tit soup. "It's time to go home."

Chapter 17

"You look ridiculous with those on indoors." I'm referring to the sunglasses Wavonne is wearing. We're in the kitchen of Sweet Tea getting ready for Sunday brunch. To say several cross words were exchanged this morning when I made her get out of bed and come into the restaurant with me would be an understatement. But I had no intention of rewarding last night's behavior with a morning off.

I've placed Wavonne on pepper-cutting duty this morning. What we call our "Technicolor Omelet," featuring chopped red, orange, and yellow peppers along with diced onions, cheddar cheese, and a touch of garlic powder is one of our most popular breakfast entrées, so Wavonne will be busy for quite some time, slicing peppers into little match-size strips that add a nice touch of zest to the eggs. The omelets really are a thing of beauty when they slide perfectly out of the pan onto a dish already prepped with home fries and a little garnish made with purple cabbage, half a cherry tomato, and some parsley. I love to see this entree go out to customers. The mix of hues on display—the yellow eggs . . . the bright-colored peppers . . . the orange cheese and purple cabbage and green parsley—they all just seem to say "Good morning! It's going to be a great day."

"Do you need to speak so loudly?" Wavonne puts down her knife and rubs the sides of her head. "Your voice sounds like a gong banging in my head."

"Did someone have a little too much to drink last night?" Tacy asks while pulling some pans from a rack hanging from the ceiling. Shortly after we open, he'll have up to four omelets going at a time throughout the morning.

I snicker. "A *little*? I'm sure she wishes it was only a little."

"So I had a good time. Sue me." Wavonne lifts her head and looks at Tacy, who's now beating a large bowl of eggs. "Can you please get those runny eggs away from me?"

Tacy laughs and moves the bowl to the counter behind him.

"I can't remember half the night. I have a vague memory of dancing with some guy. He was handsome, but I can't remember his name, or if I gave him my number."

"Do you remember his *wife*?"

"Huh?"

"Treena Simms. It was her husband you were gyrating all over last night."

"Ah . . . okay. Yeah . . . I seem to recall her gettin' all up in my face."

"Can you blame her?"

"What? Like it's my fault when a sista can't keep a man?"

"That's the same thing you said to Monique's dog last night, during your in-depth conversation with him . . . or her."

I'm about to expand on Wavonne's activities at the party when Momma comes into the kitchen.

"Hey, Momma. What are you doing here?" I ask. She usually does not come into Sweet Tea on Sundays.

"I'm on my way to church, and I thought I would stop by and see how things went with Alex last night. Should I start learning Spanish, so I can talk with my bilingual grand-children?"

"My God, Momma. How many times are we going to have this conversation? I'm in my forties. Regardless of what, if anything, happens with Alex, or *anyone* for that matter, I don't see grandchildren in your future."

"Why do you have to squash an old woman's dreams?" She points toward my midsection. "There's bound to be a viable egg or two floating around in there."

"I don't know, Aunt Celia, she's pretty old," Wavonne chides. "Practically menopausal. I saw her a minute ago, fanning herself . . . must be gettin' them hot flashes."

"I was fanning myself because I was standing over a flaming grill covered with home fries, Wavonne."

"Mmm-hmm," Wavonne utters in a "if you say so" sort of way. "Either way. I think they got all sorts of procedures they can do nowadays . . . help old hens like Halia have babies."

"Maybe she can hire one of those surrogates like those rich white ladies do," Momma jokes.

At this point the two of them are just trying to get under my skin. It's a hobby of theirs.

"All right, all right . . . enough with the old lady cracks," I say. "I'm going to check on the dining room," I tell them just to get away.

"Lawd . . . she's done got her compression stockings all in a knot," Wavonne says to Momma, and then calls behind me, "We're only playin' with ya, Halia. Come back."

"Yeah . . . and I covered for you so you could go to the party last night," Momma says. "You at least owe me some details about how things went with that personal chef fellow," Momma says.

"Later," I call over my shoulder as I exit the kitchen.

I'm barely in the dining room when I see Latasha at the front entrance, knocking on the glass. She looks distressed, so I hurry over and unlock the door.

She scurries in. "Have you heard the news?"

"What news?" I ask.

"So you haven't."

"Haven't what? What news?" I ask again.

"Monique." Latasha takes a breath. "She's been killed . . . murdered . . . shot! It's all over the TV."

Chapter 18

With Latasha following, I walk quickly toward the right side of the restaurant, grab the remote control, and flick on the flat screen that hangs behind the bar. As I change the channel from ESPN to one of the cable news stations, Momma and Wavonne emerge from the kitchen.

"I thought I heard you out here," Wavonne says to Latasha. "Come over to hear about the party last night?"

"No," Latasha says abruptly, and nods her head toward the television.

"Monique Dupree, known as the Coiffure Queen by the millions of African American women who use her products, was found dead during the early morning hours. Ms. Dupree presided over a multimillion-dollar hair care empire and was scheduled to start a nationwide tour to promote her company today," says the lead anchor on the news before cutting to a reporter in the field.

"Thank you, Leslie," says the young lady standing in front of Monique's house. "Police were called to this home in Mitchell-ville, Maryland, a suburb of Washington, DC, at twelve thirty a.m. by Ms. Dupree's husband, Nathan Tucker. We are being told that, following a social event at the house last night, Mr.

Tucker was called to the Washington Convention Center, which is currently holding the annual Unique Chic Hair Show, to handle some unexpected issues with the Hair by Monique display. Hair by Monique is Ms. Dupree's brand of hair care products, which are extremely popular with African American women and have made Monique Dupree a household name.

"When Mr. Tucker returned home in the early morning hours, he found Ms. Dupree dead via a gunshot wound to the head." The camera zooms toward a small hole surrounded by splintered glass in one of the front windows of the house. "Here you can see where the bullet went through the window."

I don't know who alerted my team in the kitchen to the breaking news, but at this point, brunch prep operations have ceased at Sweet Tea, and my entire staff is in front of the one television in my restaurant, intently watching the news of Monique's death unfold.

Before the camera pans back to the reporter, I'm able to get a muddled view of what's on the other side of the glass with the bullet hole in it. I can just make out two policemen talking to each other in front of a large television mounted over a fireplace—not a lot of detail, but when I combine it with my understanding of the layout of the house, it's enough for me to know that Monique was shot in the room Lena referred to as her den—the room she liked to relax and unwind in. This brings about a vision in my head of Monique, having changed into sweatpants or pajamas after an exhausting evening of being "on," lounging on the sofa . . . with a cup of tea, perhaps . . . when the most horrible of things happened. The thought sends a shiver through me.

"Sources are telling us that there were no signs of robbery or forced entry, and one would have to assume that the bullet that killed Ms. Dupree was fired from the front lawn, somewhere between the house and the small wooded area that offers the residence privacy from the road," the reporter adds as the camera rotates to show the layout of Monique's front yard.

Other than noting that no suspects have yet been identified, the reporter offers little additional information before the newscast returns to the studio anchor, who promises to keep us apprised as more details become available.

I turn off the TV and look around, taking in all the unsettled faces, most of which are staring at me, presumably seeking some words of posthumous acclaim for Monique or comfort for themselves. What do I tell all these people who only two nights ago were so excited to see Ms. Dupree in person and play a hand in her dining experience here at Sweet Tea? Of course, none of us were close to her, but Monique was a local girl who "made good," she was a role model for young women, and she was here, in flesh and blood, among us so recently. Her warmth made people feel like they knew her . . . like they were connected to her.

Sometimes being the boss sucks, I think to myself before trying to string some words together. "I'm so sorry we have to start the day with such terrible news. Monique was certainly one of a kind, and I feel fortunate that I . . . that *we* got to meet her in person." I pause for a moment to try to collect my thoughts and think of something more to say. "She started from humble roots right here in Prince George's County and went on to create a beauty empire. From my few encounters with her, I'll remember her kindness, her wit, and her glamourous style. She will be terribly missed. . . ." I stumble for more to say before Wavonne comes to my rescue.

"Amen!" Wavonne says loudly.

"Amen!" comes from a few others.

"If anyone needs a few moments to collect themselves or make any calls . . . or whatever, please take the time before we get on with prepping this place to open."

My staff begins to disperse, talking among themselves about the news, but Momma, Wavonne, and Latasha stay by my side as I pull out a barstool and sit down.

"Wow . . . just wow," is all I can say.

"I know," Latasha says. "I couldn't believe it when I first heard it. She was just in my salon on Friday . . . and now she's dead."

"Not just *dead*," Wavonne says. "Sista was murdered. Iced. Kevorked. Whacked—"

"We get it, Wavonne," I say. "Why would anyone want to kill her?"

"The beauty industry can be ruthless, but I've never heard of anyone getting killed over some relaxers or curling creams."

"She ran a corporation . . . all sorts of antics go on in big business. Maybe she got into some shady dealings or something," Momma says.

"Maybe," I respond. "She seemed too smart for that though."

"I don't know." Wavonne chimes in. "Maurice didn't seem to think she was so smart when it came to pickin' men."

"That's right. He did imply that Nathan was not good to Monique . . . and said something about him gambling away her money and being involved with some shifty people," I reply. "And Nathan is just plain creepy."

"Yeah, I got that, too," Latasha says.

"Me three," comes from Momma. "I did not like the way he talked to us at Latasha's salon."

"And did you see the way he was hanging all over some of the women at the party last night?" I ask.

"He was all up in the bidness of every woman at the party," Wavonne says, "except his wife's. I don't think I saw the two of them together all night."

"He does seem like an ass . . . and sort of a bully, but he doesn't strike me as someone who would kill his wife."

I take in what Latasha just said, but I'm not sure I agree. I think of how I felt vaguely threatened when he cleared just enough space to let me walk past him while he lurked in the doorway of his and Monique's bedroom. "I don't know. That man definitely has a dark side and some seriously bad energy."

"So maybe it was her scrub husband that did her in," Wavonne says. "But she and Odessa could go at it, too. I heard the two of them fighting with each other in the bathroom the night they were here. But if I'd been placing bets on who might have ended up dead anytime soon, my money would have been on Odessa for showin' up to Monique's party like she was Diana Ross instead of just one of the Supremes. Ms. Ross did not put up with that foolishness from Mary or Flo, and I doubt Monique was gonna let Odessa get away with her little stunt. You heard her as well as I did," Wavonne says to me. "She told Odessa she was gonna 'get her' when she gave her that phony hug."

"I guess I did, but as we all know, Odessa is not the one who's dead," I reply, recalling what I heard on my way up the basement stairs last night. "But you're right about Odessa having a price to pay for trying to outshine Monique. They didn't just argue here. I heard the two of them quarreling last night at the party as well . . . something about Monique telling Odessa that she was not getting any more money from her. I heard her say . . ." I let my voice trail off as I catch sight of Momma's eyes on me, her brows raised ever so slightly. Even though she's not saying a word, her message is coming through loud and clear. But I play dumb as if I don't know exactly what she's thinking. "What? Why are you looking at me like that?"

"You know exactly why. I see your wheels spinning . . .

your antennas going up . . . gearing yourself up for a challenge." Momma takes a breath. "This is not your murder to solve, Halia. Stay out of it."

I give what Momma said some thought. I have a "two for two" track record of solving murders, but what she said is true—there's no reason for me to get involved in this one. "You're right." I can see a look of surprise come across Momma's face—she's not used to me being so agreeable. "There's no reason for me to get involved. I'll leave the investigating to the police."

Wavonne laughs. "Leave it to the police? Yeah, right, Halia," she says. "Remember when we first came in this morning, and Tacy was pulling those orange cranberry muffins out of the oven, and he asked my hungover carb-craving self if I wanted one. I tried to resist—with you and Maurice forcing me into a size sixteen and all, I figure a sista's gotta get some self-control. But we all know how that little willpower test ended up . . . and we all know how this whole Monique murder thing is gonna play out. I've still got muffin crumbs in my cleavage, and it won't be long before you have your nose all up in this Monique mess. You may as well skip the resistance stage, Halia, and make like Daphne and Velma and start lookin' for clues."

Chapter 19

"I'm only going to pick up my trays," I say. I'm in the van on my way to Monique's house talking to Momma while mentally scolding myself for hitting the answer button on my steering wheel when I saw her name come up on the dashboard screen.

"Mahalia Watkins." It's never good when she uses my full name. Suddenly I'm back in middle school, and she just found my book report with the C– on it hidden under my bed. "Do you think I just fell off the turnip greens truck? Don't give me that 'picking up trays' nonsense. You're going over there to snoop around and meddle in business that is none of your concern."

"I told you, Momma, Wavonne overindulged in the cocktails and was making a fool of herself last night. I wanted to get her out of there as fast as I could. I didn't have time to collect my catering items. I'm just going to grab them and go." I know she knows I'm lying . . . and she knows I know she knows I'm lying, but this is what we do. I think it's a bit of a hobby or nervous habit for both of us.

"Oh *yes* . . . that's the first thing people do when they hear about a murder." I can almost see the sarcasm coming out of the car speakers. "They think 'I must immediately go to the murder scene, step over any pesky corpses, and fetch my party supplies.'"

"All right, all right." I give up on hiding the true intentions for my visit to Monique's house. "What's it hurt for me to poke around a little bit? See what I can find out."

"Because it's not safe, and there are other things you should be focused on."

"Like what?" Another one of my hobbies or nervous habits: asking Momma questions that I already know the answer to.

"You're not getting any younger, Halia. That young man that cooked for Monique must have some time on his hands now . . . you know, with the person he cooked for dead and all. Why don't you go over and see him . . . offer your condolences . . . take him a Bundt cake."

"I don't even know where he lives," I lie, remembering that he said something on Friday about living at Iverson Towers.

"You want to go solve a murder, but you can't find out where an eligible man lives?"

"I'll make you a deal, Momma. You get off my back, and, while I'm at Monique's, I'll see if I can find out where Alex lives and consider paying him a visit. But you need to make the Bundt cake."

Momma sighs. "Fine." She's only agreeing to my terms because she knows my stubborn self is going to do whatever I want anyway.

"I'm pulling in. I'll call you later."

I disconnect the call while I turn onto Monique's property. I stop halfway up the driveway as two police cars are blocking the rest of the way. I turn the car off and take in the scene as I get out and start walking up the drive. There are more squad cars and other official-looking vehicles on the lawn, yellow police tape around the home's front steps, and a couple of news crews packing up their vans.

"Ma'am," an officer calls in my direction. "You can't be here."

"Excuse me?" I say even though I heard him.

"This is a crime scene, ma'am."

I put my hand to my ear, still pretending I can't hear him, and keep walking.

"I'm sorry. What?" I ask when I reach the officer.

"I said this is a crime scene. Authorized personnel only."

"A crime scene?" I feign ignorance. "What happened? I catered a party here last night. I only came to pick up my supplies."

"You'll need to do that some other time. Now please step back to your vehicle and exit the premises."

I ignore his request. "What happened?" I ask again.

"Have you not seen a TV or heard a radio since you got out of bed? Monique Dupree was murdered last night."

"Murdered? What?"

"Ma'am, I have to ask you to leave. I'm sure arrangements can be made to retrieve your belongings another day."

"Okay . . . sure," I say, stalling. "But what happened? How was she murdered?"

"She was shot." He points toward the damaged window. "Bullet went right through that window. Now, Ms. . . . ."

"Watkins. Halia Watkins."

"Ms. Watkins. I need for you to be on your way."

I'm about to ask more questions, when I see the front door of the house swing open. Nathan steps outside with a tall gentleman I recognize as Detective Hutchins, from the police force. The detective and I have a bit of history. I've helped him solve two local murder cases and he . . . well, he hasn't really helped me do anything. He mostly regards me as a busybody who's had some dumb luck with crime solving, but I think he has some level of respect for me; otherwise, he wouldn't have followed up on some of the leads I've given him in the past.

"Ms. Watkins!" Detective Hutchins catches sight of me and simultaneously groans and rolls his eyes toward the sky. "*What* are you doing here?" he asks as if I've just shown up to a party without an invitation. "I know you fancy yourself PG County's answer to Jessica Fletcher, but this is a real crime scene, not a television set."

"I only came to pick up a few things. I had no idea Monique had been murdered."

Much like Momma, he is able to let me know he doesn't believe me with only his eyes. "Why do you have things to pick up from here?"

"She says she catered a party here last night," the police officer says.

"Yes, I did. Ms. Dupree told me I could come back today to pick up my chafing dishes and whatnot."

"That's true," Nathan says quietly, his eyes sort of vacant and blank. He looks more toward the ground than at any one of us. I'm not getting the intimidating, almost oppressive vibe from him that was so apparent during our last few meetings. He appears to really be in a state of quasi-shock following the death of his wife . . . or he's a very good actor. "She helped with the . . . um"—he stumbles as if too much is going through his mind to recall details—"the buffet . . . she helped with the buffet last night."

"Did you see anything out of the ordinary when you were here last night . . . anything suspicious?"

I want to say that the only odd thing I saw was Nathan cavorting with a bunch of women who were not his wife, but given that Nathan is standing right in front of me, I say, "No. Not really."

"Okay. Well, an officer may be in touch—"

"Wait," I interrupt. "I guess I did hear Monique quarreling with Odessa before I left, but it didn't sound like anything someone would get killed over."

"What were they quarreling about?"

"I'm not sure. I happened to overhear a little of their argument when I was coming up the stairs from the basement." I fail to mention that I would have eavesdropped longer if other guests hadn't started coming up the steps behind me. "Monique said something about how she was not going to pay Odessa any more . . . or give her any more money . . . or something like that."

"Odessa!" Nathan says, his voice swelling. He looks up from the ground and at Detective Hutchins. "I saw her . . . after the party last night . . . I saw her coming back toward our house on my way to the convention center."

"Why were you going to the convention center after the party?" I ask.

Nathan looks at me as if he's irritated by the question, but decides to answer anyway. "Monique got a call from the company that manages the building. One of the sprinklers in our display room, Monique's House of Style, went off. Monique was exhausted, but we were having a press conference there in the morning to launch her tour, so I went downtown to see how bad the damage was and what fixes needed to be ready for the cameras in the morning. Shortly after I left the house, about ten thirty, I saw Odessa headed back this way. I recognized her car, mostly because of the personalized license plate. It says 'good hair.'"

"'Good hair'?"

"Well . . . G-D H-A-I-R," Nathan says, spelling out the letters, more focused than when he and the detective stepped outside. "This road dead ends. There is no reason for her to be on it headed east if she wasn't coming back to our house."

"You think she came back here and shot Monique?" I ask.

"You can leave the questioning to me, Ms. Watkins," Detective Hutchins scolds. "It's really time that you leave. I'm sure Mr. Tucker will see to it that you get your plates or trays . . . or whatever it is you pretended to come over here for." He turns toward Nathan. "Let's go back inside and discuss this further." He gestures for Nathan to follow him, and they both turn back toward the house. When they reach the front step, Detective Hutchins flips his neck around and flings a "What are you still doing here?" look in my direction. I decide not to test the detective's patience any further, figuring I can question Nathan when I come back at a later date to get my supplies.

As I watch the detective and Nathan enter the house and close the door behind them, the police officer who's been standing next to me the whole time angles his head toward me. Clearly, he's about to tell me to skedaddle, too, but I don't give him the chance.

"I'm going . . . I'm going," I say, but as I walk back to my van, quietly, under my breath . . . in my best Arnold Schwarzenegger accent, I add, "I'll be back."

Chapter 20

I headed over to Monique's house when the brunch rush was slowing down and am just getting back to the restaurant now. When I swing open the door, I see that we're still pretty busy. I smile and wave to a few regulars before I step behind the bar and check in with Melissa, one of my bartenders, to make sure we have enough liquor stocked for the dinner crowd that will be filtering in soon. For the most part, I have a great staff and try to hire carefully, but I've had some issues with employees stealing alcohol in the past, so I keep limited amounts behind the bar. The rest is in a locked closet, which can only be opened by me and my assistant manager, Laura.

I'm about to retrieve some vodka reinforcements when I see Wavonne hurrying toward me with a look on her face that I recognize as her "Girl, I've got some gossip!" expression.

"Sista girl had a 'fro!" she declares when she reaches the bar.

"What? What are you talking about?" I ask.

"Monique Dupree. The queen of all things straight hair . . . she had an Afro."

I just look at her with my eyebrows furrowed. What she's saying isn't registering with me.

"Apparently, it wasn't a big poufy Foxy Brown type of thing . . . or like that dude in the Harlem Globetrotters cartoon that used to pull all sorts of gadgets outta his Afro." She's excited, so she's talking quickly. I feel like her words are buzzing past me. "It was more Lupita Nyong'o . . . or Viola Davis at the Oscars the year she lost. A TWA . . . that's what it was . . . a TWA."

"TWA?" Nothing she's saying is making any sense. The only thing coming to mind when she says TWA is an airline that went bust almost twenty years ago.

"Teeny-weeny Afro."

"Sit down, Wavonne." I pull out a barstool. "Now, take a breath and tell me, *slowly*, what the hell you're talking about."

"It's all over the news." She grabs the remote control that was sitting on the bar and turns up the volume. "Turns out 'Becky with the Good Hair' was actually 'Becky with the Nappy Afro.'"

"Why is the television set to a news station?" I ask, annoyed. I have a strict policy about only showing sports on the bar TV during open hours. There's never anything good coming from the cable news networks—it's all politics and disasters and scandal. I don't want that kind of energy in my restaurant. I resisted having a TV in Sweet Tea at all for years—I wanted my guests to focus on my food and one another rather than whatever was beaming from a squawk box. But I recently relented and put one, and *only one*, flat screen behind the bar for my customers who apparently would rather die than miss a Redskins game.

"I'm sorry, Halia," Melissa says. "We all wanted to keep an eye on the Monique story. I thought it might be okay in this case, so I left it on the news today."

"Shhh . . . would both of you shut it." Wavonne points toward the television.

"There has been a new development in today's lead story about the apparent murder of hair care products maven Monique Dupree, who was found dead from a gunshot wound in the early morning hours," says the same talking head who was on the screen this morning. "According to a source at the crime scene, Ms. Dupree, who made her fortune selling hair care products and was most famous for her straightening cream—and often used her own lustrous tresses as a key marketing tool—was found to actually have closely cropped short curly hair."

"Oh Lawd . . . the white lady is afraid to use the word 'Afro,' " Wavonne bemoans.

"What's wrong with the word 'Afro'?" I ask.

"Nothin', but she don't know that. She's probably afraid to say 'kinky,' too."

The woman on the news does seem to be handling the subject matter a bit awkwardly, and maybe rightfully so. People are uncomfortable with things they don't understand. And trying to get a white woman to understand the black hair experience is like trying to get a man to understand what it's like to have breasts.

"The source, who wishes to remain unnamed, as he is not authorized to speak to the press, said that when Ms. Dupree was discovered, slumped on the sofa with a gunshot wound in the back of her head, she did not have the flowing long hair for which she was famous. Instead she was found with a short Afro."

"Mmm-hmm," Wavonne says. "Someone must've told her through her earpiece that she can say 'Afro.' "

"Shhh." Now it's me doing the shushing.

"A search of the house found an entire closet off the master bedroom filled with wigs. There was an extensive—"

The anchor puts her hand to her earpiece and is quiet for a second or two. "We are getting word that Jenna Summers has caught up with Ms. Dupree's hairdresser. Let's go live to Jenna in Washington, DC."

The program cuts to a reporter in front of a brick row house in the city. "Thank you, Leslie," she says. "We believe that is Maurice Masson, Monique's hairdresser and personal stylist, approaching us now." The camera shifts toward the sidewalk, and I see Maurice—he's hard to miss in salmon-colored pants and a yellow shirt. His bright choice of clothing, however, does not match his demeanor. He's walking slowly with a troubled expression on his face that only intensifies when he catches sight of the reporter and her camera operator.

"Mr. Masson, do you have any comments on the murder of Monique Dupree and the allegations that she led her adoring public to believe that wigs were her natural hair," she asks when Maurice is within earshot.

Maurice refuses to acknowledge her as he picks up his speed and quickly strides past her to open the creaky iron gate that separates what I assume is his property from the sidewalk. The reporter keeps flinging questions at him as he walks up his front steps and puts a key in the door. He continues to ignore each one until she hurls a final inquiry in his direction.

"Mr. Masson, do you know who killed Monique?" This question seems to strike a nerve, prompting Maurice to turn around.

"Of course I don't know who killed her, but the police need to be looking at her husband as the prime suspect. He was emotionally and physically abusive to Monique."

"Abusive?" the reporter asks.

"Yes," Maurice replies. "Abusive." He had a steadfastness about him when the reporter first approached, but I can see that unraveling, and it strikes me as almost cruel for this reporter to be hounding him when he just lost someone to whom he was very close. "I begged her to leave him time and time again, often while I was helping her cover her bruises. But she always refused." I can see his face faintly contorting, the way one's face does when someone is trying to keep from crying. "He had some sort of sick hold on her, and she was afraid of the damage a messy divorce would do to her image."

The reporter takes it upon herself to open the gate and join Maurice on the steps. She puts one arm around him, and it would almost be a moment of kindness—one stranger comforting another—if it were not for the fact that she uses her other arm to make sure there is a mic in front of Maurice's mouth.

"But she finally seemed ready to leave when she found out he had bought a gun. Yes, Nathan had a gun, and Monique was afraid he might kill her!" Maurice starts to completely break down. "I should have pushed her harder. I should have somehow forced her to leave. But I didn't," he says through heavy breaths. "And now she's dead." He continues to breathe deeply. "I have to go," he says, and quickly lurches away from the reporter, stepping inside his house and closing the door.

The reporter goes on to say something, but I'm not really listening anymore. All I can think about is how I came upon Monique last night in her room and found her applying concealer around her eyes . . . how she tried to explain away the bruise with a story about plastic surgery—it seemed to make perfect sense at the time, but now, not so much.

My attention vaguely goes back to the television as they return to the news desk, and I hear something about how no arrests have yet been made and the gun that shot the offending bullet has not been found.

"Okay . . . enough." I use the remote to switch the television to ESPN and turn the volume down. "We'll check the news later for any updates. Back to work."

"Yeah, yeah," Wavonne says, and starts walking with me as I head toward the storage closet. "So you didn't tell me what happened over at Monique's house?"

"I didn't really get any good information." I refrain from mentioning what Nathan said about Odessa driving back toward the house after the party. Wavonne is all wound up and distracted as it is. I don't need to add to her state when we have a restaurant full of customers who need waiting on. "The police were there, and they told me I'd have to come back another day for my stuff."

"Can I go with you, when you go back?"

"What for?"

"Oh . . . no reason," she says while unknowingly giving her wig a quick adjustment.

"Seriously, Wavonne?!" Her little wig tug gave away her motive. "The woman's body is barely cold, and you're already after her wigs?"

"I only want to see them, Halia. If I, of all people, didn't know she was showin' instead of growin', those have to be some *good* wigs."

"I suppose that's true, but even if I took you with me, what makes you think we'd get access to Monique's wig closet when we're there to pick up catering supplies?"

"I don't know," Wavonne replies. "But you'll think of something. You always do."

"I suppose that's true, too," I say. "And sometimes that gets me in trouble . . . sometimes that gets me in heaps of trouble."

Chapter 21

It's been three days since Monique's death, and I got a call this morning from Lena, Monique's housekeeper—or *former* housekeeper—letting me know I could come by and pick up my things today.

On weekdays, we close Sweet Tea for a couple of hours in the late afternoon to give us a breather between the lunch crowd and the dinner service, so I'm using that time to drive over to Mitchellville and get my supplies. Truth be told, the items I left at Monique's are probably worth less than fifty dollars. Under normal circumstances, given the time and hassle involved in retrieving them, I likely would have let them go and written them off as part of my expenses related to catering the party. But, as both Momma and Detective Hutchins so keenly surmised, serving trays and chafing dishes are the least of the reasons I'm interested in returning to Monique's home.

When I turn into Monique's driveway for the third time in less than a week, I'm surprised to see that police cars are back on the property—unlike the horde of official vehicles that were around when I was here last, there are only two squad cars parked in front of the house today. I stop my van behind them. One car is empty, but there is an officer seated in the other one. He must have caught sight of me in his mirror because as soon as I put the van in park, the door flings open, and out steps Jack Spruce, a local policeman and Sweet Tea regular . . . and someone I'd probably even call a friend. We've had a mild flirtation thing going on for years, but I've always politely declined his invitations for dates—he's just not my type. He's nice enough and not bad looking, but the chemistry simply isn't there for me. I do like him as a person though, so it's not hard to engage in some friendly banter when he comes into the restaurant on a lunch break or after a shift. And, I'll admit, the little crush he has on me has resulted in a favor or two when I've needed some inside information from within the police department . . . or maybe it's the occasional complimentary slice of peach pie or sweet potato cheesecake that I offer him after a meal that keeps me in his good graces.

"Jack," I say. "Hey. Fancy meeting you here."

"Me? I'm a cop. More like fancy meeting *you* here."

"I have official business," I reply with a laugh. "I helped cater the party that was held here over the weekend."

"Yeah, I know. Hutchins told me you were here the other day."

"Did he mention how happy he was to see me?"

Jack grins. "Yeeeah . . . not so much. He's in the house now with two other officers."

"What's going on?"

"Um . . . I'm not sure."

I tilt my head and raise my eyebrows at him, giving him my "cut the crap, would you?" look. "No, really . . . what's happening? I won't tell anyone."

"I really don't know much. Since they found the gun—"

"They found the gun?"

"Oh gosh. I've already said too much."

"When did they find the gun?"

"I think I've said enough, Halia. You should probably go until we wrap things up here."

"Wrap up what?"

"Honestly, Halia, I'm not sure. I was asked to wait outside and told Hutchins would radio if he needs me."

"So he's in there with two other officers, and you've been called to the scene, too? Something must be going down."

"Probably."

I smile and sort of reprimand him, but in a joking way. "I know you know more than you're telling me, Jack. Come on, it will be all over the news in an hour, so I'm going to hear about it sooner or later."

"I really don't have all the details, Halia. All I know is that, based on the condition of her body, we've determined that Monique was shot about midnight . . . somewhere between eleven forty-five and twelve fifteen. And the team did some more searching this morning and found the gun under some leaves in the little wooded area between the road and the house. They traced it back to Monique's husband."

"Nathan shot her?"

"Not necessarily. We traced the gun to him as the owner, but that does not necessarily mean he discharged the bullet that killed Ms. Dupree."

"Huh." I try to process what I've just learned. "They said on the news that they think she was shot from the front lawn, right?"

"Yeah. I guess that's public knowledge. With all those trees along the road, the killer would not have been able to get a clean line of sight to the front of the house from anywhere else. Forensics determined the gun was likely shot from the far end of the lawn . . . either from barely inside the wooded area or at the edge. That's really all I know, Halia. Hutchins is in there now questioning Mr. Tucker. I'm just waiting around in case they need backup." Jack turns and looks at the house and then back at me. "You really should go before Hutchins comes back out. You can return another time and snoop around."

"Why does no one believe me when I say I'm here for my stuff? Why does everyone assume I'm here to snoop around?"

Now it's Jack's turn to give me the same "cut the crap" look I sent in his direction moments earlier.

"Okay . . . fine," I groan, and take a few steps toward my van, only because it actually will be better for me to come back and poke around when Detective Hutchins is not here. I won't be able to obtain any good information with the detective babysitting me. "It was good to see you, Jack. You'll come by the restaurant soon, I hope?" I open the door to my van and step inside.

"Of course."

"We've got spare ribs and fried okra on special tonight." I am hoping to entice him to come by Sweet Tea this evening, so I can find out firsthand if anything noteworthy happens after I leave here.

"Really?" he says. "That sounds so good, but I'm on until midnight."

"Okay. Swing by another time." I close the door, give Jack a quick wave, and start the ignition. The driveway is quite wide, which gives me space to turn the van around rather than try to steer it in reverse all the way to the road.

When I reach the end of the driveway, I think about what Jack said . . . about the murderer shooting Monique from the edge of the wooded area. I look both ways, and I'm about to pull out onto the street when I just can't help myself—I put the car in park, quickly hop out, and begin walking along the tree-lined edge of the expansive front lawn. I don't know what I'm looking for, but another pair of eyes scoping out the area where the fatal bullet was likely shot can't hurt.

"You really shouldn't be doing that, Halia," Jack calls to me.

"I'll only be a minute," I holler back, and continue to mill about on the grass. I'm alternating between looking down at the well-kept lawn and to my right into the trees to see if anything catches my attention. I don't see anything out of the ordinary until I notice something sparkling near my feet. At first it looks like a tiny bead or button, but when I bend over and examine the object more closely, I find the source of the reflecting late afternoon sunlight to be a single red sequin. I pick it up, give it a closer look, and immediately think of Odessa in her flashy red gown. Sequin in hand, I walk briskly back to the van, turn it around, and head back up the driveway. I'm barely out of the car when I see Detective Hutchins emerge from the house, looking, shall we say, "less than thrilled" to see me.

"Ms. Watkins! Please remove yourself from the premises now."

I don't have a chance to respond before I hear Nathan shouting, "I will sue you! I'll sue the entire police department. You have no idea who you're dealing with!" he yells as he's led out of the house by two policemen. His hands are cuffed behind his back as he rants, but he doesn't seem to be physically resisting the officers.

As the two men direct Nathan toward the empty squad car, Detective Hutchins hastily approaches me.

"I'm sorry," I say before he has a chance to read me the riot act. "Lena told me to come by today to pick up my things . . . my catering supplies. I had no idea the police would still be on the property. Really!" Nathan continues to bluster while I'm talking, so I raise my voice to be heard over his barking. "But I had a quick look around and actually did find something." I hand the sequin to Detective Hutchins.

"What's that?!" Nathan calls, squinting from the short distance to see what I'm handing the detective as one of the officers lowers him into the back seat of the police car.

"Hmm." Detective Hutchins holds the item between his thumb and forefinger and gives it a look.

"That's one of those sparkly things . . . one of those sparkly things from a dress . . ." Nathan calls, apparently unfamiliar with the word "sequin." "Odessa!" he yells. "She had that glittery red dress on the night of the party, and I saw her headed back in this direction on my way to the convention center." He looks up at the officer who's about to close the car door. "You should be going after her, not me!" He then shouts, "What other reason would Odessa Thornton have for being on the front lawn? That red twinkly thing came off her dress. Every other guest at the party was in white. It had to be her!"

When the car door finally closes, drowning out Nathan's words, Detective Hutchins takes another look at the sequin and hands it to Jack. "Bag this, please," he says.

Jack takes the sequin and walks toward his car while the other vehicle, with Nathan still raging in the back seat, begins to pull out of the driveway.

"Is that true?" Detective Hutchins asks me as we watch the squad car make a left onto the road. "What Mr. Tucker was saying about Ms. Thornton wearing a red dress with those sparkly things on—"

"They are called sequins," I say. Apparently, the detective is not familiar with the term either. "And yes, Odessa's dress was covered in them the night of the white party."

"If it was a white party, why was she wearing a red dress?"

"Because women are complicated, Detective," I respond.

"So I've learned." He shifts his eyes in a way that seems to imply that he's learned of such complications via his interactions with me. "What was the nature of Ms. Dupree and Ms. Thornton's relationship?"

"Odessa was a friend . . . or a . . . um . . . honestly, I don't know what she was to Monique. She owns Salon Soleil, which isn't far from here. She and Monique used to work together many years ago and still had some sort of business relationship. Odessa seems to have been in Monique's social circle, but at the same time, they appeared to dislike each other immensely. As I mentioned the other day, I heard them arguing about some business dealings the night of the party."

"Interesting," he says. "Thank you for the information."

"Are you going to check her out?" I ask.

"Maybe. We'll see."

"What do you mean, 'we'll see?'" I ask. "Monique was shot from the front lawn, and a sequin that could have only come off Odessa's dress is found on that lawn a few days later. It definitely seems like she should be a suspect." I regret my words as soon as I'm done saying them. I know from experience that Detective Hutchins does not like it when I tell him how to do his job.

"Oh, it does, does it?" he asks. "Not that I owe you any explanations, Ms. Watkins, but from this armchair detective work of yours, care to explain how Odessa got Nathan's fingerprints on the gun . . . or how she got gunpowder residue on his hands?"

I look at him feeling a little ridiculous. "Um . . . no. I guess not."

"Well then . . . perhaps you should get the catering supplies I've heard you mention a few dozen times and head home."

"Perhaps I should," I agree, and excuse myself before walking up the front steps to the house and knock on the door.

"Hello," Lena says. "I'll get your things. It will just be a minute."

"Thank you." The door is open just wide enough for me slip through, so I step inside despite the lack of an invitation. "Do you mind if I wait here?"

She doesn't answer my question. She simply says, "I'll be right back."

I take advantage of my brief time alone to give the foyer a quick once-over and poke my head into the living and dining rooms. All seems to be in order, but Monique was not killed in any of those rooms. What I really want to see is Monique's den.

I keep an ear out for any approaching footsteps, and when I don't hear any, I hurry down the hall to the den to take a quick peek. At first glance, I don't see anything of interest. The sofa has been removed from the room, and I wonder if it's being held somewhere as evidence, or if Nathan threw it out given the debasing it must have suffered the night of Monique's murder. If there were bloodstains anywhere else, they have since been cleaned up. I figure I'm about out of time when I see something red and fluffy on the rug next to one of the coffee table legs. I dash quickly into the room, see that the something is a red feather, and pick it up. I guess it's nowhere near as incriminating as the sequin on the front lawn—Odessa was losing feathers all over the house the night of Monique's death, but she was a guest at the party and had a reason to be in the house—she didn't have a reason to be on the front lawn at the edge of the woods . . . at least not an honorable reason.

"Ms. Watkins!" I hear Detective Hutchins call from the foyer and dart out the door and down the hall.

"I had to run to the ladies' room," I say when I reach him and find Lena standing next to him with a large box in her arms.

"It looks like your things are ready to go." He nods toward Lena.

"Yes. Thank you, Lena," I say, but before I take the box from her, I hand the feather to the detective.

"What's this?"

"I saw it on the carpet in the den on my way to the bathroom. It must have come off Odessa's dress."

"So her sequenced dress had feathers, too."

"Sequined. Not sequenced," I correct, just to give him a hard time. "And yes, it had feathers around the bottom hem. It's probably nothing. I think her dress was losing feathers all over the house the night of the party, but I thought I'd hand it over to you in case it had any significance."

"Red *sequins* and red feathers? That must have been some dress."

"It was. And Monique was not happy to be upstaged by it, either."

"Good to know." He moves his eyes from me to the box in Lena's hands with a "would you get out of here already" look on his face.

"Appreciate it," I say to Lena as I take the box from her and move toward the door.

"Not that it isn't always a pleasure, but I hope this will be the last I see of you . . . at least as it relates to the death of Ms. Dupree," Detective Hutchins says to me as I walk past him.

I look up at him, knowing that somewhere behind that stern demeanor, he has the tiniest bit of a soft spot for me. "That wouldn't be any fun for either one of us, now would it?" I keep walking as Lena kindly opens the door and holds it for me.

"I *assure* you, it would be plenty fun for me."

I turn around, smile, and then I offer him a Wavonne-style "Mmm-hmm," in a "yeah, we'll see about that" sort of tone.

Chapter 22

"**W**as that handsome Cuban fellow there?" Momma inquires as soon as I walk into the kitchen at Sweet Tea.

"He's Dominican. And no, Alex wasn't there," I respond, before asking, "What are you doing here?" It's late afternoon and Momma has usually left Sweet Tea by now.

"Like you," Wavonne interjects, "she's nosy, and came by to see if you had a rendezvous with Alex while you were at Monique's house."

"Well, like I said, he wasn't there. At least I didn't see him."

"You *are* going to reach out to him and offer your condolences, aren't you?"

"Just as soon as you make me that Bundt cake, Momma."

"Don't nobody make Bundt cakes anymore," Wavonne says. "What is this? 1972? Maybe you guys can go to the discotheque in some go-go boots while you're at it . . . you know, relive your glory days."

"The seventies were not my glory days, Wavonne. I'm not *that* old. I was a child when discos were all the rage," I protest. "Now, can we change the subject? We're opening for dinner shortly, and I still see greens that need to be chopped."

"That's my cue to leave." Momma grabs her purse from the stool next to her. "I'm going home . . . will see if I can't find that Bundt pan of mine."

I roll my eyes. "Bye, Momma."

"Later, Aunt Celia," Wavonne says.

While the kitchen door swings closed behind Momma, I walk around to the other side of the counter and examine the heap of leafy collard greens that were delivered this morning from one of the few local farms left in the county.

"They've been washed?" I ask Tacy, who's standing next to me with a chopping knife in his hand.

"Three times."

"Good. Nothing worse than gritty greens." I turn to Wavonne. "Let's grab a few knives and help Tacy with the chopping. Our supply was starting to run low at lunch, and these will take a couple of hours to simmer."

I'm sure Wavonne had planned to duck into the break room and surf on her phone until we open, but she grabs two knives, albeit very unenthusiastically, hands one to me, and keeps one for herself. The three of us begin using the knives to remove the stems from the individual leaves and lay them on top of one another in piles.

"So, what else happened over at Monique's?" Wavonne asks, and I realize why she gave me so little grief when I asked her to help with the greens—she wanted to stick around and get the gossip.

"Not much," I say. "I arrived, got my supplies, thanked Lena for them . . . oh, and Nathan was arrested."

"What?! Why didn't you tell us that when you came in?"

"Like I had a chance with Momma's hounding me about Alex and Bundt cakes."

"Girl, you better spill some tea."

"Jack was there."

"Jack Spruce? Your law enforcement admirer that you've been stringin' along for years so he'll keep givin' you inside info?"

"I have not been *stringing* him along, Wavonne. I genuinely like him. I just don't feel that *way* about him. We're friends. He's very nice."

"Very nice?" Wavonne asks. "Very nice is what you say about a dachshund or an apartment with cheap rent."

"Oh, stop. He *is* very nice, and if our friendship comes with a perk or two, then so be it." I take one of the piles of greens, roll it up like a cigar, and begin chopping. "And speaking of perks, he did share a few things with me, and so did Detective Hutchins."

"Like what?"

"They found the gun this morning under some leaves in the wooded area between the road and Monique's front lawn. It had Nathan's fingerprints on it, and his hands tested positive for gunpowder residue."

"Get out?!"

"I was there when they took him from the house in cuffs. He was ranting and raving and said he was going to sue them."

"Yeah . . . maybe when he gets out of jail in fifty years."

"It doesn't look good for him." I lay down my knife. "Why don't you guys keep chopping, and I'll get the pot going."

I continue to tell them about the rest of the afternoon while grabbing a sixty-quart pot from underneath the counter and placing it on the stovetop. I turn the burner on and drop some onions and garlic that have been sautéed in vegetable shortening and bacon grease into the pot while I tell Wavonne and Tacy, and the rest of my kitchen staff within earshot, about the sequin on the front lawn and the feather in the den, and how Nathan claims he saw Odessa headed back to the house after the party.

"Sounds like Nathan did Monique in, but who knows, maybe Odessa had something to do with it, too."

"Maybe," I agree, and turn to Tacy. "Thanks for prepping all of this," I offer, referring to the onions and garlic he had all prepped and ready to go in the pot.

Tacy, a man of few words (one of the reasons I like him so much), nods, and he and Wavonne look on as I add some chicken broth, apple cider vinegar, and water to the pots. We discuss theories about why Nathan might have killed Monique while the two of them continue to chop greens, and I diligently mix the fragrant liquid with a big metal spoon. As we mull over his rumored gambling addiction and alleged abuse of Monique, I add a few heaps of our house seasoning, which consists of paprika, salt, onion powder, black pepper, red pepper flakes, garlic powder, and dry mustard.

"There," I say, giving the pot a final stir and turning up the heat on the stove. "All ready for the greens and ham hocks."

Once we're done chopping the greens, we'll add them to the pots along with some ham hocks and simmer them for a good two hours. Then we'll pull the hocks out, remove the meat from the bone, chop it into small pieces, and return it to the pot before moving the finished product to the steam table to keep the greens hot before they are plated, topped with bits of crispy bacon, and taken out to our guests with a bottle of my homemade hot pepper sauce.

I turn back toward the counter and pick up a knife. I'm about to help Tacy and Wavonne finish chopping the greens when Sondra, one of my hosts, pops in with the portable phone in her hand.

"There's a call for you, Halia. He wouldn't tell me who he is, but he says it's urgent."

"Really?" I ask. "It's probably some dial-a-date guy Momma gave my number to." I laugh and put the phone to my ear. "This is Halia."

"Hi, Halia," I hear in a low deep voice. "Please don't hang up."

"Who is this?"

"It's Nathan . . . Nathan Tucker. I need your help."

RECIPE FROM HALIA'S KITCHEN

Halia's Collard Greens

Ingredients
4 bunches collard greens
1 tablespoon vegetable shortening
8 slices bacon
1 chopped onion
3 cloves chopped garlic
4 cups chicken broth
2 tablespoons apple cider vinegar
3 cups water
1 tablespoon Sweet Tea House Seasoning
1 smoked ham hock

Sweet Tea House Seasoning
2 teaspoons salt
1 teaspoon black pepper
1 tablespoon paprika
2 teaspoon onion powder
1½ teaspoons red pepper flakes
1 teaspoon garlic powder
1 teaspoon dry mustard

- Swish greens in a large bowl (or sanitized sink) of cold
  water to remove grit before transferring to a colander to

drain. Replace water in bowl and repeat process of swishing greens and transferring them to a colander until greens are grit free (i.e., when you do not see any grit in the water after extracting the greens).

- Stack washed greens (stalks removed) in 4 piles. Roll each pile up like a cigar. Slice into ½-inch strips.
- In frying pan, heat shortening over medium high heat. Add bacon, turning occasionally. Cook until crisp. Remove bacon, chop into small pieces, and set aside.
- Add onions and garlic and sauté in shortening and bacon grease until onions are tender (about 15 minutes). Add onions and pan drippings to a large pot. Add chicken broth, cider vinegar, and water. Stir in one tablespoon of Sweet Tea's House Seasoning, then add greens and ham hock to the pot. Bring contents of pot to a boil over high heat, cover, and reduce heat to medium. Simmer greens and ham hock, stirring occasionally, for 2 hours, or until greens are tender.
- Remove ham hock from liquid and strip meat from the bone. Discard bone and excess fat. Chop meat into small chunks. Combine ham hock meat with chopped bacon in a bowl.
- Drain greens and transfer to a large bowl or deep serving dish. Mix ham hock meat and chopped bacon into greens.
- Serve immediately so bacon stays crisp.

Chapter 23

There is something really creepy about visiting the campus of a correctional facility . . . the staid brick buildings, the tall chain-link fence topped with barbed wire, the general sense of confinement—it all just gives me goose bumps . . . goose bumps that linger on my skin as a uniformed guard asks for my name, the reason for my visit, and my driver's license. After taking down my license plate and using what looks like a very strong flashlight (even though it's daylight) to look through the windows of my van (searching for God knows what), he returns to his little booth and presses a button to lift the gate arm, allowing me to drive onto the property of the Prince George's County Correctional Center.

As I follow the signs to the building where I'm supposed to meet Nathan, I can still hear the desperation in his voice when he called me yesterday. He was adamant that he did not kill Monique, and that the police were overly anxious to close her murder case. He said they had little interest in pursuing any further investigation and were going to put him away for life without considering other suspects—namely Odessa, whom Nathan is convinced returned to his and Monique's house after the white party and shot Monique from the edge of the front lawn. The red sequin he saw me hand Detective Hutchins has only reinforced his certainty that Odessa is the killer.

Apparently, he and Monique ran in the same social circles as a now-deceased acquaintance of mine, Raynell Rollins, a former high school classmate who was killed earlier this year. She was a top-selling real estate agent in the area and the wife of a prominent former Washington Redskins player. Although she and her husband didn't have the same national celebrity as Monique, they were definitely part of Prince George's County's upper crust, so it makes sense that Monique and Raynell kept company with the same people. After meeting me, Monique must have put two and two together and realized that I was the one whose name was being batted around at cocktail parties as the person who solved Raynell's murder. At some point before she died, Monique apparently shared this information with Nathan, and he's now decided that my history as an amateur sleuth is his only hope for avoiding a lifetime in prison.

I was told I could have virtually nothing on my person when I meet with Nathan, so I shove my purse under the front seat and drop my cell phone in the glove compartment. When I lock the van and walk toward the entrance of the facility, the only things I have on me are my driver's license and my car keys.

"Yes?" says a disinterested woman behind the counter after I enter the building.

"Hi. My name is Mahalia Watkins. I'm here to see Nathan Tucker."

"Inmate number?"

I feel like responding, "I'm good, thanks for asking," but I guess if there's any place to not get smart, it's the county jail. Instead, I say, "I'm not sure. I don't think I was given that information."

She sighs as if I've asked her to go pick up my dry cleaning or mow my lawn. "I'll need to look him up. What's his name again?"

"Tucker. Nathan Tucker."

She clicks some buttons on her keyboard, finds him in the system, and scribbles a few notes on a form. She then barks more words at me, makes a copy of my driver's license, and hands me a pass.

"Security is to your left," she says. "No cellular telephones, laptop computers, tablet computers, smart watches, purses, bags, pagers . . . no food or drink, including chewing gum," she adds, almost robotically. "There are lockers before the screening area if you need to store anything."

I take the pass and say, "Thank you," to the young lady despite her groans, snappy questions, and not being bothered to make eye contact with me at any point during our interaction. From there I find my way to the screening area, deposit my keys in a little bin, and send them through an X-ray scanner. I then walk through a metal detector only to be told, once I've cleared it, to lift my arms and separate my feet. As a plump middle-aged woman with about as much warmth as the surly lady at the reception counter waves some wand thing over my entire being, I decide that if I hear the term "strip search," I'm out of here, and Nathan is on his own.

Once I'm finally cleared and pick up my keys, a guard asks me for the inmate number of the person I'm there to see. He seems just as annoyed as the lady at the counter when I don't remember it.

"It should be on your pass."

"Sorry. It's my first time here." I flip my pass upward so he can see it. He checks something off on his clipboard and leads me down a hallway that smells like both mold and bleach, to an unmarked door, which he unlocks and holds open for me. I poke my head in and see a sizable space with tables and chairs that remind me of a retro McDonald's, albeit a very stark and drab McDonald's . . . back when the tables were attached to the floor and the plastic chairs were attached to the tables.

I see a few other inmates with visitors before my eyes spot Nathan. I don't know why I'm surprised to see him in an orange jumpsuit—I guess that's what one wears in jail. But given that this is only a county detention center and he has not yet been convicted of anything, maybe I thought he would still be in street clothes or at least something less . . . I don't know . . . less *incriminating*.

I check in with yet another guard seated at the front of the room before finally getting to meet with Nathan.

"Hello," he says, extending his hand without getting up. I'm not sure if it's the circumstances of my visit or the somber environment, or his jumpsuit, but the bulk of that intimidating quality that was emanating from Nathan when I first met him is gone. At the moment he looks much more "victim" than "bully." "Thank you for coming."

"You're welcome, Mr. Tucker."

"Nathan. Please."

"Nathan," I say. "I didn't know her well, but I liked Monique, and she was such a great role model for young women. If I'm being honest, I'm only here because I feel like I owe it to her to hear what you have to say. Even then, I'm really not sure if I can help you."

"I appreciate that." He fiddles with his fingers nervously. "What I have to say is . . . is that I *did not* kill my wife."

"I'm not privy to all the relevant information, Nathan, but from what I know, the evidence is stacked against you. Word is that your fingerprints are on the gun, and your hands tested positive for gunpowder residue, which would indicate that you recently fired the weapon in question."

"Of course *my* fingerprints are on *my* gun. I had gunpowder on my hands because I went to the range the day of the party and did a few practice rounds. You can check the register at the small arms range by my house. I wanted to get in some final practice with the gun . . . make sure I knew how to use the thing before we went on the road."

"The road?"

"The tour. Monique and I . . . and Maurice and Alex were starting the tour the next day. We were going to be traveling all over the country in a very conspicuous bus. People would know Monique was on board, and she is known for being rich and wearing flashy expensive jewelry. We could have easily been targeted by thieves . . . even kidnappers. I bought the gun so we'd have some protection while we crisscrossed the country, not to kill my wife."

"Why do the police even think you would want Monique dead?"

"Your guess is as good as mine, but if you believe the talking heads on TV, I supposedly was looking to split from her, and when I did, I wanted our entire fortune, not the half of it I would have gotten if we divorced," Nathan says. "And . . . well . . . I have some gambling debts . . . some debts I owe to a not-so-nice person."

"Rodney Morrissey?"

"Yes. So you've heard about that?" he asks, but doesn't wait for me to answer. "He's been rumored to have killed clients who haven't paid him back in a timely fashion, but the feds have never been able to get enough solid evidence on him to make an arrest. He knew I was working on getting the money I owed him, though. Monique and I simply didn't have that much liquid cash—it's all tied up in the company. It was going to take some time, but Mr. Morrissey was well aware that it was coming. I didn't need to kill my wife to get the money."

"And I'm guessing you don't have an alibi or the police would not be holding you here."

"I *do* have an alibi . . . mostly."

"Mostly?"

"Plenty of people can vouch for me being at the convention center until eleven thirty Saturday night, and I was on my way back from there when Monique was shot. But the police say I had time to get home, fire the gun, and wait several minutes before calling them. They say, given traffic conditions, it should have only taken me about a half hour to get home, but it was late, and I wasn't paying attention. I missed the exit onto Suitland Parkway and had to go farther up 295 to turn around . . . and I was tired and driving slowly, so the whole trip took almost an hour. I got home about twelve thirty and called the police as soon as I found Monique."

"That's a lot to . . . um . . . a lot to believe."

"Maybe so, but it's the truth. The last time I saw my gun, it was on the top shelf of the bedroom closet. Monique could have told any number of people where I kept it. There were seventy-some odd people in our house the night of the white party. Any one of them could have snuck up to the bedroom and taken it."

"But you think it was Odessa?"

"I don't know why else she'd circle back to our house after the party. But I guess I don't know exactly why she'd kill Monique, either. They sparred with each other all the time, but I think they both got a kick out of it. They'd been . . . what's the word? Not rivals exactly . . ." He thinks for a moment. "Frenemies. They'd been *frenemies* for well over twenty years." He adjusts himself in the chair. "I don't know who else would have killed her. And you found that sparkly bauble thing from her dress. I heard you tell Detective Hutchins that you found it on the lawn."

"The sequin. Yes, it was at the far end of the lawn."

"How else would it get there if it didn't come off Odessa's dress?"

"I have no idea. Maybe I could do a little checking around and see what I can find out, but before I do, I need to ask you something."

Nathan looks back at me but doesn't respond.

"I'm assuming you have access to a TV in here. You must have seen the footage of Maurice on the news, making claims about you being abusive toward Monique. I actually saw a bruise underneath her eye the night of the party when I was up in the bedroom with her." I hear Nathan take in a deep breath. I can tell he's anticipating my question. "I have to ask: Is what Maurice said true?"

Nathan's response is a long silence. He seems to be trying to think of something to say . . . some way to spin his behavior, but I know enough to know that if the allegations were not true, he would have immediately denied them. He opens his mouth, about to offer whatever version of the truth he's concocted in his head, but I don't give him the opportunity.

"I'm not sure I can help you, Mr. Tucker," I say as I get up from the table, when what I really want to say is "I'm not sure I want to help you."

Chapter 24

"So, you really think Nathan is innocent?" Wavonne asks me from the passenger seat in my van.

"Not necessarily, but I'm not convinced he's guilty, either . . . especially given the evidence implicating Odessa," I respond as I turn into a small shopping center off of Crain Highway. "Whether Nathan actually murdered Monique or not, I would expect him to deny it. But it's the look that came over his face when I asked him about being violent toward her that makes me think he may not have killed her. When I asked him about the rumors of his abuse, he had guilt written all over his face. That look—that 'face of guilt'—was not there when he denied having anything to do with Monique's murder. I just don't think he's a very good liar."

"So you agreed to help him? That's why we're goin' to see Odessa?"

"Honestly, Wavonne, I'm not that interested in helping a man who beat his wife, but I won't be able to sleep at night if I don't at least feel out Odessa and see what I can find out. Abusive men like Nathan belong in prison, but if he didn't kill Monique, I'd like to make sure whoever did joins him there." I slide the van into an open space and move the gear shift to park. "All right, let's go see what we can find out about one Ms. Odessa Thornton," I say as we step out of the car and approach the shopping center.

"Fancy," Wavonne says when we walk into Salon Soleil.

"Sure is." I look around and take in the granite floors, sleek white furnishings, and modern chandeliers dripping with long rectangular crystals. "I hate to say it, but it sort of puts Latasha's shop to shame, doesn't it?"

"Yep. But I'm sure you have to pay for all this swank. A wet set probably sets you back seventy bucks at a bougie place like this."

"A hundred actually," we hear from a voice behind us. "Wet sets start at a hundred dollars. Bricklay rollers or flexi rods are even more."

We turn around. "Odessa! So good to see you," I say. "Where did you come from?" The woman is like a cat—I didn't see her anywhere when we walked in and, next thing you know, she's right behind us, listening to our conversation. Of course, she's impeccably dressed in a form-fitting floral print dress and suede heels.

"It's nice to see you two as well." She seems to struggle with how to physically greet us—like she doesn't know us well enough for a hug, but knows us too well for a handshake, so she just keeps talking. "I was in the supply closet doing a little inventory when I saw you come in. What can I do for you?"

"We were in the neighborhood and saw the sign. I guess we figured, after meeting you and hearing about it, we should come in and see what all the fuss is about. Salon Soleil is a charming place."

"Thank you. It's pretty much my life's work."

"You done good, girl," Wavonne says. "This place is high-class."

Odessa laughs. "So you said. I believe the term I heard you use was 'bougie.'"

"Nothin' wrong with bougie. I'd be bougie as all get-out if I could afford it."

"Thank you, Wavonne. Things around here may not be quite up to snuff at the moment. I haven't been giving my business the attention it needs the last few days . . . you know . . . with Monique's death and all. It's been hard to focus and be professional. But, when you *own* the salon, you don't really have the luxury of bereavement leave. I have to keep going. If I don't, clients will find other hairdressers." She turns her head to me. "But I guess I don't need to tell you about the trials of owning a business."

I smile. "No. I can definitely relate to what you said. Time off is rare. Sick days, snow days, vacation days . . . I haven't seen any of those in years." I let my smile fade. "I am so sorry to hear about Monique. Were you two close?"

Odessa lifts her chin and looks up as if she's pondering my question. "Close? Yeah, we were definitely close. That doesn't mean we always got along, though. Monique and I . . . we had a complicated relationship, but I've known her for more than twenty years. She was like my sister . . . sometimes more of a wicked stepsister than devoted sibling, but we met in high school and started out in the cosmetology trenches together back when box braids and the finger wave were all the rage—that's how long we've known each other. I'm honestly having trouble imagining life without her."

I'm trying to read her the same way I did Nathan when he talked about Monique, but she's not giving anything away. She doesn't seem to be stricken with grief, but she does seem to be genuinely affected by Monique's death.

"If you don't mind, I'd really rather not talk about it right now. I've got a long day ahead of me, and I don't want to get distracted. Losing focus leads to leaving the relaxer on too long or moving too slow with the hot comb. Sisters might forgive lying, stealing, cheating with their husbands, but if you screw up their hair you better get out of town and find a good witness protection program."

"Of course," I say with a chuckle. "We understand. We won't keep you. We just thought we'd take a peek at the place while we were out this way."

"I don't have a client for a few minutes. I'd be happy to give you a tour."

"That would be great."

"So this is the reception area. As you can see, we're well stocked with Hair by Monique products." Odessa points toward the shelves behind the reception counter and along the walls in the waiting area. "And that's our moneymaker," she says pointing toward a locked glass case stocked with bundles of hair. "We've got Brazilian hair, Malaysian hair, and Peruvian hair . . . sew-in extensions, tape-in extensions, clip-on extensions . . ."

"Damn, girl. That case must be worth a few thousand dollars," Wavonne says.

"Which is why it's locked," Odessa replies. "It's all one hundred percent real human hair. No fake hair added. No shedding or tangling. The cuticles are all going in the same direction for a natural look. It can be styled with a flat iron, cut, curled, bleached, and dyed any color," she adds, clearly giving us the same sales pitch she must give her clients. "Starts at a hundred dollars a bundle."

"You can close your mouth now, Wavonne," I say, catching sight of Wavonne practically drooling at the display of hair.

"I could do some damage in this place."

"I'm sure you could," I agree as Odessa leads us away from the reception area and stops in the middle of the main hub of the salon. "And this is where all the magic happens," she says, spreading her arms to showcase the two rows of styling chairs on either side of her.

I recognize some of the stylists from the convention center, and from Monique's party. Much like Odessa, they all have perfect hair and makeup and are dressed to the nines in stylish clothes and high heels. Not a single one of them is wearing a smock over their designer threads while they cut, cream, and curl.

"Your stylists are so put together. They all look like they recently stepped out of a salon after getting the works themselves."

"Thank you. I run a tight ship. They know better than to show up to work looking less than perfect. Image is very important. If you want to be the best, you have to look the part."

"I guess, but my feet hurt just looking at them. How do they work on their feet all day in those heels?"

Odessa laughs. "You'd be surprised what you can do with a little moleskin, some padded inserts, and an anti-blister stick."

Odessa continues the tour and shows us the washing stations, the manicure tables, and the chemical mixing counter before taking us down a small hallway lined with doors in the back of the salon.

"These are the treatment rooms for massages, waxings, and facials."

Odessa knocks on one of the doors and pops it open. Wavonne and I peer inside and just seeing the room gives me a sense of calm. A soft, almost misty light shines on a massage table situated against a wall paneled in a light buttery wood. Some candles (battery-operated, I assume) are flickering on the counter next to a pile of fluffy white towels while new age music plays softly in the background.

"It's so inviting. I could crawl in there and take a nap."

"I'd be lying if I say I never did that," Odessa admits. "That's pretty much the tour. Can I get you ladies anything before you go? We have a cappuccino maker, or can I offer you some sparkling water."

I decline the offer before Wavonne has a chance to say anything, and as we fall in step with Odessa back to the reception area, I try to think of a way to bring Monique up again. The tour was nice, but it's certainly not the real reason I came here. I need to determine if what Nathan said about Odessa going back to Monique's house after the party is true. If she has an alibi that would basically show Nathan to be a liar, and we can put this whole thing to rest.

"Must be hard not to think of Monique," I say when we reach the front counter, "with all her products on display." I look around at all the bright pink boxes and bottles with Monique's face on them.

"It can be, but I try to keep busy, which isn't hard around here."

"You heard that Nathan was arrested?" I ask while Wavonne steps away to peruse the glass case of hair and the shelves lined with Monique's brand of beauty supplies.

"Yes. I saw it on the news. I'm not surprised. That man was no good from day one."

"I can't say I found him terribly likable myself, but I'm not sure it's a closed case at this point. I think the police are still interviewing guests from the big white party. I guess any one of us could be a suspect. I'm glad I have Wavonne as an alibi," I joke. "I imagine the police may even come by here. I'm guessing you have an alibi as well?" I ask, and yes, it does come off as awkward and accusatory as you think.

There's a shift in Odessa's demeanor, and it's not a good one. "Are you seriously asking me if I have an alibi for when Monique was killed? Is that why you came here?"

"No . . . well, not exactly. Please don't take offense. I'm

certainly not insinuating that you killed Monique, but if I end up being interviewed by the police, I'll have to let them know what I heard the night of the party," I say even though I already told Detective Hutchins about her argument with Monique.

"What are you talking about? What did you hear?"

"I happened to overhear you and Monique arguing in the hallway near the basement steps."

"So what? Monique and I argued all the time."

"Monique said something about ending an arrangement you two had, and you didn't seem too happy about it. Clearly, the arrangement she spoke of had something to do with money."

"We were just talking business. Monique always yammered about ending our arrangement when she had a few cocktails and was annoyed with me. It was nothing."

"May I ask what this arrangement was?"

Odessa groans. "If you must know, I was one of the first salon owners to carry Monique's products. I had her stuff on my shelves long before she became a national phenomenon. She rewarded me by selling me her line at a steep discount on the wholesale price. In exchange I agreed to only carry Hair by Monique products. As you can see, there are no competing brands in my store. Whenever she got in a snit, she threatened to end our little deal, but she always came around. Even with the discount, I was making a lot of money for Monique and giving her great exposure. I run the top salon in the wealthiest majority–African American county in the country. She wanted her products on my shelves as much as I did."

"I guess that all makes sense, and I'm sure you're telling the truth," I lie—I'm not sure of anything at the moment. "But if the police start making rounds, you do know they are going to ask where you were at the time Monique was shot?"

"That's fine by me. I went out with the girls after the party. I was rockin' that dress and looked too good to go straight home. We had a nice time at Pose, didn't we, Amber?" Odessa asks one of the stylists, who's stepped behind the counter to check out a customer, an older gentleman in khaki pants and a polo shirt.

"Pose?" Wavonne says stepping back over in my direction. "I've been meaning to go there with some of my girls. What's it like?"

"Meh. Expensive drinks. Hip-hop music. Elbow-to-elbow crowds," Amber says as she pulls a few of Monique's products off the shelf and starts ringing them up for the man. "But we had a good time. Drank a few cocktails, danced a little . . . broke a few hearts. We ended up closing the place down," she adds, taking notice of the curious looks Wavonne and I are giving the products on the counter—products clearly meant for women. She points to one of the boxes, and says to the man, "Remind your wife that this is the one she should work into her hair after shampooing, from front to back. Then she can do the double strand twist I showed her last week."

"If I can remember all that," the man replies, and hands Amber his credit card, which she slides through the reader. She prints a receipt to which he adds a generous tip. Then he exits the salon with his bag of goodies.

"We should let you get back to work," I say to Monique while Amber steps away from the counter and moves on to her next client. "But can I ask you one more question?"

She offers no verbal response. Instead, she cocks an eyebrow at me as if to say, "You're really getting on my freaking nerves, but go ahead."

"The night of the white party, when you and Monique were talking, I heard her say that she wasn't the only one with secrets. What did she mean by that? Did you know about her hair? Or lack thereof?"

"If I told you about my and Monique's secrets, they wouldn't be secrets, now would they?"

"She's got you there, Sherlock," Wavonne says.

"I told you, Monique and I have known each other for decades. Of course we have secrets, but I can assure you, Halia, they certainly did not involve anything so salacious that they would lead to murder." Odessa says this in a tone that makes the whole idea of her killing Monique sound absurd. "But I will say our secrets had nothing to do with her hair—I was as in the dark about the little Florida Evans situation she had happening on her head as anyone. That was apparently a closely guarded secret."

"It sure was, but I guess the thing about secrets is . . . they always seem to come out."

"Maybe so," Odessa says. "Are we done here, ladies? I've got a client arriving any minute."

"I guess so," I reply. "Thank you, Odessa. I really hope I didn't offend you with my questions."

"I'm not easily offended, Halia. If I was, I wouldn't have stayed friends with Monique for so many years. Why are you snooping around about Monique's murder anyway? Shouldn't you just let the police do their job?"

"They seem to have decided, perhaps prematurely, that Nathan is guilty, and I must say, the evidence does point in that direction. But me? I'm not so sure Nathan is the culprit."

"You know, if you really think Nathan may not be Monique's killer, if I were you, I'd be asking questions of one Alejandro Rivas."

"Alex? Why?"

"You mentioned overhearing Monique and me arguing. Well, I overheard an argument of my own—Alex and Monique had a doozy of one the night of the party. It was after the party wrapped and Nathan had gone out back to smoke a cigar. I was the last guest still there. I'd said my good-byes, and they thought I'd left, but I made a quick run upstairs to the ladies' room. On my way out, I heard Alex begging Monique to 'reconsider.' I don't know exactly what he wanted her to reconsider, but my guess is that she was ending an affair with him, and he was trying to talk her out of it . . . to no avail, apparently. I remember Monique's words very distinctly. She said, 'It's over. I can't do it anymore. Let it go, Alex.'"

"What did he say?" Wavonne asks.

"Nothing. He just stormed out of the kitchen, through the dining room, and out the door."

"So you think he and Monique were having an affair?"

"It sure sounded like it from the way they were quarreling. I don't think he saw me, but I caught a glimpse of his face as he took off. He was mad as hell. Perhaps mad enough to kill Monique."

"Wow. I had no idea." I hope the disappointment doesn't show in my face. I liked Alex, and I was starting to entertain the idea that maybe he actually had been flirting with me over the last few days. I hate to think of him having a fling with Monique, and I really hate the idea of him possibly having something to do with her death. "Thanks for sharing that with us, Odessa. It's good to know." I turn to Wavonne. "You ready? We should let Odessa get back to work."

We say good-bye to Odessa again, who seems slightly less irritated by me, now that she's directed my suspicions elsewhere, and I compliment her salon a final time before we leave.

When we step outside, I see the man who purchased some Hair by Monique products while we were talking at the counter. He's smoking on the sidewalk in front of a Starbucks a few doors down from Odessa's salon. He takes a last puff from the cigarette, throws the bud on the ground, and stomps it out. Then he pulls out his car keys and heads toward the parking lot, making a quick pit stop before stepping off the curb onto the blacktop to lift his Salon Soleil bag of hair care products and toss them in one of the public garbage cans.

"What's that about?" I ask as Wavonne and I watch him make his way to his car. "Why would he throw away a few hundred dollars' worth of creams and conditioners?"

"Beats me," Wavonne says, her eyes on the man of interest. She waits until he's inside his car with the door closed before speaking again. "But wait here while I go fish them out."

Chapter 25

"This smell of fried chicken is making me hungry," Wavonne says. We're back in the van after making a quick stop at Sweet Tea to check on a few things and fix a plate for Alex. Wavonne and I are on our way to pay him a quick visit. I'm having trouble even considering the idea that he and Monique were having an affair or that he could have been involved with Monique's death, but if someone throws a lead my way, I can't help but follow up on it. And, if I'm being honest, it's as good an excuse as any to see him again. Maybe it's wishful thinking, but much as I denied it to Wavonne and Momma, I did feel like there was a spark between Alex and me, and I simply can't imagine that handsome man, who seemed so kind the few times I've met him, could be a killer. My guess is he's actually quite broken up about Monique's death and could use a condolence visit from some friendly faces, so Wavonne and I will make a social call and, if I can somehow bring it up in a much less awkward and accusatory way than I did with Odessa, I'll see what I can glean about his whereabouts when Monique was killed.

"I figure Alex will be happier to see us if we bring him

some goodies—everyone is happier to see you when you come with a plate of fried chicken, mashed potatoes, and collard greens. He's probably hungry. I doubt he's in the mood to cook at the moment."

"Yeah . . . instead of cookin', he's either grievin' Monique's death or, if Odessa's story holds any water, afraid the po po are about to show up at his door with an arrest warrant," Wavonne says. "How'd you find out where he lives, anyway?"

"He mentioned that he lived at Iverson Towers the night he was at Sweet Tea, but I don't have his apartment number. I'm hoping there will be a directory or something."

"I think that's it . . . right up there on the right." Wavonne points to a high-rise apartment complex, or at least what we call a high-rise in suburban Maryland . . . maybe ten or twelve stories tall. "I think a friend of mine lived there a few years ago," she adds, picking up the shiny plastic Salon Soleil bag from the floor while I turn into the parking lot of Alex's building. "Why do you think that man at Odessa's salon bought all this stuff only to chuck it a few minutes later?" She pulls out a few bottles of hair potions.

"I've been wondering about that, too. I have no idea. Odessa's salon probably caters to wealthy people, so maybe throwing away expensive hair products is no big deal to them, but I'm still not sure why he'd do it."

"Oh well . . . whateva . . . I got the hookup now. I can give this hair milk to Tanya for her birthday. I think Aunt Celia uses this conditioner—I'll sell it to her at half price. And I'll keep this detangler for myself."

"Sounds like you've got it all figured out," I say as we step out of the van and walk toward the glass doors that lead to the lobby of Alex's apartment building.

Wavonne pulls on one of the door handles. "They're locked."

There's a call box next to the entrance, but you need to know the apartment number of the person you're visiting to reach the appropriate tenant and have them buzz you in.

I put my hands up to the glass to block the glare and look inside. "There's a clerk at the front desk. Maybe she can help us."

Wavonne peers through the door as well. "She doesn't look too friendly, and sometimes these places won't give out people's apartment numbers."

"If that's the case, maybe she can call Alex and tell him we're here."

"Sometimes apartment buildings won't even confirm if someone lives there at all. At least that's what happened when I was trying to track down that lady with the pop-up wig shop on H Street in the city . . . the one that sold me what was supposed to be a genuine Beverly Johnson human hair wig that turned out to be some fake-assed Vivica Fox pile of polyester. If this building is anything like hers, they won't tell you nothin'," Wavonne says. "Come on. Follow my lead."

I don't have a chance to agree with whatever scheme she has come up with before Wavonne starts knocking on the door and waving for the clerk to let us in. The unpleasant-looking woman presses a button, and Wavonne hurries in front of me toward the desk.

"*Cómo estás,*" Wavonne says to the lady. "My brother . . . my *hermano*, Alex Rivas lives here . . . you know, *aquí* . . . but I don't remember his apartment number." I think she's trying to do a Dominican accent, but she comes off sounding more Jamaican. "He's been sick . . . you know, *embarazada.*"

I don't know much Spanish, but I do know that *embarazada* means pregnant.

"I'm Juanita." Wavonne nods in my direction. "And this is my sister, Rosario. We're Dominican, ya know . . . we brought

Alex some food . . . when he's sick he only eats Dominican food, so we made some tacos and burritos and guacamole," she says, lifting the plate in her hand.

The clerk shifts her eyes from Wavonne to me and gives me a "is this chick for real?" look. She then leans heavily in her chair and directs her gaze back at Wavonne. "So, let me get this straight. You're bringing your pregnant Dominican brother some *Mexican* food . . . *Mexican* food that smells like fried chicken?"

"Ah . . . um . . ." Wavonne stumbles as she tries to think of something to say.

"Wavonne here is a little . . . what's the word?" I ask while Wavonne still struggles for words.

"Extra," the woman says.

"Yes, *extra*. She's a ham . . . always putting on a show," I say. "May I ask your name?"

The woman gawks at me, as if she's sizing me up. Then she turns her head in Wavonne's direction and seems to decide that, at least in comparison, I'm relatively sane. "Tanesha," she says.

"Tanesha, I'm Halia and this is Wavonne. We're trying to find a friend of ours, Alex Rivas. He recently lost someone dear to him, and we wanted to check on him and bring him a little something to eat. I know he lives in this building, but I don't know his apartment number. Maybe you could help us with that?"

"You're his friend, and you can't call him and ask him for his apartment number yourself?"

"Maybe 'friend' wasn't the right word. We just met several days ago. We catered an event together last Saturday night. We never exchanged phone numbers."

"You're in the catering business?"

"She's the owner of Sweet Tea, the best—"

"Sweet Tea?!" Tanesha exclaims before Wavonne has a chance to brag. "No way?!"

"Yes way," I say with a laugh.

"I love that place! It's a bit out of my price range, so I've only been a few times . . . on some special occasions. The fried chicken and waffles were my favorite . . . and the sour cream cornbread . . . Oh. Em. Gee!" She looks at the plate in Wavonne's hand again. "Is that your fried chicken under the foil?"

I nod and reach for my wallet and find a business card. "How about I give you my card, and you can send me an e-mail. We'll set up a time for you and a guest to have lunch at Sweet Tea, on the house." My offer should go on to include "if you help us out," but we both know it's implied, and it seems impolite to actually say it.

"Four twenty-three," Tanesha says, taking the card. "Alex . . . he's in apartment four twenty-three."

"You know where tenants live by heart?"

"I know where single male tenants who look like Alex live by heart. That man is handsome as hell. But I don't think he's home. In fact, I'm not sure he lives here anymore."

"What?"

"He was moving a bunch of stuff out the other day, and I haven't seen him since. I asked him about it, and he said he was just getting rid of a few things, but he was probably afraid I'd tell the property manager if he admitted he was moving. He still has five months left on his lease."

"Wow, you've really kept tabs on Mr. Rivas."

"I'm partial to Alex because he's single and good-looking, but I don't have that much to do all day, so I keep an eye on a lot of the residents. I know who's sneaking cat litter into this no-pets-allowed building, I know women who regularly go up to their apartments at lunchtime with men who are *not* their husbands, I know who came through last night with a big box of wine even though she came through with a big box of wine the night before and the night before that. Most people are actually very interesting if you just pay attention."

"I suppose that's true," I agree, and try to steer us back to the subject of Alex. "Do you recall what day it was that Alex was moving things out?"

"Um." She puts a finger to her cheek and thinks for a moment. "I remember him, boxes in his hands, sidestepping other residents in their church clothes, so it must have been Sunday morning."

"Really? That's good to know, Tanesha. Thank you for your help," I reply. "Doesn't sound likely, but do you mind if we pop upstairs and see if he's home?"

"Be my guest." Her eyes veer toward the plate in Wavonne's hand. "If he's not at home, you're not going to throw that fried chicken away, are you?"

"If he's not home, you've got first dibs on it," I offer, and Wavonne and I set off for the elevator.

"So Alex may have skipped town the morning after Monique was killed," I say once the elevator doors close, realizing I may have to actually begin entertaining the idea of putting him on my suspect list.

"Sounds like it," Wavonne agrees as we exit the elevator and walk down the hall to Alex's unit.

I knock on the door several times and when there's no answer, I try the knob and find the door locked. "I guess the chances of getting Tanesha to open the apartment are pretty slim. We could try to bribe her with the fried chicken."

"Or," Wavonne says, reaching for her wallet and pulling out a credit card, "we could try this." She lifts the card and finagles it into the doorjamb. "This will only work if the deadbolt isn't locked." She quickly slides the card down toward the floor and, just like that, the door pops open.

"I don't even want to know where you learned that," I say, and pop my head into the apartment to see the living room. Its only contents are a sofa and a bulky coffee table. "Hello. Alex?" I call, before pushing the door open wider, and stepping inside with Wavonne to take a closer look. We can see where a flat-screen television has been removed from the wall and some indentations in the carpet where some small end tables used to be.

We start to move through the space and come upon a table and chairs in the dining room and a virtually empty kitchen—almost nothing on the counters or in the refrigerator or cabinets. There's a bed and a dresser in the bedroom, but the dresser is empty, as is the closet.

"Clearly, Rico Suave left town in a hurry."

It takes me a moment to respond, as the idea that Alex was not who I thought he was really starts to settle in. "It sure seems like it. I think he took everything he could fit in his car and just left the rest."

"You think Odessa was right about him?"

"Maybe. Maybe he did kill Monique in a fit of rage after she ended their apparent affair and left town before the police would have a chance to question him."

"So, what now?"

"Hell if I know. The police think Nathan killed Monique. Nathan thinks Odessa killed Monique. Odessa thinks Alex killed Monique. I've got as many suspects as Jennifer Lopez has ex-husbands."

"That's a lot of people who might have wanted someone dead. If anyone wants me dead, I hope it's only one person . . . two at the most." Wavonne kids. "And that sucks about Alex. He seemed like a good guy, and I know you had a thing for him."

"I did not have a *thing* for him," I lie.

"Mmm hmm," Wavonne drones. "I guess it was a disappointin' day for everyone."

"I don't know about that." We step out of the apartment and close the door. "With Alex MIA, at least Tanesha at the front desk is getting herself some of the best fried chicken in town."

Chapter 26

"It was very nice of you to invite me, Halia, but I'm afraid your wonderful menu is simply going to be wasted on me. I'm only doing lean proteins and steamed vegetables until I drop thirty pounds," Maurice says, having just walked through the door of Sweet Tea. "And, quite frankly, I'm miserable, but I can barely get these pants buttoned, and I refuse to buy any more new clothes that go up yet another size. I'm going to get back into my thirty-two-inch-waist Bonobos if it kills me. I only stopped by to say hi and thank you for the offer. I'm in the neighborhood anyway to touch base with Latasha about a business opportunity."

I invited Maurice to Sweet Tea a few days ago. I wanted to thank him for taking Wavonne and me shopping last week and, yes, I also want to pump him for information about Nathan and Odessa. And, as it appears that he has skipped town, I'm particularly interested in anything Maurice may know about the relationship between Alex and Monique.

"It's me who wanted to thank you. Who knows what I would have worn to the party if you had not intervened. Fashion is so not my thing."

"You?" Maurice runs his eyes over my outfit. "In those LL Bean khakis that are completely devoid of any tailoring and that Eddie Bauer wash-and-wear no-iron shirt? No way," he kids.

"I guess I'm a 'function over form' kind of girl when it comes to clothing, especially at work. And how did you know exactly where I bought my clothes?"

"I'm a stylist. I can tell you where most of the people in this restaurant bought their clothes."

I'm tempted to tell him to go for it, but I'm thinking it may not be the best idea for him to start pointing at my customers and calling out their apparel choices. Instead, I say, "Please. Stay and have some lunch. It's not what we're known for, but we have a few low-calorie options. Why don't you take a seat, and I'll get you a menu." He seems agreeable to my suggestion, so I grab a menu and show him to a small booth along the wall. "And how about a glass of our Purple Rain iced tea to start with? It's lightly sweetened with stevia and a touch of honey, so it's only about thirty calories a glass."

"How can I turn down something called Purple Rain iced tea?"

"We used to call it Purple Passion, but we happened to have it on special the day Prince died in 2016, and one of my servers started calling it Purple Rain, and it sort of stuck."

I give Maurice a few minutes to peruse the menu before returning with a glass of purple tea made from an organic blend of hibiscus, rosehips, and stevia leaves that we mix with puréed blueberries, a few drops of honey, and a squeeze of lemon. We normally bring out a pan of our famous sour cream cornbread with the drink order, but, clearly, Maurice is trying to stick with whatever program he is on, so I decide not to tempt him.

He takes a sip of the tea. "Very refreshing."

"Glad you like it. What can I get you for lunch?"

"I'm going to behave myself and have the grilled chicken salad."

"Sure. It will go nicely with the tea."

Our grilled chicken salad is a fine offering—mixed greens, chicken, red onions, poached pears, and goat cheese tossed in a homemade balsamic vinaigrette that we sprinkle with candied pecans and fresh ground pepper . . . but a salad is a salad is a salad. It's a necessity to offer a selection of them on my menu for my calorie-conscious diners, and I try to make the best of it, but I'll be the first to admit my heart is not really in those particular menu items. My passion is for hearty soul food, so salads are sort of the redheaded stepchild of my menu—I offer them, but not with a lot of enthusiasm.

I depart the table to key in Maurice's order, and when I return several minutes later with a heaping plate of greens and a pitcher of tea to refill his glass, he's looking at his phone.

"Here we are." I set down the plate and begin to refill his glass.

"Looks very nice," he says, which is a far cry from the mouth drops, "wows" and "oh my Gods" I get when I set down a plate of my fried chicken and waffles or macaroni and cheese topped with bacon in front of my customers, but even the best salads are like my clothes from Eddie Bauer and LL Bean . . . practical and high quality, but they mostly just make you go "meh."

"Mind if I sit with you for a bit?"

Maurice puts his phone down. "Of course not, but I hope you'll have some lunch as well."

"I'm not hungry at the moment, but I'd love to chat." I take a seat across from him. "How have you been . . . you know, with the loss of Monique?"

"I'm trying to put on a brave face and get on with things. I've even got a new business venture brewing, but it's hard to keep it together sometimes. I worked with Monique for years. We were dear friends and confidants, and I should have *somehow* made her leave Nathan." There's a change in his demeanor or his mannerisms . . . or *something* when he talks about Monique. The sardonic quality that usually abounds in his voice is absent, and there's a look of longing or regret on his face. "He'd hit her as recently as last week. I had to help her cover a bruise when I did her makeup before the white party. She told me that Nathan had gotten a little 'handsy' with her in the elevator back in their apartment building in New York a few days earlier. She would always say that he got 'handsy' or 'was in a snit and didn't know his own strength' or that 'he meant to hit the wall' and it was her fault that she didn't get out of the way—she had a whole stable full of excuses to explain her bruises, but they all meant one thing—that Nathan had beat her. I know she would have killed me if I went to the police, and I'm sure she would not have cooperated with any investigation. But I will always wonder if she might still be alive if I had done something more than just encourage . . . push . . . sometimes *beg* her to leave Nathan."

"Realistically, how could you have made her leave Nathan . . . or made her do *anything*? People have been trying to get women to leave abusive relationships since the beginning of time. It sounds like you tried, but sometimes you simply can't help people who are not ready to be helped."

"I guess," he says, his eyes still distant. "But once she told me about Nathan buying a gun, I should have reported his abuse to the police . . . or . . . I don't know, done *something*. She just would not hear of leaving him." Maurice pokes his fork into the plate of leaves and takes a bite. As he chews, I catch him staring longingly at a plate of chicken and dumplings as it travels past him on the way to another table. "God, I am so hungry," he says quietly to himself more than me while stabbing a piece of grilled chicken with his fork.

"Why wouldn't she leave him?"

"I don't know. She always said she was afraid it would hurt her image . . . her brand, if her customers found out about her tumultuous marriage, but I'm not sure if that was really why she . . ." Maurice lets his voice trail off. "You know, I really shouldn't be talking about Monique's business right now. The police asked me to keep what I know on the QT."

"So you've spoken to the police?"

"Yes, they saw me talking about Nathan on the news and then showed up at my house asking questions."

"What did you tell them?"

"Same thing I told the reporter—that Nathan was abusive and should be the prime murder suspect, and that . . ." He stops midsentence a second time. "I really need to shut up, Halia. I'm not supposed to be talking about this stuff."

"Sure. I understand."

Once again, his eyes wistfully follow a plate of food bound for another table—this time it's our smothered pork chop platter, the same one we had on special the night Monique dined here. I think he actually frowns when his gaze leaves the gravy-laden chops paired with fried apples and coleslaw and returns to his salad.

"Why don't we talk about something else," I suggest as he grudgingly lifts another forkful of lettuce to his mouth. "How about Odessa?"

"What about her?"

"I'm curious about her relationship with Monique. Do you think she could have had something to do with Monique's murder?"

"No. I don't think so. It seems pretty clear that Nathan is the killer, but I probably shouldn't be running my fat mouth about Odessa, either."

"So the police told you to keep quiet about her as well? Do you think maybe they haven't closed the book on Nathan? Maybe they are looking into Odessa as well?"

"Really, Halia. I'm sorry, but I just can't talk about it." He slightly lifts his nose. "What is that wonderful smell?"

"I think it's the pan of cornbread that was just delivered to the table behind you."

I watch as Maurice takes in the scent of cornmeal and butter and sour cream, and that's when I get an idea. "You know, maybe I will have some lunch," I say, and signal for Darius, one of my long-time servers, to come over and ask him to bring me today's special.

"What sides can I bring with it?" Darius asks.

"Surprise me," I respond. "Maybe bring some cornbread as well."

I make small talk with Maurice about our shopping trip and the white party . . . and the weather, until Darius returns and sets down a cast-iron pan of piping hot cornbread and a plate stacked with two breaded and fried pork chops covered in a rich gravy seasoned with salt, black pepper, onion powder, garlic, paprika, allspice, and a touch of cayenne pepper to give it a little heat. I'm also treated to some side plates of thick-cut fried sweet potato wedges and collard greens.

I can't help but feel sorry for Maurice, his half-eaten salad in front of him, as I see his mouth ajar while I use my knife to slice into the cornbread and lift a piece to my plate. It settles into the gravy as I cut off a little portion. Maurice's eyes follow my fork, heavy with gravy-covered cornbread, as it moves from my plate to my mouth. He looks like a hungry puppy waiting for a crumb to drop from the table.

"Monique really liked my cornbread when she was here last week." I start to cut into one of the pork chops, through the thin coating of flour into the tender meat, and, from the way Maurice is looking at my plate, you would think there was a million dollars in cash on it. "Odessa did as well. Wavonne and I went to see her the other day."

"Oh," he replies, and I can tell my little plan is working—he is clearly distracted by the sight and fragrance of my food.

"She mentioned rumors of an affair between Monique and Alex. Do you know anything about that?"

"Between who?" he asks, a little dazed, too fixated on my plate to hear what I'm saying. He's wearing the same expression I've seen on Wavonne's face when she's on whatever silly diet plan she's signed up for (and sticks with for all of about three days). It's the look she gets when she's eating some prepackaged nonsense from Jenny Craig or Nutrisystem in front of the television, and a Red Lobster commercial comes on. I guess it's the look anyone would get when they're forcing down something healthy and low calorie while the TV is showing plates of fried fish and snow crab legs being cracked open and dipped in drawn butter.

"Alex and Monique? Do you think they were having an affair?"

"Probably," he says, watching me lift a sweet potato wedge and dip it in some sour cream. "Who wouldn't have an affair with Alex if given the chance? I stumbled upon them a time or two when they abruptly ceased conversation as I walked into the room. In those moments I always got the feeling that whatever they were discussing did not have to deal with meal planning or other chef duties." His mouth is now hanging open as he stares at me while I pop a sour cream–covered piece of crispy sweet potato in my mouth.

For the next few minutes, I continue to eat my lunch and ask Maurice questions while he's too busy trying to keep from drooling to have his wits about him. He observes my every move . . . from my plate, to my fork, to my mouth, and back again. Feeling like I've more than adequately distracted him from the police instructions to keep quiet about Monique, I decide to inquire about the topic I'm most curious about.

"So . . . if I may ask, what was the deal with Monique's hair . . . or lack of hair? You had to know about it if you were her hairdresser."

"Of course I knew, but I'm about the only one who did. And she wanted to keep it that way. That's why I was the only person who styled her wigs. And the only person, other than herself, who did her makeup . . . she didn't want any other artists getting that close to her face and detecting any mesh."

"Why did she wear wigs . . . you know, instead of using her own products to straighten her hair and wear it long?"

"She never would give me the full story on that. She said it just took too much time and work to manage long hair for all her appearances, but I always sensed there was something more going on. It was convenient though—her not having to be present when her hair was styled. I could coif her wigs while she was off doing one of any number of things and then take a few minutes to switch them out, place them properly, and give them a quick touch-up . . . no fuss, no muss."

"You said you were *about* the only one who knew about Monique's situation. Who else knew? Nathan had to know. Anyone else?" I ask, realizing I've finished my entire lunch and am out of culinary diversions. "Did Alex know? Odessa?"

Maurice, now free of the quasi-hypnotic spell I had him under, halfheartedly stabs his fork into the salad he's largely been ignoring up until now. "I think I've already said too much," he says. "Why all the questions, anyway?"

"I'm just a curious person and, honestly, despite all the evidence pointing in Nathan's direction, I'm not one hundred percent convinced he killed Monique."

"Really? Why is that?"

I take a breath. "You shared some information with me, so I'll do the same for you. I went back to Monique's house a few days ago, and it's a bit of a long story about how I ended up at the edge of the front lawn, but while I was there I came across a red sequin in a spot that could have very likely been where Monique's fatal shooter fired the gun."

"A red sequin? Like the ones all over Odessa's dress the night of the white party?" he asks. "Hmmm . . . very interesting."

"When I saw Odessa the other day she claimed to have an alibi at the time Monique was killed . . . that she and some of her stylists went to a club in the city after the party. They said they stayed until closing. I think the club was called Pose."

"Pose?" Maurice questions. "That tired club closed months ago."

"Seriously?"

"Yes. You know how it is with nightclubs in DC. They come and go with the wind."

"Not really. My nightclub days are long gone, but that's very interesting that the club Odessa used as her alibi is out of business."

"Interesting and quite suspicious."

"Indeed," I say, and I'm about to start with my questions again, but if I'm going to get any good information out of Maurice, I need to bring out the big guns.

Once again, I wave for Darius. When he arrives at the table I motion for him to stoop down, and whisper in his ear. Shortly thereafter, he returns to the table with a heaping slice of Momma's warm pineapple upside-down cake topped with a scoop of vanilla ice cream. I look on as Maurice glances down at the remnants of his salad, before lifting his head and eyeing the warm golden cake as the ice cream begins to ever so slightly melt on top of a lightly browned, glazed pineapple ring.

"You've been so good and had the salad for lunch. If you feel like treating yourself, please, have some." I scoot the plate closer to him, feeling a little guilty for playing him like this, but it seems to be an effective way to gather information from him. And it's not like I'm enticing him with dessert to get some juicy gossip or fashion tips—this is murder we are dealing with.

Maurice licks his lips, moves his fork in the direction of the cake, and then pulls it back again. "I really had better not."

"Okay. I admire your discipline," I compliment, before taking advantage of his altered state of mind and asking more questions. "So, do you happen to know anything about any *secrets* between Monique and Odessa? Odessa claims she didn't know Monique was wearing wigs." I scoop up a spoonful of my dessert, careful to get a little bit of cake, pineapple, and ice cream on the spoon. I hold it in front of my lips, about level with Maurice's eyes.

"She did, did she?" His gaze is glued to the tip of my spoon.

"She said she was as in the dark about Monique's lack of hair as anyone." I scoot the plate toward him again. "Are you sure you don't want any?"

He tries to resist for another second or two, but his hankering gets the best of him. He grabs my plate and slides it all the way over to his side of the table.

"Well, Odessa is lying," he blurts out as he uses his fork to hurriedly slice off a hefty scoop of cake and shove it in his mouth. He shuts his eyes and a look of pure delight comes across his face. Then he swiftly attacks the cake with his fork again . . . and again . . . and again. "Of course she knew Monique was wearing wigs."

Chapter 27

"If Nathan didn't do it, *someone* needs to find out who killed Monique soon because I can't keep leaving the restaurant trying to chase down information," I say to Wavonne from the passenger seat of my van. I asked her to drive so I can poke around on my phone on the way to making a second visit to Odessa's salon.

"I know you think Sweet Tea will crumble to the ground if you ain't there for an hour or two, but I suspect it will still be standin' when we get back." Wavonne adjusts herself in the driver's seat. I always insist that she wear her seat belt and seat belts were simply not made for women with breasts as abundant as Wavonne's. "So, per Maurice, Odessa knew that Monique was totally frontin' with that bogus straight hair? How'd he know that?"

"He didn't say. I tried questioning him further, but once he devoured the pineapple upside-down cake, he regained a little self-control and wasn't so free-flowing with the information anymore. That's why I want to go back to Salon Soleil. I checked, and Maurice was right—the club Odessa said she was at when Monique was killed closed back in August. So not only did she lie about her whereabouts when Monique was shot, if Maurice is telling the truth, she also lied about not knowing that Monique was going au naturel under some wigs."

"Some *really* good wigs. I don't know much . . . but I *know* wigs. And the ones Monique wore were grade A. I had no idea she had a mesh cap full of hair from some bald-headed chick in China on her head. Although Monique had some coin, so maybe she got the really good Eastern European stuff." When I don't respond, Wavonne turns her head away from the road toward me. "What are you looking for?" she asks while I scroll through the screen on my phone.

"I'm poking around for some information on Maurice. I got to thinking about him after he left our little lunch, and I remembered that, when we went shopping, he was pretty keen to gossip, but I had to practically put a spell on him with my food to get him to talk about Monique yesterday. I'm wondering if his being so tight-lipped was really about instructions from the police, or if maybe he's not completely innocent when it comes to Monique's murder, and he didn't want to say anything that might implicate himself. He was awfully quick to throw Nathan under the bus, and he admitted to knowing there was a gun in the house. But, at the moment, I'm not aware of any motive he'd have for killing Monique. He seemed to genuinely like her, and she signed his paychecks. I can't think of a reason he would want her dead." I put the phone in my lap.

"Did you find anything?"

"Not yet."

"See if you can find out where he learned to style wigs. I'd like to pay that place a visit."

I pick the phone back up and start pecking on the screen again. "You raise a good point. It might be interesting to know where he went to cosmetology school."

"Maybe I can find a hairdresser who went to the same

school as Maurice and get a few of my wigs styled like Monique's. I'd call up Maurice himself, but I doubt I can afford whatever he charges. I do the best I can with my wig comb and spritz bottle, but some professional styling would be nice. And I could use some wigs that are a bit sturdier and stay in place better," Wavonne says while I continue to try to dig up whatever information I can on Maurice. "They can be very compromisin' in certain *situations*. Sometimes when I start gettin' busy with a date, I've got to tell him to take it down a notch, unless he wants to pay to have my wig detangled. Remember Jerome . . . that guy I dated for a few months who used to work at the sporting goods store a few doors down from Sweet Tea?"

"Uh-huh," I respond, not really paying attention to what she's chattering about.

"One night me and Jerome were, you know . . . kickin' it on the sofa . . . messin' around a little bit . . . things got a little heated," she says. "Next think I knew, my wig came loose against the sofa arm. I spent the next ten minutes trying to act all eager and enthralled when what I was really tryin' to do was shimmy my way back into my wig without him noticing it came off."

"Lovely story, Wavonne." I'm still only half listening as I toggle through websites for cosmetology licensing agencies.

"Not goin' through that again. Now I make sure I got a comb in the back of my wig, and that the straps are pulled nice and tight. I think I might get me one of those wig gripper thingamajigs, too." Wavonne looks in my direction as she turns the van into the parking lot in front of Odessa's salon. "You're not listening to a word I'm sayin', are you?"

"Bits and pieces," I respond, still skimming the screen on my phone. "You were 'kickin' it' with Jerry or Jason . . . Johnathan? Your wig came loose . . . something about 'shimmying' and a 'wig gripper.' " I put the phone down. "Other than his current and a few former home addresses, I can't find much of anything on Maurice . . . no history at any salon, no Facebook page, no Twitter account. And I can't find any record of him even having a license as a hairdresser," I say as Wavonne and I step out of the van. "That seems odd, don't you think?"

"Which part? The no Facebook page? The no Twitter account? The no license part?"

"All of it, I guess," I respond as we step up to the sidewalk in front of Salon Soleil. "Oh well . . . whatever. We're here, so I guess we'll turn our focus over to Odessa," I add, opening the door and holding it for Wavonne. "Let's see what we can find out."

Chapter 28

"You are paying for this, right?" Wavonne confirms as the door to Salon Soleil swings shut behind us. "I can't afford a bottle of nail polish at this uppity place."

"Yes. I'm paying . . . but only for a roller set . . . don't get all crazy and stay away from the hair extensions display case. I'm not made of money."

"Well, hello," Odessa says with a smile when we reach the counter. "I saw you guys on the books. What can we do for you today?" she asks, looking at us curiously.

Odessa's no fool—I'm sure she's aware we are really only at her salon on a fact-finding mission and getting our hair done is just an excuse to be here, but she's playing along for now.

"We were so impressed with the salon last time we were here, we figured we'd treat ourselves. I'm just looking for a trim, and Wavonne wants a wash and set."

Odessa comes around to our side of the counter and looks closely at my hair. "May I?" she asks, stopping just shy of touching my hair.

"Of course."

She runs her fingers through my hair. "I had you scheduled with Andrea, but I have some time between clients. I can do the trim. How about we add a little volume while we're at it? No extra charge."

"Sounds good to me."

Odessa moves on to Wavonne. "Hmmm," she muses, reaching for a lock of Wavonne's hair and running the frayed ends through her fingers. "You're scheduled with Amber. How about I ask her to do a quick dry cut to clean up these ends, and then we'll have you spend some time under the steamer before we start with the curlers."

Wavonne looks at me. "You paying for all that, moneybags?"

Odessa answers before I have a chance to. "No extra charge. Consider it a freebie for your first of what will, hopefully, be many visits."

Odessa calls Amber over and discusses the details about what she wants her to do with Wavonne's hair. Amber then asks Wavonne a few questions while walking her over to a styling chair, and Odessa escorts me to the washbasins.

"Use Monique's Sheer Volume shampoo and conditioner," Odessa says to the shampoo girl, and then turns to me as I get settled in the chair. "I'll see you in a few minutes. Tracy will take good care of you."

After Tracy washes and conditions my hair, and gives me a scalp massage like I've never had before, she accompanies me to Odessa's chair, lays a smock over me, and snaps it behind my neck.

"Naturally straight hair, eh?" Odessa says as she gently towel-dries my head and starts running a comb through my hair. "Much as natural curls are becoming more popular, women with hair like yours are the envy of most of my clients. Why do you keep it so short?"

"It's not *that* short," I protest with a smile. It's not like I'm sporting a crew cut or a Grace Jones flat top—I've got a good six or seven inches of length before it starts tapering on the sides.

Odessa laughs. "It's very nice . . . sort of Robin Roberts . . . or Angela Bassett on that *9-1-1* show. It's just that I have clients spending hundreds, sometimes thousands of dollars to have hair attached to their head that you could simply grow."

"I'm too busy for long hair. I need something I can run a hair dryer over, give it a little spritz for hold, and get out the door. Maybe when I retire, I'll grow it out."

"Okay . . . and if you ever get tired of it, you can cut it off and sell it," Odessa jokes. "For now, we'll just clip off the tips and give it a little more bulk."

"Is the Hair by Monique shampoo and conditioner Tracy used supposed to help with that?" Of course, I'm only asking to try to steer the conversation toward Monique, and question Odessa a little more gracefully than I did last time.

"Yes. The shampoo is great for clearing any residue that can weigh down your hair and the conditioner has silk powder in it, which helps to separate hair for increased fullness. They're great products. If you like them, we have them on sale. The smaller bottles are fifty dollars."

"Each?" bounds from my mouth almost involuntarily. I'm used to spending about four dollars a bottle on shampoo.

"Yes, but, you'll see . . . once we're done. These products are worth the price."

"I guess that's the reason Monique was worth millions."

Odessa chuckles. "Part of the reason anyway."

"What do you mean?"

"Her products are great. I'd carry them even if she didn't give me a deal on them, but there's plenty of high-quality brands on the market," Odessa says. "You were at the hair show last week . . . you saw the thousands of products out there . . . many of them are just as good as Hair by Monique.

Monique's genius was in the marketing. She sold herself as much as her products."

"She did know how to grab the spotlight, so to speak. Was she always like that?"

"A drama queen who hogged all the attention? Yes. She's been like that since I met her."

"You met her in high school, right?"

"Yes. We went to high school together, cosmetology school together, and worked at the same salon for a few years."

"What happened after that?"

"Nathan," Odessa says, as if something in the room suddenly smells bad. "Nathan happened. She met him at a nightclub . . . Classics in Camp Springs . . . back in the nineties."

"Oh my God. I remember Classics. That was back in the day when I had the time and energy to get all gussied up and go out to the clubs."

"You probably crossed paths with Monique and me on more than one Friday night then." Odessa gives my hair another comb, runs a lock through her index and middle fingers, holds it in place, and shears the ends. "She hooked up with Nathan there one night. He was visiting from New York. One thing led to another and, next thing I knew, she up and moved to New York with him. We gradually lost touch . . . you know, those were the days before texting and Facebook. It was harder to keep track of out-of-town friends back then." Odessa releases a big dollop of mousse into one hand and works it into my hair. "I hadn't seen or heard from her in years until I came upon her at the Bronner Brothers show in Atlanta when she was first launching her product line. I had recently opened Salon Soleil. We were at a smaller location in Largo back then. We talked, and I agreed to sell some of her first products, one being Sleek, her straightening cream that became so popular."

"If Sleek worked so well and was such a success, why do you think Monique chose not to use it on her own hair?"

"I have no idea. Maybe, much like yourself, she didn't have time to style long hair every day."

As Odessa reaches for the hair dryer, I roll my shoulders back in the chair and lift my head so my eyes meet hers in the mirror. "Did you *really* not know Monique had been wearing wigs for the past several years?"

"I answered that question last time you were here, Halia."

"I know, but you told me some other things last time I was here as well . . . at least one of which turned out not to be true."

"And what was that?"

"You said you and your friends went to Pose after the white party. Apparently, Pose closed a few months ago."

"Did it?" Odessa asks. If being caught in a lie has unnerved her, she sure isn't showing it. "I guess it wasn't Pose. Who can keep the names of nightclubs straight? Maybe it was Bliss or Ultrabar. One of the girls picked it. I just went along. I'd spent a small fortune on my dress. Seemed a shame to go straight home from the party. I was keen to go anywhere."

"Speaking of your dress, can I ask you another question?"

"I'll take one more question, Halia. Then I'm turning this hair dryer on to drown out the sound of anyone."

"I'm sure this seems like a strange thing to ask, but, by any chance, were you on Monique's front lawn the night of the party?"

"Her front lawn? No. Why?"

I inhale deeply, and let it out, buying time to figure out how to politely bring up what I want to ask her about. "I found a red sequin, like the hundreds of red sequins on your dress the night of the white party, on the front lawn . . . at the far end, close to the road. Do you have any idea how a piece of your dress might have ended up there?"

"No. Can't say that I do."

"So you weren't, at any point in the evening, on Monique's front—"

"I said *one more* question, Halia."

Odessa flicks on the hair dryer.

"Fair enough," I call over the loud roar.

"Looks very nice, if I do say so myself," Odessa says once she's done drying my hair and has given the style a spray to hold it in place.

"It really does," I agree as she unsnaps the smock and lifts it away from me. "How come I can never get it to look this way at home?" I ask, wondering if maybe I should invest in a hair dryer like the one she used. "Where can I get a hair dryer like that?"

"This a prototype Monique's company was developing. It hasn't gone on sale yet, and I'm not sure what will happen with it now that Monique is . . . is no longer with us." Odessa lifts the hair dryer from the cabinet next to her and gives it a look. "It's really something, though . . . 1,875 watts of power, and I think the airflow reaches eighty or ninety miles per hour."

"I'm not sure my van goes that fast," I joke following her back toward the reception area. "I'll take a seat in the waiting area until Wavonne is done."

"I hope you're happy with the cut and style," Odessa says, before pausing for a moment. "Though we both know that getting your hair cut is the least of the reasons you came here."

I smile awkwardly, but don't say anything.

"And just to confirm," Odessa says. "No, I was not on Monique's front lawn at any point during the night of the white party. I have no idea why there was a red sequin in the grass . . . maybe her landscaper bedazzles his mower or something. And yes, I got my nightclub names mixed up, but I assure you I had *nothing* to do with Monique's death. And why are you still nosing around about Monique's death anyway? The police wouldn't still be holding Nathan if they were not convinced that he did it. Word on the street is that it was *his* gun with *his* prints that killed her . . . and his hands tested positive for gunpowder residue."

"Thank you, Odessa. I appreciate the information and do really like the haircut. You're very talented," I say, trying to make nice rather than actually answer her question.

"You're welcome," Odessa says. "It was nice to see you again, Halia. Amber can check you and Wavonne out when they're done."

After Odessa steps away, I read through a few magazines and am about to toggle through my phone again to see if I can find anything more about Maurice when I see a young man who just finished up with one of the stylists perusing the shelves in front of me. I watch as he grabs four bottles of the same shampoo and four bottles of the same conditioner and takes them to the register. He cradles them between his left arm and his chest to get them to the counter. I look down at my phone, but I'm still listening when I hear his stylist say, "That comes to three hundred and thirty dollars."

Seems odd that he's buying so many bottles at once, but I guess three hundred and thirty dollars is what a gaggle of designer shampoo and a haircut costs at a place like this. I briefly wonder how long it will take a man with short hair to use so much product, but after he pays via credit card and exits the salon, I switch my attention back to my phone and try a few different queries: "Maurice Masson hairdresser," "Maurice Masson cosmetology," "Maurice Masson Monique Dupree." But it's not until I type in "Maurice Masson wigs" that a new site comes up. I hit the link to www.mmmwigs.com and find myself staring at a web page with a banner at the top that reads: MAURICE'S MAGNIFICENT MANES.

"What's got you so focused that you aren't lookin' at my new 'do?" Wavonne asks as I stare down at my handset.

"Look at this." I hand her my phone.

Wavonne takes a look and begins reading from the web page. "The styling genius behind the flawless wigs of Ms. Monique Dupree is pleased to introduce Triple M Wigs, your exclusive resource for high quality human hair wigs engineered with Maurice Masson's patented technology—wigs so natural-looking, no one will ever know it's not your own hair." Wavonne hits a few links within the site. "Girl . . . I gotta get me one of these wigs." She continues to scroll through the site, taps on the phone a few times, and lets out a gasp. "Thirty-five hundred dollars?!"

Odessa hears Wavonne's yelp, steps over to see what the fuss is about, and looks over Wavonne's shoulder at my phone. "Well. Isn't that *interesting*," she says.

"How so?" I ask.

"Oh . . . I don't know . . . considering Maurice was one of the only people who knew Monique was wearing wigs, I imagine she would have made him sign some sort of airtight agreement to keep his mouth shut about it. Seems a little suspect that he's launched an exclusive . . . and likely *highly lucrative* wig business on the heels of her death, doesn't it? He never could have done that if she were still alive."

"If that's true, it does seem awfully convenient that he had a website for his business ready to be up and running barely a week after her death," I say.

"So Monique bites the big one," Wavonne says, "and word gets out that she's got about as much hair as a freshly sheared poodle . . . and the dude that's been makin' the world think she had one of the best heads of hair in the country launches his own wig line a few days later . . . that is some shady bidness right there."

"Can't say I disagree. Talk about cashing in on someone's death," I say. "I can't imagine someone would murder another human being merely to get a wig business off the ground, but people have certainly killed for lesser reasons."

"That's for sure," Odessa says. "So now maybe you can go bark up Maurice's tree and leave me alone."

"Maybe I can," I reply before turning toward Wavonne. "Let's check out and get going." I take my phone back from her, look up Maurice's number from when he texted me the day of the hair convention, and press the call button.

RECIPE FROM HALIA'S KITCHEN

Halia's Purple Rain Iced Tea

Ingredients
5 hibiscus blueberry tea bags
8 quarts of water
2 tablespoons of honey
½ cup frozen or fresh blueberries
1 lemon

- Heat four quarts of water to a rolling boil. Pour over tea bags. Let tea bags steep for seven minutes.
- Add honey to hot tea. Stir until dissolved.
- Use a blender to puree blueberries in remaining four quarts of water and mix resulting liquid with hot tea.
- When cool, pour over glasses filled with ice, and garnish with a lemon wedge.

Tip: This recipe used "The Republic of Tea Hibiscus Blueberry Superflower" tea bags, which contain stevia. If using a berry tea without a sweetener in the tea bags add additional honey.

Chapter 29

"Look at you all hoochied up," I say to Wavonne as I step inside the ladies' room at Sweet Tea. She's in front of the mirror in a snug pair of black jeans, a glittery green top, and a pair of shiny four-inch black heels. "Where are you off to?" I ask as she applies some makeup. It's after ten and, although we are open until eleven on Saturday nights, the crowd started to thin out at about nine thirty. So I, at her request, cut Wavonne from the floor about a half hour ago. She's been in here ever since, changing clothes and getting what she calls "club ready."

"Me and Melva . . . and Linda are goin' downtown . . . to Club Timehri for some mango martinis and reggae music . . . and then probably to Black Cat or The Park for some dancin'. Don't wait up."

"Club Timehri, eh?" I respond, as if I know anything about it . . . or *any* nightclub, and quickly scan her and her flamboyant outfit. "I thought maybe somehow we were back in 1982, and you were off to dance on *Solid Gold*."

"Ha ha." Wavonne rolls her eyes at me as she grabs a small brush from her bag and applies some sort of gel or glue to her eyelid. She then dips the same brush in a little jar of green glitter and paints it over the gel. "Don't be hatin' just cause you're goin' home to watch reruns of *The Golden Girls* while I go out."

I laugh as that is likely what I would be doing if I didn't have something else in mind this evening. "I'm not sure I'll be home in time for *The Golden Girls* tonight."

Wavonne puts her brush down dramatically and turns to look at me straight on instead of via the mirror. "You have plans after work on a Saturday night?! A late date? Please tell me you have a date."

"Afraid not. I'm just going to do a little exploring . . . investigating."

"Related to Monique, I assume. If you worked half as hard at catchin' a man as you did nosin' around in dead people's bidness, Aunt Celia might have you married off by now." Wavonne turns back toward the mirror and starts glittering the other eye. "Where are you goin' exactly?"

"I've been trying to reach Maurice since we left Salon Soleil this afternoon to find out more about this new wig business of his. He won't answer my calls. I found his address online, so I'm going to let Laura close the restaurant tonight so I can drive by his house, and see if he's home."

"This can't wait until daylight?"

"I suppose it could, but I'm anxious to talk to him, and if he's not home tonight, maybe I can shine a flashlight through a few windows, and see if I see anything suspect." I'm silent for a moment while I shift my weight on my feet. "But I'd really prefer to not go alone."

Wavonne puts the brush down again. "I got plans, Halia."

"Maurice's house is in the city. You can come with me, and then I'll drop you off at that Club Tim Tom or Black Bear or wherever your friends are."

"It's Club Timehri and Black Cat." She pulls out a tube of lipstick and runs its bright red balm over her mouth. "The girls will be here any minute to pick me up . . . although Linda's probably still shovin' some day clothes in her purse, so she doesn't have to go home from wherever she wakes up tomorrow in a strapless black mini. She ain't got no standards, so she hooks up a lot. Last time she got lucky, she had to go home the next day in her club clothes—her Uber driver thought she was a day shift stripper. He was all set to give her a ride to the Royal Palace or Good Guys Club. Can you imagine? It's bad enough bein' mistaken for a stripper," Wavonne says in a way that makes me think it's happened to her. "But one that works the day shift? Those are the bottom-of-the-barrel heifers."

"Sometimes you overshare, Wavonne. A simple 'Linda may be running late' would have sufficed." I'm trying to make my reflection in the mirror look sort of needy and pathetic, hoping she'll take pity on me. "I just need to check in with Laura and make sure she and the team can manage the few customers still here and help the kitchen staff shut everything down. You and I can be out of here in a few minutes, and I'll have you with your friends in no time. I'll even give you a few bucks to buy a round for the girls, assuming you have a designated driver."

"No one has designated drivers anymore, Halia. That's what Uber and Lyft are for." She turns around, looks at me, and then starts digging through her makeup bag again. "Fine," she says, running a black eyeliner pencil along her bottom lash line. "Give me a few minutes to finish my face, and I'll run your little fool's errand with you, but you've got to have me at the club by midnight. And I need fifty bucks for a round a drinks . . . martinis cost a lot more than they did in your day."

"Agreed," I say. "I'll go check in with Laura and then we can go."

"I need some time. I think I want to pop on my party wig.

I am not sure my new 'do from Odessa's salon today works with my outfit. I need something with more flair . . . more . . . what's that French word?"

"Panache?"

"Yeah, that. I need something with more of that."

"Okay. I'll meet you at the front door in about twenty minutes," I say, and head out the door.

By the time I wrap things up at the restaurant and Wavonne styles her wig, it's almost eleven o'clock when we cross the line into DC and approach Maurice's house.

"That's it," I say as we turn onto a residential street off of Rhode Island Avenue. "I recognize it from when he was on the news."

"So are we just goin' to park and go knock on his door at eleven o'clock at night?"

"I'm not sure. Let's drive by first and see if it looks like he's home."

"Oh, he's home, all right." Wavonne catches sight of him walking past a bay window as I slowly move the van along the street in front of the old, but well-maintained, row house.

"Okay. So we know he's home."

"You mean he *was* home." Wavonne's got her head turned around looking out the back window after we pass his house. "He's steppin' outside."

I pull the van over, put it in park, and turn around myself to see Maurice tossing a few things into the back seat of his car before settling into the front seat. We lay low while he pulls out of the parking space and wait a few seconds after he passes to pull out ourselves.

"This is some Dick Tracy stuff right here," Wavonne says. "Can I say it? *Please* can I say it?"

"Go ahead," I respond, not taking my eyes off of Maurice's vehicle.

"Follow that car!" Wavonne calls, and we both start to laugh as we tail Maurice. We follow him along a few side roads to Fourteenth Street and onto Massachusetts Avenue as he makes his way over to the Southwest Quadrant of the city. After about twenty minutes or so, we end up on South Capitol Street near the Nationals stadium, and Maurice makes a few turns that lead us into a mostly industrial neighborhood. It's here that he slides his car into an open spot on the street.

I pull the van over a few car lengths from where Maurice parked, and Wavonne and I look on as he emerges from his vehicle, grabs some garment bags from the back seat, and approaches what appears to be a nightclub with the name ENIGMA spelled out in bright neon lights on the side of the building. There is a line of people waiting to get inside, but Maurice bypasses them, exchanges a few words with one of the club's bouncers, and goes inside.

Once Maurice is out of sight, I pull up closer to the building. "Well, I guess this was a wild goose chase. I don't think we're going to learn anything related to Monique's death in there."

"Maybe . . . maybe not. But, what the hell. We're here, and I've never heard of this place—I'm curious," Wavonne says. "Let's go in. You could use a drink . . . a cocktail would do your tight self some good," she insists. "Maybe we'll meet some men."

"I think we'll meet some men all right." I point at the line waiting to get into the club. It's about fifteen people deep, and I only see one woman. "I don't think any of those guys are buying what we're selling, Wavonne." I nod toward two young men holding hands.

"Huh. I should've noticed." Wavonne takes in the nearly all-male line in front of the club. "That's an awful lot of hair gel and tight shirts," she says. "At least we won't feel bad if we don't get any attention when we're in there."

"You really want to go in? Don't you want to meet the girls?"

"The girls will be there next week. Let's check it out. It will be an adventure."

"Fine." I let out a long exhale and step on the gas to find an open parking spot on the street.

"I feel incredibly out of place," I say to Wavonne once we've parked the car and walked a couple of blocks to join the line outside the bar. Unlike her and her flashy club clothes, heavy makeup, and wig that she teased up a good five inches from her head, I'm still in my work clothes. "I'm a middle-aged woman in a pair of khakis, a plain navy blue shirt, and slip-resistant kitchen shoes in line at a nightclub for twenty-somethings. To say I don't fit in here is quite the understatement."

"You're fine. Like you said, ain't nobody buyin' the little piggies we're bringin' to market in there, so what's it matter?"

It takes a good ten minutes to reach the front of the line, pay a ten-dollar cover charge, and walk inside, where we find an expansive and well-appointed space. There's a long bar on a raised landing that overlooks a much larger lower area, which is set up like a Vegas lounge with small tables arranged around a dance floor. There's a second bar to one side of the dance floor and a stage to the other. It must be peak time because the place is really crowded—all the tables are occupied and people are standing all around them.

"Let's get some drinks," Wavonne says over the loud music, and we *maneuver* more than walk our way through all the people to get to the upstairs bar where Wavonne orders both of us gin and tonics, which, of course, I pay for. We've barely taken a sip of our drinks when the music abruptly stops, a spotlight begins to shine on the stage, and an unseen announcer asks us to, "Please welcome the Hostess with the

Mostess . . . the grande dame of the evening: Ms. Mable Devine!"

Wavonne and I watch as a mature thickset black woman graces the platform from a side entrance. She's wearing a metallic-looking dress covered in silky fringe that unfurls like a few dozen helicopter propellers as she spins toward a microphone to the beat of Donna Summer's "Hot Stuff." It's only when the performer is done with a dazzling lip sync performance, actually turns the microphone on, and begins speaking to welcome all of us to the *Ladies of Illusion* showcase that I realize *she* is a *he*.

Chapter 30

"Oooh girl, this is a drag queen bar!" Wavonne calls into my ear over the loud club noise.

"Apparently so." I look around the room as Mable Devine entertains the audience. Aside from a small but rowdy group of young ladies who appear to be out for a bachelorette evening, the club goers are almost all gay men, a handful of them dressed in drag themselves.

Ms. Devine ends up being quite amusing. She has some fun banter with the crowd and brings the bride-to-be from the bachelorette party onstage with her. Her questions to the inebriated young woman, while a bit vulgar for my taste, are funny, and she gets lots of laughs from everyone.

After thoroughly embarrassing the soon-to-be-wed woman, Mable ends her monologue and introduces the next act, a very tall performer in a Tina Turner wig and short gold dress. As we watch her "Rolling on the River" routine, Wavonne starts to really get into the whole thing and works in a few calls of "Sing it, girl!" and "Shake what your Momma gave ya!"

We're having such a good time, I almost forget our reason for being here in the first place, but by the time the fourth drag queen appears onstage, I'm starting to get tired and my feet are beginning to hurt.

"Why don't we see if we can find Maurice?"

"Okay, but let me get another cocktail," Wavonne says, turning back toward the bar and placing an order.

"Do you happen to know Maurice Masson?" I ask the bartender while he hands Wavonne her drink, and I hand him my credit card.

"He's backstage getting ready for his number." The gentleman points toward a door several feet to the left of the stage.

"Thank you." I sign the receipt, motion for Wavonne to follow me, and we work our way through the crowd. We're about halfway down the steps to the lower level of the club when a highly intoxicated young man looks Wavonne up and down.

"Girl! You slayin' all dayin'!" he says, snapping his finger.

"You know it," Wavonne replies as if she hears this sort of thing all the time.

"Fierce!" the gentleman, a stocky white guy, calls, reaffirming his admiration of all things Wavonne. He stands at nearly six feet, but when you factor in her heels and wig height, Wavonne is taller than him. I should probably also mention the man is wearing a cheap wig, an ill-fitting leather skirt, and a spandex tube top.

Wavonne smiles as if to say "Don't I know it!" before the man introduces himself. "I'm Margaux Laveau," he says. "What name do you go by?"

"Go by?" Wavonne asks.

He ignores the question while his eyes continue to scan her from head to toe. "You've got to help me out with some tips," he demands. "Your look is flawless! The wig. The heels." This Margaux character is truly excited by Wavonne. "And the breasts. Amazing!" He stares down at his chest. "They look so much better than my foam falsies. What do you have stuffed in there?"

My mouth drops as I realize the assumption Ms. Laveau is making and brace myself for Wavonne to go off on him for mistaking her for a drag queen. But, to my surprise, Wavonne doesn't seem at all bothered.

"Girl, you gotta go with the chicken cutlets . . . you know, the gel pads. And you're just gonna have to gain some weight if you really want those boobies to look authentic with a low neckline. Get a little fat upstairs, and then all you need to do is squish the flab together with some duct tape . . . and voilà, you got yourself some cleavage," she says. "Duct tape . . . it's a broke girl's Wonderbra."

"That sounds painful."

"You think all of this"—Wavonne points her finger from her toes up to her neck—"comes without pain? If bein' fierce were easy, everyone would do it."

"What else? What else?" the young man asks eagerly. "Any wig tips?"

"My first tip would be to bury the one you got on your head because, girlfriend, it's dead," she advises. "You gotta go to Lolita's Lavish Locks in Capitol Heights. Mrs. Sagong will hook you up . . . she's a mean little Asian woman, but boy can she throw down with some wigs. And you got to get the real hair. No nylon . . . if some chick in India or China ain't walkin' around bald because of your wig, it ain't worth puttin' on your head."

"Duct tape. Lolita's Lavish Locks. No nylon. Got it," Margaux says.

"And the clothes," Wavonne adds, shaking her head and pursing her lips while looking at his outfit. "I'll be straight with you, Margaux . . . you look more 'transvestite' than 'drag queen.' You ain't never gonna be Lady Chablis if you keep dressin' like Lady Project Ho. You gotta hit the sample sales at—"

Much as I'd like to help Margaux up his drag queen game, we didn't come here to play fairy godmother to some RuPaul wannabe . . . and my dogs are barking big time, so I interrupt Wavonne. "I'm sorry, Ms. Laveau," I say. "But we have to go backstage. Perhaps the two of you can continue this discussion later?"

"Yeah . . . sure," he says. "Thanks for the tips . . . ah . . . ah," he adds, waiting for Wavonne to tell him her name.

Wavonne looks away for a moment and sees a bottle of champagne en route to the bachelorette party. "Champagne," she says. "Bubbles Champagne."

Wavonne is better at wading through a crowd than me, so she leads this time. Fortunately, we encounter no further interruptions on the way backstage. Unlike me, who would have probably knocked and waited God knows how long for a response, Wavonne opens the door next to the stage with no permissions given, and we walk into a cramped room with six dressing tables, three on each side. We find Maurice at the middle table on the left side. He's wearing a wig cap and his face is adorned with thick concealer or maybe foundation.

He sees us as we come into view in his mirror, but he finishes pressing a fake eyelash on his lid before saying anything. I'm expecting a curt "Who let you back here?" but instead he says, "Well hello, ladies. What can I do for you?"

I smile and take in Maurice for a second or two. His mirror has a little nameplate on it that says BRIGHTINA GLOW. There are two performers adjusting wigs and reapplying makeup on either side of him. Their mirrors are labeled DIXIE CRYSTAL and DOMINIQUE DEVERAUX. Maurice notices me looking at their nameplates.

"Dixie is from the South . . . and she likes sugar." He turns his gaze to the man on his other side. "Dominique is a *Dynasty* fan."

I nod and give a quick wave to Dixie and Dominique as Wavonne and I inch closer to Maurice, who doesn't seem at all startled or unnerved by our presence. And he certainly doesn't seem embarrassed for us to find him about two-thirds of the way to an alternate gender. He does, however, seem to become annoyed when, after offering a few pleasantries and not even bothering to try to explain how we found him here, I start asking him questions. But I sense that his irritation may have more to do with me delaying his readiness to perform than with any insinuations I'm making about him possibly being associated with Monique's murder.

"I apologize if we're in the way, but I tried to call you a number of times and didn't have any luck reaching you," I say. "Forgive all the questions, but I'm just trying to make sure the police really have the right guy locked up. I'm sure as someone who cared about Monique, you want that, too."

"Of course I do. But I, unlike you, have no doubt that Nathan killed her. I've known that man to be evil to the bone for as long as I've known Monique."

"And how long is that?" I ask. "How long *have* you known Monique?"

"I met Monique right here about ten years ago. She came to Enigma to catch the show with a bachelorette party and sought me out after my performance."

"Really. Why?"

"Because she was just starting to launch Hair by Monique, and she was impressed with the quality of my wigs, and how they were virtually impossible to discern from a real head of hair." Maurice applies some blush to his cheeks. "We all now know that Monique did not have a lot of hair. As her products began to take off, she planned to make infomercials to really push her business to the next level. If she was going to be hocking hair care products in an age of HD television, she needed her wigs to be flawless." He quiets for a moment, stares at himself in the mirror, and applies a bit more pink powder to his face. "So, Monique and I came to an agreement. I'd make her wigs . . . and position and style them for any important occasions . . . and, most important, I'd keep her secret."

"And what did you get out of the deal?" I ask.

"Money," Maurice responds. "A lot of money."

"So, if you're so good with wigs," Wavonne says, "how come Halia can't find any record of you having a cosmetology license? Why would Monique trust a person with no formal training with something so important to her career?"

"No formal training!?" Maurice says, more riled by this question than any having to do with Monique's murder. "I've been working with wigs since I was old enough to reach the one on my momma's dresser."

He pulls a wig from a foam head on his dressing table, lowers it on his head, and begins to describe how he learned to make "truly exquisite" wigs and adhere them in a way that makes them undetectable through years of trial and error as a performer. He explains concealers and lace fronts and wig clips . . . and knot bleaching . . . and edge control . . . and the creative use of a toothbrush for baby hairs . . . and eyelash glue to hold things in place. By the time he's done with his spiel, and Wavonne is finished taking notes on her phone, I'm more than convinced of his talent and understand why Monique entrusted him with something so important to her. But I'm still wondering about his new line of wigs, and if it translates to a motive for wanting Monique dead.

"It does look pretty amazing," I compliment, eyeing his wig as he dabs some concealer along the part near his forehead.

"Thank you," he says. "One never wants one's wig to look . . . well, *wiggy*."

I chuckle. "May I ask you about one more thing, Maurice? Then we'll—"

"Get out of your hair," Wavonne says, and laughs and

laughs, quite pleased with herself, but also annoyed that neither Maurice nor I found her quip as amusing as she did. It's
one of those things that must be funnier after two gin and
tonics.

"What?" he asks, touching up his wig with a big plastic
comb.

"Triple M Wigs," I say. "We came upon the new website
for it this afternoon."

"What did you think? I've been working on it for
months."

"So it was in the works before Monique died?"

"You're a business owner, Halia. You, of all people,
should know you can't launch a business, especially one with
an interactive website, in a week."

"So Monique knew about the business?"

"Yes. It took some serious negotiating, but she eventually
gave me her blessing as long as I stayed behind the scenes and
didn't market my wigs under my name or in any way that
would publicly connect them to her."

"But the business has your name all over it . . . and
Monique's, too."

"Yes. Yes, it does, but only now that Monique has passed
on." He stands up from the table and reaches for a garment
bag hanging from a hook on the wall. "I had not planned to
launch the business for several months and, I swear, it was
only after Monique died that I hurried to get the business online and use my history with her as a marketing tool." Maurice
unzips the bag and pulls out a short yellow dress made of lay-
ered chiffon. "Yes, it's ill-mannered to use Monique's death to
promote a new business venture. I admit I was . . . am trying
to profit from her death, but I never would have betrayed her
like that when she was alive. I only tried to benefit from her
secret once it was . . . well, no longer a secret. I'd like to think
Monique would approve. She was clearly one to take advan-

tage of every opportunity to market her products. I don't think she'd have had a problem with me doing the same." He holds the dress against his body and looks at himself in the mirror. "It's pretty nice, isn't it?" he asks. "I really do need to get into it."

"Of course," I say. "We'll go."

"Before you do, let me be the one to ask a question," he says. "At first, I thought you were here to see if I could help you identify any suspects other than Nathan, and maybe Odessa, but I'm starting to think you might actually have me on your list. Is that true?"

I swallow. "I wouldn't say you are exactly on my list, but—"

"From what I've heard on the news Monique was most definitively shot between eleven forty-five p.m. and twelve fifteen a.m.," Maurice says, interrupting me. "I go onstage every Saturday at twelve thirty." He lays the dress on the chair and turns to look at us. "Do you have any idea how long it takes to go from Maurice Masson to Brightina Glow? Do you? Any idea at all?"

Before my "no fuss/no muss" self can answer that, in fact, I do not, Wavonne looks in his mirror and adjusts her own wig. "Oh . . . I think I have some idea."

Maurice turns back toward the mirror and looks at Wavonne's reflection. "Then you know there is no way I could have been at Monique's house at the time she was killed. I'm always here by eleven thirty. It takes a full hour to pluck, tuck, and glitter all of this," he says, pointing from his feet up to his wig, "to be ready to go onstage, which is where I was at twelve thirty last Saturday night. An entire club full of people can verify that I was here."

"Glad to hear it. I guess you're in the clear then," I say. "The dress and the wig . . . they really are quite nice. Thank you for your time, Maurice." I turn to Wavonne. "Come on, *Bubbles*, let's go."

"Oh ladies," Maurice calls right before we reach the door.

"I may be a shameless opportunist when it comes to making money, but I really did care about Monique. I'm hosting a sort of memorial for her next Saturday. I can send you the details if you'd like to attend. Nothing somber or morbid. I want it to be upbeat like Monique . . . a gathering . . . a party, even . . . to celebrate her life and her memory."

"Yes, please," I respond. "I'm not sure we'll be able to make it, but we would appreciate the information."

As Wavonne and I step out into the main club and try to make our way to the exit, my mind attempts to put a few pieces of the Monique murder puzzle together. Maurice has a solid alibi, so unless any other persons of interest make themselves known, my suspect list, aside from Nathan, is down to Odessa and Alex. Did Odessa really just mix up the name of the club she supposedly went to after the white party? And, if she didn't kill Monique, how did a piece of her dress end up on the front lawn? But at the same time, if Alex didn't kill her, why did he skip town immediately after her death?

I'm trying to sort it all out in my head, when I hear Mable Devine introduce Brightina.

"We gotta stay for this," Wavonne says.

I'm exhausted and really want to go home, but I guess I'm also a little curious about Maurice's showmanship and, I must say, he does not disappoint. As Katy Perry's "Waking Up in Vegas" blares from the speakers, Maurice emerges onto the stage looking like a Vegas showgirl—albeit an unusually plump Vegas showgirl, but a showgirl nonetheless. The yellow dress we saw backstage is nice, but his real pièce de résistance is an intricate feather headdress constructed from a mix of yellow and white feathers.

"Girl," Wavonne says as she and I hover near the exit on the upper level, looking over the crowd as Maurice jaunts about the stage. "I bet he's got some Spanx working overtime under all that."

"Maybe so." I laugh. And then it happens . . . a moment

of insight when I notice some feathers that have fallen off his headdress onto the floor of the stage.

"What?" Wavonne asks me. "Why do you have that look on your face . . . like someone just shouted bingo and you've got the winnin' card?"

"Oh . . . nothing . . . enjoying the show," I lie as I carefully consider what I've just realized.

Chapter 31

"We need to leave for the restaurant a little early tomorrow. I want to go by and see Odessa beforehand, assuming she's open on Sunday mornings."

We're back in the van a few miles from home. The clock on the dash reads 1:10 a.m.

"Huh?" Wavonne says, distracted by some flyers and newspapers she grabbed on the way out of the club.

"Are you listening to me?" I ask as she lifts a slick piece of paper from the pile in her lap. "What's all that?"

"Nothin' . . . a couple of news rags . . . some promo stuff from Enigma . . . looks like they're havin' an amateur drag contest next week . . . maybe we should go back and watch," Wavonne suggests, before stuffing the flyer between the seat and the armrest and starting to flip through a copy of the *Washington City Paper*.

"It was fun," I admit. "But I think I've had my fill of drag queen bars for a while."

"Well, at least the visit wasn't for nothin'. You got to scratch Maurice off that suspect list I know you got goin' in your head."

"I guess I did," I say as we start to pass the shopping center that houses Odessa's salon. It stands out from the other merchants as it's the only storefront that still has lights on inside. "Look. The lights are on in the salon. Do you think she leaves them on all night as a security measure or something?"

"I dunno. You want to pull in and take a closer look?" Wavonne asks as we pull up to a traffic light and stop the van. "There's someone coming out," she adds, keeping watch on the building as a man, carrying a plastic bag, exits Salon Soleil.

"What the . . . ?" I say more to myself than to Wavonne and steer the van into the lane that turns into the shopping center. When the light changes, we drive into the lot and park the car in front of the salon.

"Should we call the police?" Wavonne asks. "You think it's a robbery?"

"The man leaving a minute ago didn't seem like he was stealing anything. He only had the one bag on him."

"Maybe he's the janitor or something."

"Maybe. But he didn't lock the door behind him when he left." I sigh, turn off the ignition, and open the car door. "There's only one way to find out what's going on."

When we reach the main door, I give it a little tug. It's unlocked, so I pull it all the way open and see Odessa. She's grabbing some women's hair care products from the shelves and handing them to a gentleman, whom I assume is a customer.

"What are you doing here?!" she asks, startled.

"We were driving by and saw the lights on . . . and a man leaving the premises. Seemed odd for so late at night. We thought we should check it out."

"Everything is fine." She walks the man over to the register and begins ringing up his purchases. She's clearly still unnerved by our intrusion and seems at a loss for more words.

"We're . . . um . . . open late some days . . . for customers, like this young man, who can't make it in during regular hours."

She catches me looking inquisitively at the products she selected for the man as she puts them in a bag. He's a white man with short straight hair, and Odessa is bagging three boxes of Sleek, Monique's hair relaxing cream, and a large container of edge-controlling gel. "For his wife," she says.

"Seems to be a lot of men buying products for their wives here," I say with a raised brow as the man pays for his items and moves to exit the salon. He opens the door to leave only to hold it for yet another man on his way in.

"Hello," the newest arrival, who is much older than the one who just left, says to Monique.

"Hello, Jim," Odessa says. "Janelle is ready for you in room three."

Wavonne and I watch the man head toward the referenced treatment room and exchange knowing looks with each other as it becomes clear what is going on here.

"I don't know what sort of . . . um . . . *business enterprise* you really have going here, Odessa . . . with men meeting women in 'treatment rooms' well after midnight." I do the air quote thing with my fingers when saying "treatment rooms." "But I suspect—"

"Well, I know," Wavonne says. "Sista girl is runnin' a whorehouse."

I shift my eyes to Wavonne in a way that tells her to "shut up" and then move them back to Odessa. "Like I said, I don't know what you have going on here, and honestly, I really don't care. But what I do know is that you went back to Monique's home after the white party. Nathan was telling the truth when he said he saw you driving back to the house on his way to the convention center."

Odessa neither confirms nor denies my accusation. She just quietly returns my gaze and waits for me to elaborate.

"I can't believe I didn't think of this before, but Wavonne and I just came from seeing a . . . I guess you'd call it a *show* . . . and it involved a feathered headdress . . . it was yellow . . . not red, but it made me think of your red dress with all the feathers at the bottom of it. Did I mention last time I was here that I found one of the feathers from your dress in the little den where Monique was shot?"

"No, but what does that have to do with anything? Why wouldn't you find some feathers that may have fallen off my dress? I was a guest in the house . . . I was at that party for hours."

"True . . . true . . . but I found this particular feather in a room no one was socializing in during the party. Aside from the TV, there wasn't much more than a sofa and a couple of chairs in there . . . all of which were covered with coats and wraps. The only reason anyone went into Monique's den during the party was to either drop off or retrieve their jacket."

"Okay. So what?"

"I remember you making a grand entrance into Monique's foyer when you arrived at the party. I remember your beautifully styled hair, and that stunning red dress . . . and the strappy black heels. But you know what I don't remember, Odessa?" I question. "A coat. Your entrance would have been way less dramatic with one covering that dress."

"Which means girlfriend had no business being in that little room durin' the party," Wavonne says.

"It also means," I say to Wavonne before fixing my eyes on Odessa, "that she likely came back to the house in that sequined feathered red dress after the party and had words with Monique in the den. Could those words have gotten so heated that they made you want to kill her?"

Odessa's eyes go wide, and she takes in a long, deep breath. "For goodness' sake," she says, and lowers herself down on the stool behind the counter. "You've worn me down, Halia," she adds, looking tired and just sort of *over it*. "I may as well tell you the truth."

Chapter 32

"Yes, if you must know, I did go back to Monique's house after I'd left the party. I wanted to have it out with her," Odessa says. She looks tired, like the last week has really taken its toll on her. "I thought perhaps I had taken things too far by showing up at her house in a flashy gown, and that maybe this time she was serious about ending our little discounted pricing arrangement."

"What do you mean, 'too far'?" I ask.

"It's hard to explain. Let me give you some backstory," Odessa responds. "Since Monique and I met in high school and became friends, we've had a kind of unspoken agreement." Odessa looks up at the ceiling. "How should I put this?" she ponders. "Monique was not *unattractive*, but she was always a big-boned girl who was, shall we say, 'prettier from a distance.' I was always, if I do say so myself, better looking than her. It may sound arrogant, but it's true. We all know that Monique was highly competitive, and she dealt with me being the 'pretty one' by defining herself as the 'glittery, flamboyant one' . . . the one with the big personality. And it was understood that I was not to compete with her on that level. Of course, we jabbed at each other all the time and had our share of blowouts—we've been doing that since high school—but I respected our little pact for decades. That all went south the night of the white party."

"What made you let it go after so many years?"

"You know what, Halia . . . I'd just sort of *had it*. The green-eyed monster got the best of me. Monique had arrived at my salon the day before in her own tour bus . . . her own freaking tour bus! Then, at your restaurant, I had to listen to her talk about her Bentley and Nathan's Tesla . . . and her apartment in New York. Do you know how much apartments in New York cost? She was there with her *own* personal stylist and her *own* personal chef. And she only added fuel to the fire when she, once again, threatened to end our business arrangement. But do you know what really pushed me over the edge?"

"What?" Wavonne asks. "Let it out, girl."

"That damn purse . . . that Fendi Aubusson-Print Chain Shoulder Bag. I'm still on a waiting list for it, and she *had it*! She had it right there next to me . . . in her possession. Suddenly, being prettier than her was not enough." Odessa rearranges herself on the stool, and it's almost as if I can see her body relaxing . . . like holding on to all this information had tightened her muscles for days, and now that she's telling her story, the tension is finally starting to dissolve. "I'd had a white dress picked out for the party. It was very nice: form-fitting . . . taffeta . . . floor-length . . . lovely, really, but . . . I don't know . . . it was ordinary, and the night before at Sweet Tea I was so over *ordinary*. Unbeknownst to her, as I was sitting right next to Monique while she gobbled up her banana pudding, was surfing the Neiman Marcus and Lord & Taylor websites for the most ostentatious dress I could find. That's when I came across the red gown—it had everything: a bold color, sequins, feathers . . . any more glitz, and I would have needed to connect it to an extension cord. I went to the mall the next day and bought it."

"So the dress . . . the dress is what you think you may have taken too far?"

"Yes. I thought that maybe this time she was serious about cutting me off and taking away the discounts she gave me on her products. My entire business model depends on those discounts, and I knew I wouldn't be able to sleep that night if I didn't get the whole thing resolved and make sure our arrangement was intact."

"So, let me get this straight," I say. "Monique had given you preferred pricing on her products to reward you for carrying her line for years. She had been threatening to end the arrangement for almost as long, although she never did. But this time, you thought she really meant it?"

"That's mostly true."

"Mostly?"

"Monique *was* giving me discounts, but not to reward me for anything. Truth is I blackmailed her for those discounts."

"Ooh . . . this is gettin' good now," Wavonne cackles. "Like some Wendy Williams Hot Topics."

"I was not completely honest . . . well, honest at all about my knowledge of Monique's hair situation. With a murder investigation going on, I figured the less I admitted to knowing about anything related to Monique the better, but I knew she was wearing wigs, and I threatened to tell the world about it if she didn't make a deal with me. Besides, she owed me. We invented the cream she eventually marketed as Sleek, the product that put her on the map, *together*."

"What? Really?" I ask. This really is getting good.

"We started out working on hair potions together in her momma's kitchen. In fact, it was my idea to reduce the amount of lye and add a natural straightening ingredient called guanidine carbonate that we learned about from a chemist at our cosmetology school. Apparently, it comes from mushrooms or something. The addition of guanidine carbonate allowed for a lesser amount of lye, and less lye means less burn and scalp irritation. We also added some coconut, avocado, and olive oils to the formula to further reduce stress on the hair. At first, it worked great. It straightened our hair beautifully without the burn of most relaxers. . . ."

"But?"

"Well, I never had any issues, but after a few uses, Monique noticed her hair thinning. I think it was about the fourth time that she used our concoction that she started losing clumps of hair. That was some twenty-plus years ago, and, while much of it grew back, her hair never fully recovered. She had no choice but to keep it cropped. It never got back to a healthy enough condition for her to grow it out.

"So, of course, when it ruined Monique's hair, we stopped making it. After that, we kind of lost interest in creating our own hair creams. Monique met Nathan and was busy with him and eventually moved to New York. And I was putting in a lot of hours, saving up money to open my own shop. There simply wasn't much time for it anymore. And that was the end of it, or so I thought."

"I sense you're about to get to the juicy part," Wavonne says, eager to hear the rest of the story.

"You can imagine my surprise a little over ten years ago when I was walking around the Georgia World Congress Center in Atlanta at the Bronner Brothers show and came across a small stall for a new line of beauty products called Hair by Monique. While I was looking at some of the bottles and boxes on display I heard a familiar voice yammering about a straightening cream called Sleek to another attendee. I lifted my head, and there she was—Monique Dupree peddling her wares—telling a young lady about how nicely Sleek worked on her hair—hair that I could tell was not her own.

We caught up a bit . . . she told me I looked too thin and that I needed a better lotion for my ashy skin . . . I told her she'd put on weight and needed to spend more than $4.99 on her wig . . . you know, just like old times. Then she went on to tell me how she and Nathan had been working to get Hair by Monique off the ground. She bragged about how they were starting to make some good money, and I boasted about my new salon . . . the usual deal of us trying to one-up each other. All was good until I started examining the ingredients in Sleek and saw it was made from the exact same formula we developed together years earlier."

"She was selling the same formula that made her hair fall out?"

"Yep. She said that when she moved to New York, Nathan convinced her to try the cream out on a few customers. It worked well for them, so she used it on more and more of her clients. They loved it. Who wouldn't love a quality relaxer that doesn't burn? Monique claimed that only a very small minority of patrons reacted badly to it, and if she noticed their hair starting to thin, she would switch them back to a traditional relaxer. I told her that was all fine and good, but I also asked her, now that she was marketing Sleek for mass distribution, if she warned buyers of the possibility that it could cause massive hair loss. Her response was to show me some bogus warning label on the box about how the product could have adverse effects, how a small amount of hair should be tested prior to full use . . . blah blah blah. You needed a magnifying glass to read it, and you still do.

"At first, I thought it was pretty sleazy of her to be selling a product that she knew, firsthand, could ruin a woman's hair for life. But the more she rationalized her decision by reminding me of how the full-lye and no-lye relaxers we use every day have, on occasion, done the same thing, the more I thought it was even sleazier of her to be making money off a product we developed *together* without giving me a cut.

"Of course, I belittled her wig with my $4.99 comment just for my own amusement, but it actually was a fairly respectable wig—nothing like the masterpieces Maurice has been making for her over the past few years. But decent nonetheless. A layperson may not have known it wasn't her real hair, but most of us in the business could probably tell she was wearing a wig. I think she was afraid I might have snatched the thing off her head right there in public if she lied to me, so she was honest when I asked her if the hair under her wig had finally recovered. When she told me it was still too thin for her to grow it out, I knew I had my trump card."

"So exactly how did you play it?"

"After I told her she had better get some nicer wigs if she was really planning on passing them off as her real hair so exquisitely straightened by Sleek, I said I wanted in on the action. Monique was a stubborn thing and reasoned that, even though I was involved in developing the formula, she and Nathan had done all the countless hours of legwork to take something we invented at her momma's kitchen table to the commercial market; therefore, I was not entitled to any of the profits. And I did admit that she had a point—maybe I was not entitled to an equal share, but I deserved something. And if I didn't get it, I threatened to shout far and wide what was going on under her wig. We eventually agreed to the deal we've had in place for years. I order whatever Hair by Monique products I want and pay way below the standard wholesale price."

"That seems fair enough," I say as yet another man steps inside the salon.

He seems a little unnerved to see Wavonne and me at the counter.

"Hi, Eric," Odessa says to him. "These are some friends of mine. Tamara is waiting for you in room one."

The man nods, and there's an awkward silence as the three

of us watch him walk to the back of the salon, knock on one of the doors along the hallway, and step inside.

"So, I'm guessing these discounts from Monique, and the men we've seen buying her products, tie together in some way?"

"At this point, I clearly have nothing left to hide, Halia, so I may as well tell you," Odessa responds. "Yes, they do, in fact, tie together. Shortly after I . . . shall we say *diversified* Salon Soleil's services, the IRS started snooping around. Back then, I only accepted cash from my clients that utilized our . . . our *extracurricular* services, so I didn't have to report it. But at some point, my tax returns triggered some interest from the feds . . . something about my reported income not amounting to sufficient funds for my personal living expenses. Fortunately, the auditor they sent out was a man, and I was able to sweet-talk my way into paying a small amount in back taxes.

"If I didn't want the tax man coming around again, I had to find a way to launder the money coming from all the gentlemen paying for the female company we offer here—that's where Hair by Monique comes in. I buy her products for a steal and then mark them up a few hundred percent. Rather than pay the full fee for their time with my girls, clients are informed to come to the register and spend a predetermined amount on products after their session. We can only charge so much for a 'massage' without raising suspicions." It's now Odessa's turn to do the air quote thing with her fingers. "So we tack on some overpriced beauty products to the bill to even things out. It all gives me something to show the IRS for . . . for *services rendered*. Stock coming in, stock going out, receipts for it all. Everyone's happy—me, my girls, my clients, and the IRS."

"So you had this whole complex scheme in place for years, and you were afraid Monique was going to pull the plug on it?"

"I was. I had dared to compete with her in the glamour game . . . I took attention away from Monique at an event that was supposed to be about nothing other than *Monique*.

It may not seem like such a big deal to most people, but if you knew her well, you knew there was nothing worse I could have done."

"But you were blackmailing her," I say. "Why did she feel like she could cut you off if you knew her secret?"

"She figured our secrets canceled each other out. She got wind of my little side business and threatened to report me to the police if I ever dared spill the tea on her wigs," Odessa says. "And that's why I drove back to her house the night of the white party. To remind her that I knew about more than just her wigs, and she had better think twice about messing with our arrangement."

"What?" Wavonne asks. "What more did you know?"

"I knew that Nathan was one of my best clients . . . that's what I knew. I told her if she reported me to the police, the first thing I would do after telling the world about her teeny-weeny Afro was tell the police and the general public about her husband's penchant for paid trysts with my girls. Maintaining her image as this jovial beauty titan with a perfect home life was very important to Monique, and a husband that's running around paying for sex with other women doesn't exactly fit in with that narrative."

"You make it sound like she knew about Nathan and your . . . your *girls* when you went to see her after the party. She just didn't want the rest of the world to know about them?"

"Of course she knew. That's how she found out about my operation to begin with. She confronted me about it weeks ago . . . said she had someone tail him one night when he supposedly left for the gym. He's such an idiot. What a stupid excuse. I mean, they have a full gym in their home."

"What did she do when she found out?"

"The same thing she always did when Nathan treated her badly—nothing."

"Get out!" Wavonne says.

"I'm not kidding. She didn't even ask me to drop him as a client. She said if he was going to run around with . . . well, the term she used was not very nice, but she indicated that she preferred that Nathan's indiscretions happen with my girls who at least adhere to certain health and safety protocols."

"That is *messed up*," Wavonne says.

"Several years ago, if you had told me that a smart successful woman like Monique, who is probably turning over in her grave hearing me call her smart and successful," Odessa says, "would stay with an abusive man, I'd had said you were crazy. But now, based on her story and some of the women I employ and whose hair I cut, it no longer surprises me. I've learned that the idea that women only stay in abusive relationships because they are financially dependent on their men is a total myth. I knew that Nathan was an ass and encouraged her to leave him more than once, but I was not aware of the physical abuse—she hid that well. Monique and I quarreled and traded barbs all the time, but she knew I would be there for her if she left Nathan. It was just not something she was ever going to do." Odessa takes a breath and sighs. "I've gone on and on, but what this all amounts to is that by the time I left Monique's house last Saturday night, she was well aware that, unless she knew how to explain why I have Nathan on security camera footage coming in and out of my salon after midnight on a few dozen occasions, she would keep our deal in place. So you see, I had no reason to kill her. I knew our arrangement was secure at that point. I already told you how important Monique's image . . . her brand was to her. You can imagine how afraid she would be about word getting around that the husband of the charmed Ms. Monique Dupree was getting busy with . . . with . . ."

"Hookers? Hos? Ladies of the evening?" Wavonne says.

"Ladies of the evening. Let's go with that one," Odessa replies.

"Not that I'm judgin'," Wavonne says. "What you and your girls do ain't no worse than what my friends Melva and Linda were probably gettin' into last weekend . . . at least your girls got a few bucks to show for it."

"Can we get back to the subject at hand?" I ask, giving Wavonne the stink eye. "So, it appears you didn't have a motive for killing Monique. But, I have to say, you claiming to have been at a club that has been closed for months when she was killed still raises some eyebrows."

"I made up the story about the nightclub because I didn't want to have to explain to anyone where I really was when Monique was killed, which was here. Being at my salon at midnight would lead to questions that I didn't want to answer. But, if push comes to shove, the same video camera that has Nathan on tape as a regular visitor also has me on tape right here managing our evening activities when Monique was killed. Of course, I'd rather not have to share such footage with the police to confirm my alibi. But if it comes to that, rather than being brought up on murder charges, I'll confess to running a . . . a . . ."

"Cat house?" Wavonne says. "Again, I ain't judgin'."

"I'll confess to running a *gentlemen's club*."

"This is all a lot to take in. But I do thank you for sharing all the information. What is it now? Like two a.m.?" I pull out my phone and look at the time. "I'm too tired to even process it all right now. I think I'll just say good night. I hope the rest of your evening . . . or morning or whatever goes well, Odessa." I turn to Wavonne as it occurs to me that I just told Odessa that I hope her hooker business goes well. "I think we've taken up enough of Odessa's time. Why don't you drive home, Wavonne? I'm exhausted."

"See ya, girl," Wavonne says to Odessa as we turn to leave.

As we step out of the salon onto the sidewalk, we pass yet another one of Odessa's late-night clients on his way into the building. He's a tall, lanky man with a weathered face and dark hair.

"Hi there," he says, stopping to speak to Wavonne. "How do I get on your client list?"

Wavonne is quiet as it takes her a moment to realize what he's asking.

"You *don't*," I declare, grabbing Wavonne's hand and pulling her away from the man.

"Was he insinuatin' what I think he was insinuatin'?" Wavonne asks me as I click on my key fob to unlock the car doors.

I don't respond, which I guess is really the same as saying, "Yes."

"So, over the last few hours I've been mistaken for a drag queen and a hooker," Wavonne says once we get in the van. "All in all, not my worst Saturday night."

Chapter 33

"Pretending to turn it up or down?" I ask Wavonne as I see her fiddling with the thermostat by one of the ordering stations.

"Down," Wavonne says. "Those bougie hos at table fourteen said it's too hot in here."

"Okay. I was coming over to act like I'm turning it up. The couple at table six said it's too cold." I smile at my customers at table six and gesture toward Wavonne to imply she is turning the thermostat up. Truth be told, you need to punch in a code before you can adjust the temperature, so multiple times a week, I or my servers . . . or the hostess . . . whoever . . . head over and press a few buttons without typing in the code. If we actually adjusted the thermostat every time a customer asked, we'd vacillate between a hot yoga studio and a walk-in refrigerator. I keep the restaurant at a comfortable sixty-eight degrees year round. I want it to be warm enough for my customers to be comfortable, but also cool enough for my servers who, with the exception of Wavonne, who is not known for moving quickly, race around for hours taking orders, fetching drinks, delivering food, and clearing tables. If I let it get too hot in here, I'd end up with servers breaking a sweat, and as Wavonne would say, "don't nobody need to see that."

I'm about to walk over to table six and tell them that it should be warming up shortly, when I see a familiar face come through the front door. I know I've seen her before, but it takes me a moment to recognize who it is. As she approaches the host station, I realize she's Tanesha, the woman who worked at the reception desk at Alex's apartment building. On my way over to her and a friend she has brought along, I vaguely recall her sending me an e-mail asking if she could come in one day this week for that complimentary lunch I promised her. But I've been so busy running around this week trying to find out everything I can about possible murder suspects, Tanesha's visit fell off my radar.

Things are mostly back to normal at the moment. I haven't lost interest in the case or suddenly decided that Nathan is definitely guilty, but I don't really have any solid leads that I can follow up on at this point. Maurice and Odessa have solid alibis, and I have no way of finding Alex. He may have gone back to the Dominican Republic for all I know. I'm sure the police have access to databases that could tell us where he last used his credit card or if he boarded a plane recently, but I have no way of getting that information on my own, so I called Detective Hutchins and told him Alex skipped town the morning after Monique's murder. He said he'd look into it, but I'm not sure if he really intended to do so or if he only said he would to get me off the other end of his phone.

"Tanesha," I say warmly. "I'm so glad you came by."

"Thank you for having us," she says. "This is my friend Sheila."

"Hello," I say to Sheila. "Welcome to Sweet Tea."

I fetch a pair of menus and lead the two women to a table.

"Our iced tea of the day is apple spice, and on special this afternoon are Cornish game hens with an apple, cranberry, and sausage stuffing. We brine them for eight hours so they are super moist. I'll let you look over the menus, and a server will be with you shortly." I set the menus and a wine list down on the table. "Thanks again for your help the other day," I say to Tanesha. "We're still concerned about Alex. As far as I know, no one has heard from him in more than a week or even knows where he is."

"Ah . . . I know where he is," Tanesha says.

"You do?"

"Yeah. He came back to the building yesterday, but I still think he was lying about purging stuff from his apartment because he seemed to be moving everything he took out back in again."

"Is that so?" And, just like that, my investigation wheels start spinning again. "May I ask you one more favor?"

Before Tanesha can respond Wavonne sidles beside me, stopping off on her way to another table with a pitcher of tea in her hand. "Did I hear someone say Rico Suave is back in town?"

Tanesha and her tablemate laugh. "He is indeed." Tanesha looks up at me. "What's the favor?"

"When you get back to the apartment building, can you look up Alex's phone number and e-mail it to me?"

"I don't need to go back to work to do that." Tanesha pulls her phone from her purse, taps on the screen a few times, and hands it to me. "I confess. Sometimes I press star six seven and dial his number just to hear him say hello or listen to his voice mail greeting. That deep voice and that Dominican accent send me over the edge."

"That is some serious stalker stuff right there," Wavonne says to me under her breath as I step back from the table, holding Tanesha's phone in one hand and typing Alex's number into my own with the other. "Girlfriend is cray cray."

"Probably so," I agree before I inch back toward Tanesha

and return her phone. "Thanks. I want to call and check in on him." I spin around toward Wavonne. "Can you take care of these lovely ladies once they've had a chance to review the menu?" I ask. "I've got a phone call to make."

"What did you tell him?" Wavonne asks me as we walk toward Iverson Towers. We've made a quick trip over to Alex's building during Sweet Tea's midday closure.

"I told him I wanted to see how he was doing since Monique died. I didn't let on that I knew he'd left town for several days. I asked if we could come by to say hi and check on him. When he hesitated, I promised to bring him some treats from Sweet Tea and offered to give him a few leads on restaurant jobs—something that should be a welcome gesture, given that one of his two employers is dead and the other is in jail."

Now that we know his apartment number, I look it up on the console and press the appropriate button that sends a call to Alex's phone. He answers and immediately buzzes us in without saying anything.

"Hi there," I say when he opens the door.

"Hi, Halia," he responds. "Good to see you, Wavonne."

"Back at ya," Wavonne says, shamelessly admiring Alex's physique in a tight white T-shirt and basketball shorts as we enter this apartment.

"We brought you a little something." I hand him a bag filled with Sweet Tea takeout containers.

"It looks like more than 'a little something.'"

"Yeah . . . it's a whole spread . . . fried chicken, mashed potatoes, collard greens, and some cornbread. Oh, and a slice of Momma's chocolate marshmallow cake."

"Sounds wonderful. That's so nice of you." He walks over to the dining area and places the bag on the table. "Please. Have a seat."

Wavonne and I move toward the sofa and sit down.

"Are you looking for something?" he asks, taking notice of me slowly turning my head to search the room.

"No. Just checking out your place. It's very nice." In reality I'm trying to see what's different from the last time we were here. I come upon several things—there's a TV back on the wall where one was obviously missing earlier, the legs of two end tables are filling the little depressions in the carpet they left behind when they were likely hastily removed last week, and there's a couple of boxes in one corner of the living room, probably full of stuff he brought back yesterday and hasn't had a chance to unpack.

"Thank you. I've only been here a few months. Can I get you anything? Some coffee or water?"

"No, thank you," I respond, and settle into the sofa. "So how are you doing? I'm sure Monique's death must be hard on you."

"It is. She was a nice lady. I'll miss her." He sounds somewhat unaffected by her death, but I feel like he's acting . . . like he's holding back. "She was a good friend and a good employer. I had planned to be touring the country with her . . . and Nathan and Maurice at this time."

"That would have been quite an experience. How long was the tour supposed to last?"

"We had planned to be gone for five weeks. We were supposed to hit thirty-seven different cities . . . more than one hundred salons."

"Wow. You would have gotten to know each other really well."

"Assuming you didn't know each other really well already," Wavonne says.

"What do you mean?" Alex asks.

"Do you want to ask him or shall I?" Wavonne says.

"Ask me what?"

"So it's a bit of an awkward question, but . . ." I inhale deeply and cross my legs. "Did you and Monique have more than . . . more than just an employer/employee relationship?"

"I'm still not quite sure what you mean?"

"She means, were you and Monique gettin' freaky?"

"What? No! Of course not," he says. "Why would you ask that?"

"To be honest, Alex, more than one person in Monique's circle has floated around the idea of the two of you having an affair. I probably shouldn't say who, but someone actually heard the two of you arguing the night of the white party."

"When? I barely saw Monique that night. She was busy mingling with guests."

"It was at the end of the evening after Wavonne and I had left. Apparently, she was overheard telling you 'it' was over. What exactly was she telling you was over?"

"I don't know. I can't remember everything she said to me that night. At some point after everyone left, she came into the kitchen while I was cleaning up and putting things away. I have a vague memory of her sitting at the table and pulling her heels off. I think she did say something like 'it's over, I can't do it anymore' when she was taking off her shoes. She was talking about the party being over and how she could no longer stand to walk around in five-inch heels."

"And you never stormed out of the kitchen and left the house?"

"I left the house when my work was done. I was late meeting a friend for a drink, so I may have been moving quickly, but I certainly didn't *storm* out of the house." Alex looks directly at me. "Why do I feel like I'm being interrogated?"

"I'm sorry," I say. "I certainly don't mean for you to feel that way. It's just that when you combine the idea of you and Monique having an affair with the fact that you skipped town the day after she was murdered, it raises some questions."

He looks at me curiously.

"Yes. We know you left town . . . or at least this apartment. We came by here last week and saw all your stuff was gone."

"How did you get up here . . . and in my apartment?"

Wavonne and I look at each other trying to figure out how to respond.

"I bet it was that busybody at the front desk who keeps calling my phone and hanging up. Did she help you somehow? Tamara? Tameeka?"

"Tanesha," Wavonne says. "I'd watch out for her if I were you," she adds. "Not that I'm sayin' she helped us, but girlfriend's a little whacked."

"Never mind about that," I say. "Where did you go, Alex?"

"Oh my God! This is all so ridiculous. Where I went doesn't matter. I was not having an affair with Monique," he declares before taking a breath and calming himself. "Look. I like to flirt and have some fun with women . . . and maybe I have a fondness for older women like Monique and . . ." He lets his voice drop, but it's pretty clear from the way his eyes veered in my direction that he was about to refer to me.

"So that's why you were all up in Halia's bidness. You've got a thing for cougars."

"Maybe I do," Alex replies. "But I'm not interested in getting involved with married women . . . especially one married to Nathan, who is clearly dangerous . . . and now we know just how dangerous. I have no idea what someone overheard between Monique and me, but I assure you there was nothing going on between us beyond friendship. And even if there were . . . even if I had some motive for wanting to kill Monique, I was nowhere near her house after the party."

"Oh?"

"It had been a long day. I met my friend Javier for a couple of beers. Look," he says fumbling with his phone and handing it to me. "He posted a photo."

I look at his phone and see a photo of Alex with his friend on Facebook or Instagram or one of those sites. They are both smiling with beers in their hands.

"That's awfully convenient that the photo is date- and time-stamped about the time Monique bit the dust," Wavonne says. "It could've been taken six months ago."

"I guess," Alex says. "But Javier will vouch for me."

"So if the photo is legit, and your friend can give you an alibi, then why did you skip town after Monique was killed?"

"I have my reasons."

"Which are?"

"I'd really rather not say, but they have nothing to do with Monique."

"Let me give you some advice, Alex. Halia here can be a big fat pain in the behind when she wants to be. And if you don't tell her why you left town, she's gonna nose around until she finds out anyway, so you may as well tell us," Wavonne advises. "Besides, if you have nothin' to hide, what's the problem?"

"I didn't kill Monique, but that doesn't mean I don't have anything to hide." Alex looks down at the floor and then back in our direction. "I didn't . . . don't want the police nosing around . . . because . . . well, I'm not exactly in the country legally. When I heard Monique was killed, I was afraid they'd be reaching out to people close to her, looking for information to find the killer. Even if I can prove I didn't kill Monique, if they run a check on me, I'll be in a mess of trouble for overstaying my visa. That's why I left town."

"So why did you come back now? I'm assuming your immigration status is just as tenuous today as it was when you left."

"I saw on the news that they arrested Nathan. I figured it

was safe to come back . . . for a little while at least . . . enough time for me to get the rest of my things and settle some affairs. I doubt the police will be digging into my business now that they have identified Nathan as the killer."

The three of us are quiet for a moment until Alex breaks the silence. "You seem like nice people. If I hang around for a few days, can I assume you will not turn me in to immigration?"

"Your immigration status is the least of my worries, Alex."

"Oh, please!" Wavonne says, giving me the eye. "Girlfriend's got a kitchen full of illegal immigrants workin' for her."

"I do not!" I respond. "I have Social Security numbers and copies of every employee's driver's license on file."

"Whateva, Halia . . . let's swing by the 7-Eleven on Branch Avenue on the way back to Sweet Tea, and we can get a few more 'driver's licenses' for you to keep on file. Some guy named Hector that hangs out in the parking lot sells them out of his trunk for fifty bucks."

Chapter 34

"I'd marry his fine self and make him legal," Wavonne says as we get back in the car. "But given his proclivity toward women of a certain age, it seems he'd prefer you do the honors. Go on, Halia," Wavonne jibes. "Get yourself a lil boy toy."

"Maybe I'll consider it once I've cleared him of murder," I joke.

"He's got an alibi, just like Odessa and Maurice. Seems he's in the clear, too."

"I guess. Which means there is no one left on my list. I suppose I could ask around and see if anyone knows of who else might have a motive for killing Monique, but at the moment, I guess Nathan stays in jail until he goes to trial. I saw on the news that the judge wouldn't grant him bail. Not that I'm crying any tears for him. The man belongs in jail whether he killed Monique or not."

"Got that right," Wavonne says before she turns up the radio and starts rifling through the papers that she left in my van the night we went to Enigma. She flips through the news rags, which are mostly just ads for bars and restaurants, occasionally mentioning something about a happy hour she wants to keep in mind.

On the way back to Sweet Tea, I half listen to the radio and half listen to her talk about how Bar Charley's happy hour offers six-dollar cocktails and two bucks off any glass of wine . . . or how Colada Shop has two-dollar empanadas from four to seven on weeknights . . . and something about DC Reynolds having a BOGO special. Before I know it, we're almost back to the restaurant.

"Take all that stuff in with you, would you?" I ask, pointing to the newspapers and magazines she has in her lap. "They've been cluttering up my car for days."

"Yeah . . . yeah," Wavonne responds, organizing the papers in her lap and reaching for the flyer she picked up at the club and had stuffed down past the armrest. "Girl, these men have better wardrobes than I do." She eyes the shiny piece of paper advertising Enigma's amateur drag contest. "I love this green dress," she says, and flips the flyer toward me.

I turn my head from the road for a quick second—long enough to see that the promo sheet gives some details about the contest and includes some photos of Enigma's current lineup of drag queens.

"What about this black one . . . with all the fringe?"

As I turn into the parking lot in front of Sweet Tea, I turn my head toward her for another quick second to sneak a peek. That's when my eyes immediately stray from the black gown Wavonne is referring to and land on Maurice . . . or should I say, Brightina Glow. "Whoa, whoa . . . wait a minute." I pull the van into a parking space. "Give me that." I grab the flyer from Wavonne and give the photo of Maurice—and his dress, in particular—a closer look. It's a long gown with thick straps and a low neckline cinched at the waist with a wide belt . . . and the entire thing . . . the *entire* dress is adorned from top to bottom in red sequins.

"I can't believe you didn't tell me that Maurice had a red-sequined dress," I say to Wavonne as we walk through the front door of the restaurant.

"What's this about a sequined dress?" Momma asks. She's sitting at the bar with a cup of coffee.

"We were talkin' about Maurice, Monique Dupree's stylist . . . and his sequined red dress," Wavonne says. "He moonlights as a drag queen. We went to see him—"

"Went to see him?" Momma asks. "Good grief, Halia." She glares at me. "A few billion men in the world, and you're going to see the only one who owns more makeup and pantyhose than Wavonne? That is not how you land a husband!"

"Don't nobody wear hose anymore, Aunt Celia," Wavonne says. "Even drag queens."

"Oh, I think drag queens still wear hose," Momma says.

"Nope. None of the drag queens we saw last Saturday night had hose on."

"Well, I'm not giving up my hose. In style or not, I like the way they make my legs look. And at my age, I need all the help I can get. I think—"

"Oh my God! Would you two stop talking about pantyhose," I snap at both of them, before looking at Wavonne. "Again, why didn't you tell me about the dress Maurice is wearing in the photo on the flyer?"

"I didn't notice," Wavonne says. "I didn't look at it that closely. I liked the green dress that Dominique Deveraux was wearin' better. What's it matter anyway? Maurice was clearly at the drag club when Monique was shot."

"But was he?" I question.

"What do you mean?"

"He said he couldn't have possibly shot Monique as he has to be at the club by eleven thirty to be ready to go on stage by twelve thirty. But what if he 'Brightina'd' himself earlier in

the evening, crept back to Monique's in full red-sequined re-
galia, murdered her, and then went to the club. If he was already dolled up when he killed Monique, he could have
gotten back into the city in time for his performance . . . and
that would explain the red sequin I found on the front lawn.
If traffic isn't bad, it's probably just over a half hour from
Monique's house to Enigma . . . and how much traffic could
there have been at midnight?"

"Well, I've heard enough about drag queens and men
wearing sequined gowns . . . neither one of them is going to
get me any grandbabies," Momma says, stepping off the
stool. "I just came by to check on supplies for my baking tomorrow. I'm going home." She steps behind the bar, drops
her empty coffee mug in a little tub underneath the counter,
and grabs her purse.

"Bye, Momma," I say as she walks past Wavonne and me
on the way to the door.

"So now we're back to Maurice bein' a suspect?" Wavonne
asks as the door closes behind Momma.

"Looks like it. When you think about it, it makes sense.
Even if he was being truthful about having Monique's blessing for his wig line, how successful could it have really been
without his name . . . or her name attached to it? It would
have simply been another wig website in a sea of wig websites. The publicity he's gotten for his business because of his
relationship with Monique would have cost him millions of
dollars. I mean, I hate to believe that Maurice would have
killed Monique to make a buck, but crazier things have happened."

"I guess that's true," Wavonne says. "There was somethin'
on TV last night about that lady in Texas that wanted to kill
the cheerleader's mom so her kid could make the squad. People are nuts soup."

"That they are," I agree. "Now we only have to find out if Maurice got ready at the club just prior to his performance the night Monique was killed . . . or if he showed up to Enigma all gussied up and ready to go."

"How you gonna do that?"

"The other men . . . the other drag queens who were back-stage prepping for their performances while we were there . . . they would know."

"They must've heard him last Saturday night when he was talking to us about his alibi. If he was lyin' then, and they didn't speak up, what makes you think they will now?"

"Good point," I reply, which is not something I say very often after Wavonne speaks. "I would imagine they're a pretty tightknit group—they may be willing to lie for one an-other. If we really want candor from them, we'll have to play it like we're not snooping or looking to implicate Maurice." I sit down at the table where Wavonne and I laid the papers we brought in from the car. The flyer about the amateur drag contest is on the top of the pile. I give it a look, and it gives me an idea. "Who would a drag queen be more open to . . . more willing to talk to than anyone else?"

Wavonne stares at me waiting for me to answer my own question.

"Another drag queen." I hand the flyer to her. "Look. It says the club manager is meeting with amateur drag queens who want to enter the *Ladies of Illusions* contest tomorrow afternoon. What if we went down there—"

"So what are you getting at, Halia. Are you going to go down there as a woman, dressed like a man, dressed like a woman to try and question Maurice's friends?"

"No." I straighten myself in the chair and lock eyes with Wavonne. "*I'm* not going to go down there dressed like a man dressed like a woman, but . . ."

"So what's your plan then?" she asks.

I don't answer her immediately, but it doesn't take her long to detect the wicked twinkle in my eyes. And once she does, her response is swift and resolute. But by the time I hear the words "Oh HAIL no!" come out of her mouth, I've already figured out how I'm going to convince her to do it.

Chapter 35

"I can't believe you made me do this," Wavonne says as she totters along on heels that are obscenely high even by her standards.

"I didn't *make* you do anything. You agreed," I correct.

While I *could* have, I didn't *want* to tell Wavonne that half of what she has in her closet would pass for drag queen wear without any alterations, so, in an effort to make it look more drag-queenish, Wavonne and I spent much of last night glue-gunning little sparkly plastic gems from the crafts store all over one of my old prom dresses. She's wearing our creation as we speak. She's a bit thicker around the middle than I was in high school, so we couldn't get the back of the gown fully zipped, which is why she's also wearing a velvet cape we dug out of a box of Halloween costumes to cover the back of the dress . . . we glue-gunned that sucker with plastic gems, too. And leave it to Wavonne to have a pair of six-inch metallic gold platform shoes in her closet—she's teetering on those babies at this very moment as we walk from the car toward Enigma.

"Only because I thought I might get some boss wigs out of the deal."

"And maybe you will. If it turns out that Maurice killed Monique, and Nathan gets off, I'm sure he'll let you have whatever wigs you want when I tell him the role you played in solving the case," I say, reminding her of the bargaining chip I used when I got her to agree to this little stunt. "Besides, you didn't seem to have a problem pretending to be a drag queen the last time we were here."

"That was me havin' a lil fun," Wavonne replies when we reach the club. It's closed as it's only three thirty in the afternoon, but the door is unlocked, so we let ourselves in. "And it was dark . . . and everyone in here was drunk as a skunk. It's goin' to be much harder to pass as a drag queen to a sober manager in the middle of day with all these lights on." Wavonne looks up at the light fixtures that are going at full blast at the moment. "So that's why I really teased this wig up good and laid my makeup on real heavy."

I refrain from telling her that I hadn't noticed she had done either any more than usual. Instead, I just say, "It's amazing how much different the place looks when the only sources of light are not sparkling disco balls."

"May I help you?" asks a short bald man with a lit cigarette in his hand. He looks to be about sixty, but he's one of those people whom you sense is younger than he looks . . . like he's lived hard, and it's showing on his face.

"Hi," I say. "I'm Halia. It may have been you I spoke with on the phone earlier . . . about the amateur drag contest this Saturday night."

"Yeah, it was me. I'm Lou . . . Lou Hodge," he responds in a raspy voice, switching the cigarette to his left hand, so he can shake mine with his right. "I'm the manager." He takes a drag on his cigarette.

"Isn't it illegal to smoke in here?" I ask.

"Who ya going to tell," he replies, more of a statement

than a question. "What's your name, sweetheart?" he asks Wavonne.

"Bubbles Champagne," she says in a deep voice, and extends her hand for Lou to kiss.

"Hmph," he says, ignoring her extended hand, stepping back, and taking a look at her. "So what have we got here?" He walks a circle around Wavonne like Maurice did when she and I were trying on clothes at Nordstrom. "Not diggin' the dress—looks like Hobby Lobby meets low-budget bridesmaid's dress." Another puff on the cigarette. "The cape's not so bad. You should have left it alone though . . . the plastic gems make it look like a grade-school art project."

"This is only one of my costumes. I have others."

"Sweetheart," he says. "I have to be honest. I don't think you're a good fit for Enigma." He inhales the cigarette again, turns his head away from us to exhale the smoke, and then swings it back around and looks at Wavonne. "The wig is okay and clearly you know how to beat a mug, but—"

"Beat a mug?" I ask.

"Her face . . . her makeup . . . it's not bad," he replies to me before looking back at Wavonne. "But the boobs . . . they're a bit ridiculous . . . you're trying too hard there. Whatcha got in there . . . sacks of birdseed?"

"Excuse me?!" Wavonne asks. I can see she's starting to get riled up. First he pans the dress we spent several hours decorating last night, and now he's insulting her breasts, which are all hers . . . no chicken cutlets, no falsies . . . no bags of birdseed.

"They're just too much." He lifts the side of Wavonne's cape and holds it up like he's pulling back a curtain to a bay window, and, from his facial expression, you can tell he does not care for the view. "It may be an *amateur* drag contest, but it's a big deal . . . and Enigma is for serious drag queens . . . true Ladies of Illusion." He lets the cape go, and it falls back in place against Wavonne's dress. "Your drag . . . with the teased wig and makeshift gown . . . and the overstuffed bazoombas . . . it's more comical . . . even cartoonish. Maybe you can try for a waitressing job at one of those touristy drag brunch places."

"Okay, okay," I say, before Wavonne can respond. I lightly rub her arm up and down, trying to soothe her and keep her from going all Naomi Campbell and throwing a phone at Lou. "That's great feedback . . . great feedback."

"Great feedback my ass!" Wavonne dramatically tilts her head to one side and unfastens an earring. "You best take back what you said about my—"

"Just chill, Wavonne . . . um I mean, Bubbles." I grab her by the elbow and pull her a few feet away from Lou. "Calm down," I say quietly. "Remember the real reason we are here. Now take a breath."

Wavonne takes in a long inhale.

"Let it out . . . slowly . . . slowly."

Wavonne does like I tell her, and we repeat this exercise a few more times until I think it's safe for her to be near Lou again.

"Now, come on. Help me out here . . . play along," I say as we move closer to him.

"Bubbles can be a little sensitive to criticism, but we really do appreciate your candor, and your taking the time to meet with us," I say to him. "We were here the other night and saw Brightina Glow. She was wonderful. That's who Bubbles ultimately wants to be like. Right, Bubbles?"

"Yeah, I so want to be just like Glowtina Bright," Wavonne mumbles with an utter lack of enthusiasm, clearly still harping on Lou's earlier comments.

"Brightina Glow," I correct, and direct my attention back to Lou. "We were talking on the way over here about how fabulous she looked and how long it probably takes her to get ready for a show. Does the performer who portrays Brightina usually get ready here or does he arrive at the club all ready to perform?"

"He gets ready here . . . they all get ready here. We have a communal dressing room backstage."

"Really?" I say. "The reason I ask is I can almost swear I saw Brightina coming into the club . . . not this past Saturday, but the Saturday before, already in full dress," I lie, seeing if Lou bites.

"Huh," Lou says, lighting another cigarette. "I wasn't really paying attention. I've never known him to come to Enigma in costume, but he may have."

"Do you happen to remember what he wore for his performance that night . . . about a week and a half ago? It wasn't, by chance, a dress with red sequins, was it?"

"Oh hell . . . couldn't tell you what Maurice wore yesterday. I've got five performers onstage every Saturday night. It's all a blur of glitter, and ruffles, and spandex."

I'd like to say, "Well, you're no help at all," but instead I ask, "Are any of the other Ladies of Illusions here at the moment? Maybe Bubbles can get a little advice from them before we go."

"I don't need no more advice," Wavonne says.

"No, not at the moment. But some of them work the crowd between shows, so you can come back after we open and talk with some of them."

"Okay," I say. "Then I guess we'll be going. Have a good day, Mr. Hodge."

"Said my drag was comical," Wavonne says as we clear the front door. "What would be comical is me punchin' him in his fat face."

"There will be no punching of anyone," I say. "Let's just go."

"Fine, but let me take these things off. They're killin' my feet."

"Very classy, Wavonne," I say to her as she leans against the building and pulls off a shoe.

As she pries off the other one and unties her cape, I see a sinewy black man approaching the club. He's holding a garment bag in one hand and a wig box in the other.

"That's the guy who was getting ready next to Maurice the other night," I say to Wavonne, who's now standing next to me a few inches shorter than she was a second ago. "Dominique Deveraux."

"Excuse me, sir," I say, approaching him as Wavonne hangs back and starts looking at her phone. I suspect she may be afraid he'll critique her look like Lou did, so she's keeping her distance. "You work here, right?"

"I prefer the term 'perform,' but yes," he says. "You two were here the other night . . . asking Maurice all sorts of questions."

"Yes. That was us," I say. "My name is Halia."

"Nice to meet you," he replies. "Jeffrey."

I recall Wavonne and I talking about how the other drag queens could have spoken up last time we were here if Maurice had been lying to us about his whereabouts the night Monique was killed. But I figure this gentleman may be willing to talk truthfully with Maurice out of earshot, and decide to ask him a few questions. "I guess you overheard us asking him about Monique Dupree."

"I did," he says. "The way you were talking to him . . . it was like you thought he might have actually killed the woman."

"I was just doing some investigating. I've been asking a lot of people close to Monique questions. Maurice was one of many. Besides, it sounds like he has an ironclad alibi." I look the man in the eye. "He was telling the truth, wasn't he? He *was* here . . . at Enigma getting ready for his show from eleven thirty to twelve thirty the night Monique was murdered, right?"

"I think so. I don't really pay that much attention to his comings and goings."

"So the Saturday before last, you don't remember him showing up to the club already clad in a red-sequined dress, do you?" I reach in my purse, grab the drag contest flyer with Brightina's photo, and show it to Jeffrey. "This dress."

He lets out a quick laugh.

"What's funny?" I ask.

"The idea of Maurice in that getup . . . that's what's funny." He looks down at the photo with a smirk still on his face. "I can assure you he did not arrive at Enigma in that dress anytime in the recent past."

"Because?"

"Because his fat ass couldn't fit in it." Jeffrey points toward the photo. "Look how much thinner he was in that picture. That photo is from a couple of years, and if I may say, a few too many plates of biscuits and gravy ago."

"What's this about biscuits and gravy?" Wavonne asks, looking up from her phone and moving closer to us.

"Nothing," I say. "But talk of them reminds me that we need to get back to the restaurant." I turn my attention back to Jeffrey. "Thank you for the information."

"You're welcome," he replies, and gives Wavonne a once-over. "You got potential, kid . . . keep at it," he adds, and makes his way to the door.

"Come on, Bubbles," I say to Wavonne. "Let's go."

"I think Bubbles is dead," Wavonne replies as she catches sight of her reflection on the glass side panel of a covered bus stop. In the broad daylight, the dress really does look like what it actually is—an old prom dress with some cheap sparkly titbits glued to it. She stares at herself, flat-footed with her cape in one hand and her shoes in the other . . . and I think one of her false eyelashes has fallen off. "Maybe that

Lou guy was right," she says. "I look like a *quinceañera* on crack."

I laugh. "I wouldn't quite say that. It's not *that* bad. Maybe you can repurpose it as a Glinda the Good Witch costume for Halloween," I advise. As we approach the van, I can't help but think how only Wavonne could get praised as a drag queen when she's *not* trying to look like one and ridiculed as a drag queen when she *is* trying to look like one.

Chapter 36

"I think I have to let it go at this point. I've got a restaurant to run, and I haven't found any smoking guns for any of them . . . Odessa, Maurice, Alex. They all have alibis. The only one without a solid alibi is Nathan, and a man like him should be in jail anyway."

"True dat," Wavonne says.

She's sitting at the bar with me halfheartedly marrying ketchup bottles while I figure out the specials for next week and what ingredients we'll need on hand to make them.

"Good," Momma says. "Now you can put the moves on that handsome Alex fellow."

"We saw him the other day, Aunt Celia," Wavonne says. "He admitted to having a thing for old hens like Halia, so she's got a shot."

"Is he going to be at the service tomorrow?"

"It's not really a service, Momma. I think it's more of a get-together. We're just going to swing by and say hello. Maybe it will give me one last chance to find any new leads. As soon as I . . ." I let my voice trail off as I catch sight of the television behind the bar and see a photo of Monique on the screen. I reach for the remote and turn up the volume. A narrator on one of those midmorning tabloid shows is speaking about Monique's rise from a local Maryland hairdresser to a national hair care products guru as various photos, some going back to her childhood, appear like a slideshow on the screen. Then the broadcast goes back to the show's host, who further introduces the program.

"Today we'll explore the salacious details of Monique Dupree's rise to fame and fortune . . . her years as the reigning Coiffeur Queen . . . and her untimely and scandalous death," the host says. "We'll delve into the crushing secret she hid from the world that could have taken down her entire beauty empire and her rumored tumultuous relationship with husband Nathan Tucker, who is currently behind bars awaiting trial for her murder."

"My God, the woman has not even been dead for two weeks, and they're already producing this kind of garbage about her?" Momma says.

"Honestly," I reply. "I'm surprised it took this long."

"Oh yeah . . . like the two of you ain't gonna watch every minute of it," Wavonne says.

"I didn't say anything about that." I turn up the volume a bit more, and the three us can't help but give our full attention to the show. For the most part, it doesn't tell us anything we don't know already. We hear about her growing up in District Heights and graduating from Suitland High School, a little about her time working at the local HairPair, and how she got her company off the ground with a homemade relaxer called Sleek, eventually parlaying the success of that product into a multimillion-dollar business.

I'm actually starting to get bored when the show moves on to talk about Nathan. While the host speaks of him, the program shows what appears to be cell phone camera footage of Nathan being cuffed in front of his house while I was there last week. It looks like the video was filmed from inside the window, which makes me think that Lena, Monique's maid, may have taken it, and sold it to the tabloid show for a few bucks.

"Halia's on TV!" Wavonne calls out when she catches a glimpse of me in the background watching Nathan being escorted to a police car as the host continues to speak of his gambling debts and the allegations of his abuse toward Monique.

"Eeh," I moan, hating the way I look on the screen.

"Don't worry . . . the camera really does add ten pounds," Wavonne says. "But I got nothin' when it comes to your hair or your clothes. That's all on you."

"I'm always telling her she needs to wear more makeup and pay more attention to her hair," Momma says to Wavonne as if I'm not in the room.

"Shhh . . . both of you. I'm trying to hear this."

In addition to the amateurish cell phone video that aired earlier, the television producers have gotten their hands on some of the footage Monique's camera team had been taking for her infomercials or the documentary she may have had in the works . . . or whatever she was planning to do with all the video clips she was having made while she was still alive. There's video of her getting her hair—well, her *wig*—done by Maurice . . . of her showing off her new tour bus . . . of her visiting both Latasha's and Odessa's salons. But it's when they show some footage of Monique hamming it up as the grande dame within Monique's House of Style at the hair convention that I grab the remote and press rewind and then pause.

"Hmmm." I take a closer look at the screen before pressing play and letting the program run again.

"What? What do you see?" Wavonne asks.

"Nothing," I respond, and watch the scene unfold again. It's yet more video in which I'm present, but this time it was taken right after Wavonne, Momma, and I had just bypassed the long line, with some help from Odessa, and made our way into Monique's House of Style.

"Oh my God. If they show any video of me without my wig, I will sue someone," Wavonne says as the camera takes in the three of us along with Monique and my whole band of suspects . . . Nathan, Odessa, Alex, Maurice . . . but now, as the video zooms out, a fifth person of interest comes into play. I barely have time to process the new information when the video cuts to shots of Monique's white party.

I watch intently as the white party unfolds on the television, looking for any more persons of interest. Nothing seems out of the ordinary, until there's a close-up of Monique and Nathan posing for photos next to the cake that Alex made. In true sensational journalist fashion, the program freezes this scene into a still and begins to expound upon how, underneath the beautiful mane of what everyone thought was Monique's hair, was, in fact, a shortly cut Afro. And, in what is clearly an attempt to up the "salacious" factor, the program depicts what Monique actually would have looked like without her wig. As much as I'm sure they tried, it seems they couldn't get their hands on an actual photo of her wigless, so the producers digitally altered the still of her and Nathan in front of the cake. They erased her wig and superimposed a closely cropped head of hair on her. And this is when it all comes together—this is when I figure it all out.

"What's goin' on?" Wavonne asks me. "Why do you look like Lucy when she's finally figured out how to worm her way into Ricky's show?"

Chapter 37

"Thank you for coming," I say to Detective Hutchins. He just stepped out of an unmarked car in front of Maurice's house. Wavonne and I have been waiting for him to arrive before going into the gathering. Maurice had mentioned earlier that he had been approached by police, so I confirmed with the detective that he was not involved in that meeting. Otherwise, I don't think there's much chance that anyone else at the gathering will know who he is.

"I'm not happy about this, Ms. Watkins," he says. "I've told you a million times to leave the police work to the *police*. We have a solid case against Nathan, but we are following up on other leads. There was no need for you to do that. I came more for your protection than any other reason. I'm a little afraid for your safety—if you start hurling allegations of murder at people, you may find yourself in a 'more than you bargained for' situation."

"I appreciate your concern. I'm grateful . . . *really*," I say. "Did you bring what I asked?"

Detective Hutchins pats his front pocket. "Yes."

"Thank you. We'll introduce you as a friend of ours."

We walk up the front steps and knock on the door.

"Hello," Maurice says, looking down at my hands, and then back up at me. There's a brief look of disappointment on his face, and I realize that he may have expected me to bring some food. I thought it was a bit odd that he invited Wavonne and me to a gathering for Monique's close friends, as we barely knew her, but now it makes a bit more sense— he was likely hoping I'd show up with a few pans of corn-bread. And, now that I think about it, I probably should have at least brought a bottle of wine with me or something. But this is my first time at an affair like this—part memorial service, part party. I'm not sure of the etiquette for such a thing.

Maurice is dressed a bit more conservatively than usual in a pair of tan khakis, a white shirt, a pink bow tie, and a plaid patchwork blazer that's a mix of pastels. "Please forgive me for wearing spring fashions in the fall, but Monique loved this jacket . . . it complemented the pink of her product packaging so nicely."

"You look great. Very smart," I say. "This is our friend . . ." I stumble for words. I can't believe that after all I've been through with Detective Hutchins over the years, I've never learned his first name.

"Hi," Detective Hutchins says. "I'm Robert. I'm a friend of Halia's. Forgive me for tagging along, but we have plans in the city afterward, so they invited me."

"No problem. Please come in."

Maurice's home is a narrow row house, so when we step through the door there is no foyer or hallway. We come through the threshold right into a living room/dining room combo and find about twenty people present, either seated or milling about, some with small plates of food or a drink in their hands.

"How about I get you each a glass of sangria?" he asks, before narrowing his eyes at Wavonne. "Wavonne, sweetie, I thought we had come to an agreement about the tight clothing," he adds, referencing the very snug leopard print dress she's wearing. "Rule of thumb: If we can tell you're an 'innie' or an 'outie' through the fabric, you need to go up to the next size, dear."

"This is a new dress, Maurice. I got it off my Wish app for seven dollars," she says. "I'm still breakin' it in. It will loosen up as the day goes on."

I have to laugh when Maurice gives Wavonne one of her very own "mmm-hmms" before leaving our little group to fetch our drinks.

I scan the crowd and see Odessa on the sofa talking with another woman I don't recognize. I also see Alex, looking dapper as ever in a pair of tapered chinos and a fitted gingham shirt. He's standing by the dining room table, helping himself to some cheese and crackers.

"Your boyfriend's here," Wavonne says to me.

"I see him," I say. "And he's not my boyfriend."

"That's Alex Rivas," Wavonne says to Detective Hutchins. "He's Dominican . . . and he's got a thing for *chicas viejas.*"

"Old girls?" Detective Hutchins asks.

"Wavonne's just being silly," I say. "Why don't we sit down."

The three of us have barely started toward the sofa when Maurice comes back with our drinks. He quickly passes them to us and then begins clapping his hands. "Okay, everyone. Why don't we get started?"

The room quiets as Maurice grabs a stool and sits down. "I'm so glad everyone made it today to honor Monique and her memory. I honestly feel this is the kind of memorial she would have wanted—a gathering where the people closest to her can celebrate her life away from throngs of fans and press that were at her funeral. I thought we could introduce ourselves, as I'm not sure everyone has met before, let others know of our connection to Monique, and share stories or anecdotes."

Maurice starts the sharing process by telling everyone how he was Monique's personal wig dresser and stylist. He talks of how they met at Enigma years ago before she was a household name, and how they became friends as well as business associates. He starts to tear up when he speaks of how he regrets not taking more aggressive action to get her to leave Nathan. He then shares a few touching stories about Monique, the charity work she did, and how well she took care of her mother.

A few other people share stories about how they met Monique and what she meant to them before Odessa's turn comes around. "I don't even know where to begin with Monique," she says. "We met in high school when we were Biology lab partners. I had spent the morning trying to make my hair look like Paula Abdul's when she was in Janet Jackson's "Nasty" video, and the first thing Monique said to me when we were paired in class was, 'That side ponytail looks stupid.' I responded with the first thing I ever said to her: 'No one watches *Dynasty* anymore. Perhaps you should lose the shoulder pads.' Of course, I knew she wasn't wearing shoulder pads . . . and she knew she'd met her match. From then on we were friends . . . sisters . . . sometimes nemeses. We had our ups and downs, but through it all, I think we always respected each other's ambition and drive. The world . . . *my* world will be a much less interesting place without Monique. I'll miss her."

The room is still until it becomes clear that Odessa is finished.

"Who would like to go next?" Maurice asks.

"I can go," Alex says, and clears his throat. "I met Monique last year when I was working at a little restaurant downtown. I'm proud to say she enjoyed my food so much that she asked for me to come out of the kitchen, so she could meet me. She—"

"Um," I utter, interrupting Alex. Detective Hutchins and I have been exchanging looks while guests have shared their stories, and I can tell he's getting inpatient and wants me to move things along. "I'm sorry to cut into your story, Alex, but I'm curious—what restaurant was it that you worked at when you met Monique?"

"Oh . . . it was just a small restaurant here in the city . . . it's out of business now," is his response. "They couldn't make it when I left to cook for Monique," he adds with a laugh.

"Did you have a favorite thing to cook . . . a specialty at the restaurant?"

"No . . . um . . . just different things."

"So you made 'different things' at an unidentified restaurant?"

"I guess I did . . . yeah. Why all the questions?" Alex asks, and from the looks on the faces of everyone else in the room, they want to know why the rude lady is asking "all the questions" too.

"I think you know why, Alex," I say. "There was no restaurant, was there?"

"Of course there was. It was—"

I cut him off. "And you're not a chef, either, are you?"

He doesn't answer, but I can tell I've unnerved him.

"When I let you tour my kitchen at Sweet Tea, and one of my employees called 'behind you,' the first thing you did was *back up*. Anyone who's been around a commercial kitchen knows 'behind you' means *don't* back up. I didn't think much of it at the time—perhaps you'd been away from the hubbub of a busy restaurant kitchen after signing on with Monique and had gotten rusty about the workings of such a place."

"Yes. Maybe I did."

"Maybe so," I respond. "And I guess I can forgive the lack of knowledge around restaurant kitchen protocol, but the more I thought about it, the more I realized that no real chef would have served the . . . for lack of a better word, 'crap' that you prepared for Monique's House of Style and for her white party. There was nothing about the spreads you prepared that said 'professional chef.' Even Wavonne here"—I gesture toward Wavonne—"can make spinach dip and meatballs. And now that I think about it, those mini quiches that looked fresh from the freezer at the white party probably *were* fresh from the freezer."

"What do you mean, 'Even Wavonne'?"

I ignore Wavonne's inquiry. "Besides, I looked you up, and L'Academie de Cuisine has no record of you ever attending. But my Internet search did dig up a few other records for one Alejandro Rivas. It wasn't that long ago that you worked as a masseur at the Gold Door Spa in Bethesda . . . your name was mentioned in a review on Yelp. That's the same spa that I heard Monique mention going to the night she dined at Sweet Tea. I don't know how it happened . . . maybe she booked a massage with you, kept coming back for more, and that's how the affair started. Who really knows . . . but the affair *did* start, didn't it?"

"This is ridiculous. I never had a romantic relationship with Monique."

"Of course you did. And she couldn't bear the thought of going on the road for weeks without you. I'm guessing Nathan would not have been too keen on his wife bringing a handsome young man on tour with them whose only job would be to give his wife regular rubdowns. So she hired you as a personal chef . . . or I guess I should say, to *pose* as a personal chef."

"You don't have any proof that we were having an affair."

"I'm not so sure about that, Alex," I challenge. "Women don't usually wear jewelry given to them by men who are simply in their employ at grand affairs like Monique's white party."

"From the look on your face, I'd guess somethin' about what Halia just said struck a nerve," Wavonne says, eyeing Alex. "You look like my friend Melva when she got caught stuffin' all-you-can-eat crab legs in her purse at the Korean buffet."

I give Wavonne my "shut up" glare and turn back to Alex. "Monique looked stunning the night she was killed in that custom-made blue dress. When Maurice told Wavonne and me about it before the party, he said she planned to add her usual splash of color to her annual white party with a *Larimar* blue dress, I didn't think much of it. I had never heard of Larimar. But I spend most of my days in khakis and unisex no-slip kitchen shoes—I figured he or she was some hot designer that I'd never heard of . . . but it turns out that Larimar is not a *he* or a *she*."

"Of course he is," Wavonne says. "He's dressed Tyra Banks and Iman. He's the one with that famous cat . . . Chowpeter or somethin'."

Maurice lets out a long, *loud* sigh. "That's *Lagerfeld*," he says, shaking his head. "And the cat's name is Choupette."

"So who or what is Larimar then?" Wavonne asks.

"I'm getting to that," I respond. "For reasons that are not important at the moment, I had the pleasure of glue-gunning a few hundred plastic gems to an old prom dress a few days ago. At some point as I was pressing the gems on the fabric, the blue ones sparked a memory of the necklace Monique wore the night of the big white party. I assumed it was just an accessory that she added to her gown, but in retrospect, I suspect she had the dress made to go with the necklace. I remember the piece of jewelry because it was made from a stone that I'm not sure I'd seen before . . . it was somewhere between light blue and turquoise. I did a little research on blue gems, and that's when I found out that Larimar is not a designer . . . Larimar is a *gem* . . . a blue gem . . . a gem found in only one place—the Dominican Republic."

"So what?" Alex says. "Anyone could have given her the necklace. Yeah, Larimar is from the DR, but you can buy it anywhere. She may have purchased it for herself."

"Anything is possible, I guess, but Larimar is not expensive, and Monique was not in the habit of buying cheap jewelry . . . or cheap *anything* for herself. She had necklaces worth thousands of dollars, but she chose to wear one that may very well be worth less than a hundred bucks. She would have only done that if the necklace had sentimental value . . . if it came from someone very special to her."

There is a change in Alex's eyes when I say "someone very special to her" that makes it clear to me, and to everyone in the room, that the necklace was from him.

"Speaking of the Dominican Republic, you were showing me some photos of your recent trip there at the white party. Doesn't seem like much of a stretch that you picked up the necklace for Monique while you were there, and she decided to wear it the night of the party as a symbol of your feelings for each other."

"I'm not saying any of this is true, but if it were, why are you bringing it up now?"

"Because it gets to the root of why you killed Monique."

My words are followed by a collective gasp from virtually everyone in the room, including Alex, who squirms in his chair before responding. "If Monique and I were in love, like you say we were, why on earth would I kill her?"

"I asked myself the same question when I was suddenly able to tie you to being in the very spot on the front lawn where the gun that killed Monique was likely fired." I turn to Detective Hutchins. "Do you have the sequin from the front lawn that I gave you the day Nathan was arrested?"

Detective Hutchins pulls a small plastic bag from his jacket pocket and hands it to me. I retrieve the red sequin and hold it out between my thumb and index finger.

"At first, I thought for sure it came from Odessa's gown . . . that it fell off her dress as she shot Monique from the front yard. Then I thought maybe it was Maurice . . . that he fired a gun at Monique in full red-sequined Brightina Glow drag from the same spot. But then, yesterday, I saw footage from the white party on some trashy barely news television show. That's when I realized the sequin I found on the front lawn may not have fallen from a dress . . . or any piece of clothing at all."

"Sista say what?" Wavonne cackles as I see brows go up with curiosity around the room.

"Can I borrow your shoe?" I ask Wavonne, knowing that my practical flats are not quite up to the task I have in mind.

"For what?"

"Just give me your shoe, Wavonne."

Wavonne leans over, removes one of her heels, and hands it to me. "I got these off Wish, too . . . only fourteen dollars."

I take it from her and drop the sequin on a table by the sofa.

"Sequins for clothing are typically made of metal or plastic. Giving one of those a little pounding would likely have no major impact." I take Wavonne's shoe, give the sequin a couple of good taps with the heel, and watch it shatter. "But this sequin wasn't made of metal or plastic. It smashed into a tiny pile of dust because it was made of *sugar*."

"Sugar?" Detective Hutchins asks.

"Edible luster dust, to be more exact."

"Edible? The sequin was food?" Wavonne asks.

"Yep. You can make them . . . or buy them off the shelf at any craft or cake decorating store. They would be a great resource for a man posing as a chef . . . a man with no real culinary experience who was attempting to make a pretty impressive-looking cake . . . an easy way to add a little razzle-dazzle to an otherwise very ordinary dessert," I explain. "I didn't see the cake on the night of the party. I never really made it into the living room that night, and I guess people were congregating around it, blocking my view when I poked my head in there. But when I saw the cake on TV, things started to make sense. There it was on the flat screen above the bar at my restaurant . . . a pink three-layer cake sprinkled with red sequins."

All eyes are on me and the room is obscenely quiet as Alex becomes increasingly agitated.

"When Wavonne and I arrived at the party, you had just come from finalizing the cake and were removing your chef's coat because you had gotten some icing, and apparently sugared sequins, on it. I'm all but certain you put the coat back on before you left the house, and you must have still had it on when you shot Monique from the front yard, with gloves on, I assume, so only Nathan's fingerprints would be on the gun. Maybe it was the recoil from the gun . . . or just from you blundering around, but at some point, a sequin fell off your jacket and onto the ground."

Alex is visibly shaking at this point. "That's all speculation. Why would I kill Monique?"

"Because she dumped you!" Wavonne says. "Odessa said she overheard her telling you that she was 'done' . . . that it was 'over.' "

"She didn't dump me!" Alex calls. "She wasn't telling me

that *we* were done . . . or that *we* were over. She was talking about something else." He looks directly at me. "You yourself said we were in love. If I loved her the way you said I did, why . . . why would I want to kill her?"

I see the distress in his eyes, and I can't help but feel a smidgen of compassion for him.

"I never said you *wanted* to kill her, Alex. I only said that you did." Surrounded by inquisitive eyes, I continue. "Back to the television program I saw earlier today . . . it included video from the hair convention . . . from Monique's House of Style. You're in that footage talking in Spanish to one of the maintenance workers the day of Monique's big reception. As the camera zoomed out, I recognized the worker as the same gentleman who was supposedly having a drink with you at the time Monique was killed—your alibi. Funny, how he was also someone who could make the sprinkler system 'accidentally' go off in the ballroom used to showcase Monique's product line."

"What does the sprinkler system at the convention center have to do with Monique being murdered?" Maurice asks.

"Alex wanted Monique out of the house and out of harm's way. He wrongfully assumed that she would be the one to go and check on the damage and salvage whatever was left of her displays for the conference in the morning."

"What are you getting at?" Detective Hutchins asks, trying to make sense of what I'm saying.

"Monique mentioned that Nathan's car—his Tesla—was in the shop the weekend that she was killed. My guess is that, not only did Alex assume Monique would be the one to handle the sprinkler system fiasco, but he was thoroughly assured that she had left the house when he saw her Bentley pulling out of the garage . . . even though Nathan—not Monique—was driving it."

Alex is now leaning forward in his chair with one foot

swiftly twitching. He seems to be scanning the room for a possible getaway.

"It all became very clear to me when that tasteless TV show digitally altered an image of Monique to show what she would have looked like with short hair . . . an image of her with a closely cropped Afro standing next to her husband, who also has a closely cropped Afro." I take a breath before I turn to Alex and continue. "So this is how I think it went down: You arranged for the sprinkler system to go off to get Monique out of the house. You saw her car pull out of the driveway and assumed she was out of harm's way. You then saw the back of an individual with a . . . a . . . what did you call it, Wavonne?"

"A teeny-weeny Afro. TWA."

"Yes. You came back and saw a person with a TWA sitting on the sofa. You assumed that person was Nathan. You raised the gun, aimed, and fired . . . thinking you were putting a bullet in Monique's husband. Only it wasn't Nathan. It was—"

"Monique!" Alex shouts, and hops up from his chair. "It was Monique. I never meant to kill her! I swear. It was supposed to be Nathan. Nathan should be dead. Not Monique." He quiets himself for a moment as he looks around the room at everyone staring at him. Then he begins speaking again through quick breaths. "Earlier in the evening when she said that 'it was over,' that she 'was done,' she was telling me that her plan to leave Nathan was over . . . was done. He had threatened to kill her if she left him, and we all know he had purchased a gun, and was regularly practicing his shooting skills at the range. He hit Monique . . . he beat her . . . he'd *bought a gun* for Christ's sake. If she stayed, she was in danger . . . if she left, she was in danger . . . she was damned if she did, damned if she didn't. The only way out was for him to die. It was supposed to be quick and easy. Everyone knew Nathan had gotten involved with Rodney Morrissey. Once he was found dead, the cops would've assumed that Mr. Morrissey's goons had done him in. The case would have gone cold when, like always, they couldn't get enough evidence to arrest Rodney, and Nathan wouldn't be able to hurt Monique anymore."

Alex plops down in his chair. He doesn't appear to be looking for an exit anymore. The tension that he's been carrying around for weeks appears to have left his body as he slumps into the chair and stares straight ahead and nowhere at the same time.

"But it all went very wrong," I say to him. "When you moved in for a closer look after releasing the trigger and realized what you did, you panicked, dropped the gun in the woods, and left town. The cops may have linked Nathan's death to his shady gambling habits, but Monique had no such habits. You knew they'd investigate everyone with a connection to Monique. That's why you left town . . . not because you are in the country illegally. I wanted to kick myself for not figuring that out sooner."

"How would you have known?" Wavonne asks me.

"From the photos he showed me of his recent visit to the DR . . . when he likely purchased the necklace for Monique. If he had been in the US illegally, he never would have risked going back there for a vacation. He wouldn't have been able to get back in the US." I turn from Wavonne to Alex. "You're as legal a citizen as I am, aren't you?"

"I'm not sure he's much of a legal anything at the moment," Detective Hutchins says, and pulls his badge from his pocket, lifts the side of his blazer to reveal his gun, and walks over to Alex, who stands up and does not resist as the detective signals for him to turn around and put his hands behind his back. Detective Hutchins cuffs Alex and leads him toward the door. We can faintly hear him reading Alex his rights once they are through the threshold and outside.

Everyone in the room is silent for a moment or two until Maurice speaks up. "Well, that was a bit of a buzzkill," he says. "Who would have thought such a pretty man could do such an ugly thing. Not that Nathan didn't have it coming."

"I guess Nathan will go free now," Odessa says.

"Maybe," I say. "But maybe not. I'd like to talk to Maurice about that."

"Why?"

"Because I think I have an idea."

Epilogue

"That had better not be Sleek," Wavonne jokes, as Latasha applies the relaxer to her roots.

Latasha laughs. "It's not. I don't even carry Sleek anymore. I stopped ordering it after you two filled me in on the backstory."

It's been over a month since Monique was killed, and Wavonne and I are back where it all started—Illusions, getting our hair done.

"I wonder what will happen with the whole Hair by Monique line, now that its founder and the face of the product is gone," I say.

"My guess is that one of the biggies—L'Oréal, Unilever, Estée Lauder—one of them will snatch it up. I read in some of the trade magazines that Nathan is trying to keep it going and wants to take the company public, but he can't line up any investors with Monique no longer in the picture," Latasha replies.

"With any luck, Nathan won't be 'in the picture' much longer, either," Wavonne says.

"What do you mean?"

"I mean, if all goes well, he'll go back to the slammer where he belongs."

"For what? I thought Alex had confessed to the murder."

"He did," I interject. "And the cops had to release Nathan. But Maurice and I went to see Detective Hutchins the next day. Maurice told him about the abuse Nathan perpetrated against Monique. He was sympathetic, but said there was little point in pressing any charges given that Monique had never contacted the police about Nathan's abuse and the fact that she's no longer alive to testify against him. It wasn't until after I told him that there might actually be evidence of Nathan's abuse on video that he referred us to the department's domestic violence detective and things got rolling."

"Might be evidence on video? So was there?"

"Yes, indeed there was," I say. "When I finally determined that Alex killed Monique, I was glad to have the case solved and know that he would be brought to justice, but it bothered me that Nathan would go scot-free after all he'd done to Monique . . . and have the chance to abuse other women. I played the stories of her abuse over and over in my head trying to figure out if anything I heard could provide enough evidence for an arrest. This got me to thinking about something Maurice told me when he had lunch at Sweet Tea. He said that she'd told him that Nathan had gotten a little 'handsy' with her in the elevator of their apartment building in New York a few days before the white party. Per Maurice, 'handsy' was Monique's way of downplaying Nathan beating the crap out of her. It occurred to me that there may be surveillance cameras in that elevator, and, sure enough, there are. It took a few days for the detective here to coordinate with the police in New York and get the footage into police custody, but they eventually acquired and reviewed it. I haven't seen it, but I've been told that Nathan was caught on tape hitting Monique

in the elevator . . . apparently the scene was pretty grue-
some."

"I bet the tape is leaked to TMZ before the end of week,"
Wavonne says.

"Probably so," I respond. "Apparently, whatever was on
the video was enough evidence for the New York District At-
torney's office to file charges."

"So what happens from here?" Latasha asks.

"Nathan was arrested and released. He'll go to trial sometime over the next few months. Between the camera footage
and testimony from people who were in the know about the
abuse, they are hoping to make third-degree aggravated as-
sault charges stick. If they do, Nathan could go to jail for
years."

"So Maurice is testifying?"

"Yes, and Lena, Monique's housekeeper, has agreed to be
involved. She apparently witnessed some of the abuse."

"It's funny how you think someone like Monique has it
all," Latasha says. "Then you find out what's going on behind
closed doors, and you realize that you have no idea what's
going on with *anyone*."

I'm about to agree, when we're interrupted by an older
white woman with curlers in her hair. "Excuse me," she says
from the chair next to me. She's been very quiet while one of
Latasha's stylists has been cutting her hair and has likely
heard every word exchanged between us. "Are you ladies
talking about Monique Dupree?"

"Yes," I say.

"I've been following that story in the news . . . well, not
the news really . . . *Access Hollywood*."

"Oh?" I ask.

"Yes. And something about the whole thing just doesn't
make sense to me."

"What's that?"

"On TV they said that her lover, that Alex guy, killed her

when he was really trying to kill her husband, Nathan something or other . . . that when he saw someone in the house with short hair, he thought it was Nathan and that's why he pulled the trigger."

"Yes. I believe that's how it went down."

"Shouldn't it have occurred to Alex that the person with short hair could have been Monique? If he had been intimate with her, how would he not know that she was wearing a wig most of the time?"

"Says the white lady," Wavonne calls next to me with a laugh. Latasha and I start laughing as well.

"What?" the woman says. "What's funny?"

"I'm sure you don't know this," Wavonne replies. "And why would you? But any brotha worth his salt . . . any man that has ever slept with a black woman knows you do *not* touch a sista's hair without permission. If you do and live to tell about it, believe me, it's not a mistake you make twice."

"Oh," the woman says, but still looks perplexed.

"Let me break it down for you. Sometimes we got complex sit-u-ations goin' on up here," Wavonne says, using both index fingers to point to her hair. "Wigs, weaves, tracks, extensions, clip-ons, sew-ins . . . any man with half a clue knows better than to start rummaging around all up in this bidness."

"Oh," the woman says again, but this time it's in a more "okay, now I get it" sort of way.

As the woman's stylist clicks on the dryer and begins to blow out her hair, Latasha finishes applying the relaxer to Wavonne's head and slides over to start on my cut. It takes about an hour for her to finish up with both of us and lead us to the counter to check out.

"Were you at all thinkin' what I was thinkin' while we were in there?" Wavonne asks after we've exited the salon and are walking to the van, so we can run a quick errand before going to Sweet Tea for the day.

"I don't know. What were you thinking?" I ask.

"About how much nicer Odessa's salon is than Latasha's. I mean Illusions is okay, but it's like stayin' at a Holiday Inn when you know there's a Ritz-Carlton just up the road."

"Salon Soleil is nice, but it also has Ritz-Carlton-like prices. And, call me crazy, but I really don't want to get my hair cut at a salon that doubles as a brothel. And Latasha's been a friend for years," I say. "I don't see us switching salons anytime soon."

"I guess you're right," Wavonne replies. "I wonder what will happen to Odessa's little side business now that Monique is gone. I guess she'll have to find another sparring partner, too. She and Monique could really go at it."

"Those two did have a strange relationship," I agree as we climb into the van. "One minute they were trading insults, and the next, they were talking like best friends. Very odd."

"Yeah, it was weird," Wavonne agrees, buckling her seat belt. "Your hair looks nice, by the way," she compliments.

"Thank you," I reply as I start the car and the radio comes on. It's set to a station out of Baltimore that plays a mix of everything . . . oldies, R & B, pop, rock . . . you name it.

"Listen, Halia," Wavonne cackles. "They're playin' your song."

When I realize what song is coming from the speakers, I laugh, and it occurs to me that maybe Odessa and Monique's relationship wasn't that strange after all. Their case was a bit extreme, but I guess they are not the only two who go from trading compliments to trading barbs without batting an eye. Then I turn up the radio, back out of the space, and Wavonne and I sing along to Queen's "Fat Bottomed Girls" as we drive out of the parking lot.